Heartthrob

Estalyn

Heartthrob

Dedication

A heartfelt thank you to my husband, I may have written this book before we met but never in my wildest dreams did I realize that I was writing my future. Two strangers meeting in the same school at 10 a.m. When our eyes locked, my life with you flashed before my eyes. Since that day in 2012 we have been forever unstoppable.

Will love you forever.

- *Your Moon*

Chapter 1
New Girl

I walked into the school, it was my junior year and I hated that I was having to start over yet again. I wasn't actually sure how I felt about moving to Ohio and everything changing. All in the hope that he wouldn't find us here. There was one thing that wasn't about to change though, how different I am compared to these people. I walked down the less crowded hall, mouth shut and eyes wondering. I have something none of these people do and that is a dead best friend. Only I could see him; only I could feel him. And there was also the necklace I wore that would alert me when he's nearby; the stone on the necklace would turn the same shade of ghostly blue as his eyes. With my hand on the strap of my bag I watched his blue aura shimmer amongst all the other people. He was here for me. Dave died several years ago; he got hit by a car. His spirit still roams the Earth, although he has stopped searching for answers as to why he is still here. Dave is older than eighteen-year-old me; he is twenty-five. Long out of high school but still close enough in age to care and always be here for me.

"It's okay, Skylar." He was right beside me with an arm wrapped around my shoulder. I couldn't speak back at the moment, so I just nodded my head. His icy touch sent chills through my body. We turned and I went sprinting up a flight of steps. Before I knew anything my whole body was turned around and my bag went flying down the stairs.

"Watch it, bitch." Her voice was high pitched and mocking, yet tense. My eyes traveled over to her, a blonde girl, taller than me with glossy pink lips. She wore Hollister clothes, a pair of pumps, and had three other girls with her that seemed to be enjoying watching my confusion.

She started to strut past me, the air illuminated by her high-end perfume. I watched her pink Victoria Secret bag swing as she went walking on with her friends. I sighed going down the stairs to retrieve my bag. A boy stood there picking my bag up, placing my papers back inside. I knew him; he'd been in front of my eyes before. Flashbacks emerged of him standing on the busy streets of New York that played on the theatre screen before me, a year ago. I said nothing as I took my bag from his hand. The bell rang and he gave me a crooked smile revealing those pearly white teeth. His forest green eyes watched me closely. His black choppy hair that drifted over one eye gave him that edgy style. When our eyes broke from the stare, he walked around me; his soft gray shirt sleeve brushing against my arm. The amazing smell that ran up my nose as he left me standing on the staircase caused a sense of happiness to rise inside of me. Once he was gone, Dave returned. I couldn't believe what I had just seen. The remnants of woodsy cologne with a sweet touch or bourbon remained.

"Dave, did I just–?" I stopped staring up the steps.

"You did." He confirmed with an expression of awe just like mine. Chills ran up my body, not understanding, what was an actor doing in a high school in Dayton, Ohio? A slight smile tugged at the edge of my lips wondering if he was on the run just like me. I was thoughtless, taking myself back up the stairs landing my feet on the second floor. I walked into my first period late. I was excused but all eyes were still on me. My body still trembled from having run into a celebrity only minutes ago.

"Hello, you must be Miss. Saxton?" The teacher's voice broke all the awkward stares. I nodded my head not saying a word, "Okay, well I'm Mr. Delray, please take a seat anywhere and welcome to Algebra 2." He smiled at me with a slightly impatient glare in his eyes. I sat down at a desk near the back. I noticed one of the girls that was with the blonde from earlier was in front of me. To my right side, the celebrity sat beside the blonde's friend. I swallowed hard, scared for some reason. It's not every day you walk into a new school and some movie star is sitting in your class. This was the most baffling day of my life.

Mr. Delray started talking, everyone was paying attention besides the three of us. My eyes stayed on the back of Jason Blackstone. His hair just reached the back of his shirt. His head bent down staring at his phone. As for the other girl that was with the blonde, she was on her phone as well. She chewed her gum and reached down for her designer purse. All I could stare at though was her stiletto heels. I closed my eyes, shaking my head to myself. I didn't want to come here. It was almost the end of the year, who changes schools one month before it's summer vacation? The problem is, if I tell anyone the real reason why, then they would be too scared to even be around me. That was something that never sat well with me.

"Is everything alright?" His voice sounded just like it did in the movies. Rough yet sexy, he had turned around halfway in his seat and was looking right at me. I just blinked at him with a short nod. I couldn't yet find it within me to speak back to him; I had never met anyone famous before, let alone been at the same school as someone like him. He just smiled and turned back around. My heart was racing out of control. My pen slipped from my sweaty hand. My eyes were big, as my heart skipped a beat watching his hand run down the back of his black hair. The short edges of his hair flattened under his palm. My lips fell apart, I jumped at the shrieking sound of my pen hitting the desk.

"Calm down Sky, he's not going to hurt you." Dave was beside me turning my air cold. I flipped a page in my notebook and wrote, 'I know that'. Dave chuckled in response. His arm stayed relaxed over the back of my chair until the bell rang. I got up quickly wanting to get out of there. I realized sitting at the back of the room was a bad idea; everyone got out before you did. I stopped, however, watching the preppy girl walk over to Jason. Her high-pitched giggle made me cringe as she started weaving her arm through his. He didn't seem to smile though. I walked slowly following behind, watching as they exited the room. Before I took another step, Jason looked back at me before escaping with the girl. Just a short amount of eye contact with no smile. His green eyes were almost reassuring but for what? What was it supposed to mean? His piercing green eyes stained my memory, those eyes would stay with me for the rest of the day. It was as if I'd been staring at a green light for way too long. I blinked the feeling away, feeling as though my legs were locked into place as another guy brushed passed me. I've made eye contact with a Hollywood star three times! I was also standing in the doorway like a jackass, star struck again.

One hour later, and it was lunch time. Four periods down

three more to go. I walked into the restroom where it was empty, and I could talk to Dave. I checked under all the stalls first, but his blue aura appeared with no hesitation. His body turned to normal, as if he was still alive. It always captivated me watching a dead man's soul become human again. I could physically touch him without his blue aura disintegrating into the air. I had so much to still unfold about the souls that walk among us.

"Sky, you know you should go eat lunch." He said leaning against the sink inspecting me like a parent would.

"Dave, I can't eat. This has been the craziest first day of school I've had in my whole entire life!" I was more than overwhelmed with everything. He laughed at me shaking his head.

"Yes, a movie star goes to your school, but what are the chances of you actually going out with this man?" His blue eyes pierced mine. I bit on my lip knowing he was probably right. My eyes drifted to the floor, mulling over the possibility. I never mentioned wanting to date Jason, but Dave knew me better than I knew myself sometimes. The tips of my teeth were grinding gently on my lip as I considered how many girls in this school wanted, have tried, or have dated Jason Blackstone. There was a chance that I looked like chopped liver to him. His crooked smile was still imprinted in my brain. It was as if he'd pierced my memory with a tattoo gun, tattooing the moment our eyes had first met. I blinked myself out from my thoughts.

"It's still exciting though." My voice was so low, I was speaking to myself.

"*Teenage* girls, he shouldn't even be here. He's like twenty years old." Dave laughed, closing his eyes. I narrowed my eyes at him crossing my arms. I wasn't sure of Jason's age, but I knew Dave's mocking tone towards teenage girls was grinding my gears in the wrong direction.

"When did you become my mother?" I asked him, sensing the way he was going to take this.

The restroom door came flying open and Dave was gone just as fast. The blue air disappearing along with him. I saw the blonde from earlier with her small posse. The girl from my math class came in, her high heels clicking against the floor. Her two-toned hair flowing down over her shoulders. Then there were the other two girls. They all looked like some remolded form of Barbie. It was time for me to leave the restroom.

"Oh, look what the cat dragged in." The blonde cocked her head to the side. The girls behind her started laughing, nodding their heads along with her. My body tensed knowing these were the girls that would be trouble.

"Funny the cat just conveyed the field of mice to her dinner table." I said walking around them. I heard a couple of them gasp. One was confused that I considered myself the cat instead of its dead prey.

"Did she just call us rodents?" The girl with platinum blonde hair squeaked. I laughed heading on to the lunchroom. Now I had a hard decision. Eat the mystery food, or starve? The thought of the simplicity of this one issue was soothing compared to my mountain sized issue outside of here. I found an empty round table and took a seat. I wished that Dave could show himself, so I at least had one friend to talk to. A tray came down beside me. There was a girl pulling the chair out and taking a seat. I didn't say anything, I just focused on her bright red hair. I smiled at her and she smiled back. I felt a short twist in my stomach, panic rose inside of me.

"Hi, I'm Missy." Her voice was energetic, and her posture was very chilled. She relaxed back in the chair ripping open a bag of chips. She wore a simple black T-shirt with skinny jeans and Converse shoes. Her red hair was braided but also falling out.

"Skylar." I replied, wondering why she was talking to me. No one has talked to me all day minus Jason's few short words. Then there were the snobs that I kept running into. The thought of making friends wasn't exactly at the top of my list, knowing I would have to leave again.

"Nice to meet you, so tell me, why the new school so close to the end?" She shoved a chip into her mouth. My eyes fell away from her then. I couldn't even explain it to myself. The horror of it all had left me scarred, there wasn't a chance I would be telling anyone the truth of my story. I had to lie. I didn't want to lie though; it was the worst thing to do when making new friends. There was also a chance I would just have to forget these new friends as well. Not one piece of me wanted to scare away someone from talking with me either.

"My mom got reassigned to a new position in her job." I said nodding my head. That was the best lie I had to give. That was going to be my alibi now. My mom worked a very important job, I just hope that didn't involve me going into detail. I should have thoroughly thought through my lies for why I was here.

"That's cool, so where are you from then?" She took a bite out of her sandwich.

"Florida." My voice was hushed upon catching sight of Jason and a bunch of guys walking into the cafeteria. They all laughed and had that edgy punk style to them. I watched them with their ripped-up jeans, black clothes, and cute rocker boy hair. Dave was right though, what were my chances of becoming a part of their crowd? Just having the same taste in style did not mean I would mix well with them. I'd never seen the other guys before in my life, which told me none of them were famous.

"You've spotted the eye candy of the school I see." Missy brought my attention back around to her, although my eyes stayed focused on him. The blonde girl went running up to Jason wrapping her arms around his neck. He sighed, rolling his eyes. My head tilted, seeing how unimpressed he was with the random blonde girl that I couldn't seem to get away from.

"Yeah, I have my first and third periods with him." I felt hatred inside for the blonde girl. Why was I jealous? I knew as well as Dave did that there was no chance, although Jason wasn't interested in her, that much was evident.

"Well at least you have something cute to stare at." Missy joked drawing my attention back to her. I saw her bright red braid coming down over one shoulder. Her smile gleamed, making me feel a sense of comfort.

"Yeah, until you see a snob always hanging on him." That was the truth and always would be. Missy laughed a little, while my eyes swayed back to their table. Jason pressed his back against the red chair shoving his hands into his hoodie pockets. His white teeth showing as he spoke with another guy at the table. His hoodie had the graffiti face from that Blink-182 album.

"That snob that was just hanging on him, that's his sister." She informed me shoving a grape into her mouth. My eyes opened wider then. My head swung back around watching as she sat at the same table with his group of friends and her posse. Why would she hang on him like that if he was her brother?

"Gross!" The thought made me feel nauseous. I was not ready for that abomination.

"You can say that again." Missy agreed, and our two different worlds stayed apart. For some reason I felt like I wanted to be in his world though. I wanted to know more. Maybe it was the foolish girl in me being guided by a celebrity, but I felt this urgency to watch him. There was an odd touch of comfort whenever his eyes met mine. He stayed in tune with me even if my radio was on a different channel.

School was finally over, and I was walking home. I didn't live far from the school this time around. Then again, I had also lost my car. I sighed as I remembered leaving it on the side of the road in Tennessee. We had been spotted which meant we had to ditch the car. Everything seemed so dreadful about this move, nothing felt like mine anymore. There was just one person I could call mine – Dave. Although, he didn't belong to me either. Just a dead close friend who I could keep to myself. I thought Dave would be here to walk me home, but he wasn't. I could call him but maybe I was better left without him. Sometimes I wonder if my life is better without somebody. I was just a friendly reminder of endangerment.

My phone started going off in my pocket. I reached for it as I got to the steps of my house. I saw Joey's picture. His smiling face caused memories to blossom. It's been a while since I've talked to Joey. The only true best friend I could ever really remember. I hit the decline button though. I wasn't ready to talk to him, not yet. I walked into the small, new house, shutting the door behind me; I wasn't ready for my mom to be home. Then again, where else would she be? She doesn't have a new job to allow for her to be anywhere new yet. I wanted to go straight to my room; my feet took me to the kitchen though. Mom sat at the table flipping through ads on her phone, searching for a new job.

"Hey sweetie, how was your first day?" She turned her head around.

"Alright, awkward ya know." I said going over to get water.

"Always is, *right*?" She smiled, setting her phone down.

"Yep, how was job hunting?" I no longer wanted to stay on the school topic.

"Not bad, going to apply for one tomorrow actually." Her smile was reassuring as she stood up from the table.

"What's the job?" I couldn't stop thinking about Jason going to my school. I wasn't about to tell my mom though; she would flip out. His green eyes flashed before me when I blinked. This odd ping in my heart making it skip a beat. I blushed at my own ignorance for catching feelings so fast. There couldn't be anything between us. A few moments of eye contact and he'd cleaned up my belongings, that was it. There was a high chance he would vanish from my life soon, Hollywood never stops. My eyes narrowed wondering which character he's played that is him in real life. *No, shut up! You don't like him, you can't!* I chanted at myself, in my thoughts.

"A florist." She got some tea out of the fridge. The sound of her glass clinking brought me back into the room staring at her peach shirt. I never pictured my mom as the type with a green thumb. We had a small garden down in Florida before we had to go on the run. We've spent so much time moving, that we never had any time for the little things. A small smirk arose, thinking back to a tiny carrot that Mom pulled from the garden for a salad. We joked about it for weeks because it was made for no more than one bite.

"Why not a teaching job like down in Florida?" I was confused as to why my mom didn't want to go back to teaching. Concern rose on her face. I felt lost all of a sudden.

"Have you made any new friends yet?" She switched subjects in a blink of an eye. What was up with my mom? There was something uncomfortable about her. Her body shifted to one side, and she held her glass of tea with both hands which she hardly ever did, unless she was feeling anxious.

"Not really, well there was this one girl, but things got awkward when she asked why I moved up here in the middle of the semester." I explained, feeling my insides drop. Mom's eyes grew bigger as she looked at me. There was a slight quiver in her fingers and the slightest twitch in her left eye.

"You didn't tell her, did you?" Mom was worried now. I should have never opened my mouth.

"I told her you got a new job offer." I sighed, still hating my own lies. Sure, I didn't know the girl yet and I was not going to be open with a stranger. I shuddered at my own thoughts of gaining another friend that I would have to hug goodbye. My eyes dropped down to the countertop thinking about Joey, he was my best friend in Florida. We just vanished out of thin air one day and I would never be able to explain to him why we left. No matter how many times he would ask, I would ignore him or lie about why we had been uprooted. I couldn't allow Joey to be in harm's way.

"Good, good, no one needs to know about your father." She collected herself, and her anxiety began to calm. I closed my eyes feeling mad every time she said that. I felt a raging ball of fire ignite inside of me.

"He's not my father!" My voice was harsh as I left the kitchen. I walked over to the short staircase resting my hand down on the railing. Chills ran up my spine thinking about the past with my dad. My life turned into a Lifetime movie before I could even take my next breath. I found myself shuddering at the mere thought of the man who I had once called my father. My feet skimmed the stairs as I went to my room. It was the first door on the left. Once I entered, all I saw was the two duffel bags that I still needed to unpack. We moved up here so fast; I couldn't even bring most of my belongings. Tears came to my eyes, wishing everything could have been different. I walked over to the window thinking back to how my dad had struck my mom across the face. I would never forget the shrill screams from that night. I still recall her eyes glazing over from the tears. I would have never thought my dad would ever treat her like that. I've never seen my mom so weak before. Home is never home once it becomes broken.

It's been a year since all hell broke loose in my real home. We've moved from three different states since then, but he somehow keeps catching back up to us. We moved from Florida to Colorado back to Florida then to Ohio. I wasn't even in Colorado long enough to enroll in a school. My mom had upped her game for this move though. I thought homeschooling would be best for me since we are always leaving. I thought about how we'd called the police that night. My dad was gone. He threatened to kill her if she told the police the truth about what had happened, ever since then we've never been able to settle down. I have mini panic attacks every night thinking that he will find us and come into our home. I shuddered away from the terror I had, but the fear kept growing and getting the better of me. Tears came slowly down my face, Dave turned me around wrapping me up in his cold arms. His blue aura covering me, holding me tight. His color made me feel like I was wrapped in the ocean on the Gulf Coast, yet his coldness made it feel like the Artic.

CHAPTER 2
Rich Kid

It was the next day and I was sitting in art class, letting my mind wonder. I watched the clock as I sat in my last class of the day; it's my second day of school and I've watched a lot more and noticed more things than I did yesterday. Jason's friends were in almost all my classes. I wasn't too sure who any of them were; I didn't take the time to try and get to know them. I'm not even sure why I care so much about knowing them. I was baffled by why I cared so much about knowing Jason Blackstone. He's just a rich asshole that only cares about himself. I wouldn't be surprised if he parties hard with his friends every weekend, getting drunk and doing drugs. That's what the high life is, fancy clothes, expensive sounding drugs, and drunk until the next evening.

"Looks like I have quite the artist in here." The teacher came over, looking at my drawing. My eyes grew bigger, not even realizing I was drawing Jason. I blinked a few times before crunching the paper up between my hands. *How the hell did I draw him just by thinking of him!?*

I squeezed the paper tightly between my palms feeling nervous.

"Now, why do that? That was a beautiful drawing." Mrs. King said, taking the crumpled piece of paper and straightening it back out. I was getting ready to say something back but then Jason came walking into the classroom. Her attention went to my subject of choice. She put my drawing of him back down and I smashed it back up in my hands quickly.

"Jason, you are late yet again, we are seriously going to have to have a talk about this." She told him, as he kept his cool smile on his face. I watched his green eyes stay on her. He pulled out a note handing it over to her. Jason was in my art class? Panic rushed into every inch of my body. Swallowing hard, my eyes stayed focused on him as if he was my prey. He never showed up to this class yesterday either; it would seem that there was a lot I was now curious about.

"It's okay; I have a pass this time." He said, shoving his hand back down into the pocket of his black jeans. Mrs. King shook her head, spectating the pass.

"Jason, don't you think I can tell that you wrote this?" She held it back up between two of her fingers. I smiled wondering how stupid this rich kid could be. His black eyebrows lifted. His forest green eyes glimmering under the florescent lights, his eye lids drifted down in the way I've seen them do a hundred times before on TV.

"Well, I guess you've got me then, haven't you?" He

was just as cool, calm, and collected as could be.

"Next time you are this late to my class you're getting a detention slip." She threatened him, throwing the note in the trash. His green eyes came over to me, sitting here by myself. A tiny smile came back to his face. Why was he staring at me? He said nothing back to her as he went over to the cabinet fetching his drawing out. His hips swayed as he approached my table gracefully. He took a seat on the stool across from me. What was he doing? My heart took off like a race car leaving the start line.

"You're in this class too." He smiled pulling out a sketching pencil. My eyebrows lifted, averting my gaze. He did not say it as a question but a statement. I wasn't sure how to carry on a normal conversation with him. I'm not going to lie there is a part of me that has a crush on him just like all the rest of the girls in this room, likely to be staring at him. I glanced around but no one was staring, it was only in my imagination.

"And you chose this table, why?" I asked him, getting up to go and get another piece of paper. I had to start over again. By the time I got up Mrs. King was back at the table. She reached over getting the crumpled-up drawing. *No! Don't open that,* but of course my thoughts never came out of my mouth when I needed them too.

"Skylar, we need to talk about your drawing skills." She said, turning it back around to me. Jason's eyes went up seeing the picture of him. A big smile spread across his face. His shining white teeth staring me down. I nodded my head, not wanting him to see it. Jason's lifted cheeks flushed with rose colored embarrassment. He lowered his head as he brushed his hand through the back of his somewhat messy hair.

"What about them?" I sucked in a big breath of air. He already knows, now I'm stuck in this embarrassing situation. I must keep my composure with confidence.

"Just your stroke lines, they could be a little clearer." She pointed making Jason's eyes go into a squint staring at the area she'd highlighted. My cheeks were red, I could feel them. I craved being able to read his thoughts as he analyzed those stroke lines.

"I'll try my best to make them clearer." I said while my foot bounced anxiously across from him. She walked away, and he snatched the paper. My mouth fell open.

"I must say, you did capture me quite well!" He smiled holding the picture up on his shoulder beside his head, his hand framing his jawline. A rough chuckle escaped his throat as he slid the drawing back over to me.

"Why are you here?" I shook my head starting to trace my new picture. I felt anger rising inside myself for being so stupid. This was a small school, there was a chance Jason would have another class with me. I let my guard down and when I did this, it would often lead to my heart drawing my work for me. *Come on Skylar, you have to stay on your toes!* My own thoughts were giving me a headache.

"Why are you drawing pictures of me?" He kept his

smile as things got more awkward. My phone vibrated on the table. His eyes lit up when he saw that I'd received a text. I was unsure why he would care.

"Don't answer my question with another question." I threatened him, opening my phone.

Dave: Looks like luck!

I closed my eyes smiling to myself. Why did Dave have to say that? He is always here watching every move. A quick glance at my necklace, that shined ocean blue, letting me know he was near. I wouldn't be shocked if he was right beside me on the empty stool.

"Well, the best way to get to know someone is with twenty questions." Jason laughed a little as I closed my phone.

"I don't play games." My voice was shallow with coldness, focusing on my drawing.

"Alright, who text you?" He crossed his arms on the table. My eyes wonder up to him. I laid my pencil down staring into his dreamy green eyes. It was like escaping into a forest that I've never walked through. I could almost feel the calm air welcoming me in.

"And what makes you think it's any of your business?" I wasn't sure where rich boy was coming from here. He laughed again shaking his head.

"Okay, let's try this the proper way, shall we? Hi, I'm Jason." He held his hand out for me to take. There was a smile that wanted to come out, but I held it back. I wasn't sure where he was taking this. I've watched guys like him get close to girls, they want to touch their hearts but only for it to end in unsatisfying pain.

"Hi, I'm Skylar, girl that regrets ever drawing you." I said, not taking his hand but going back to sketching instead. His eyebrows lifted; an electric shock hit the forest staring back at me.

"Ouch!" His voice was low letting his chin rest down on his hand with perplexed eyes. My phone went off again. His green eyes shot to it right away. Why wasn't he working on his project?

Dave: What is wrong with you? You wanted to get to know him!

I locked my phone back up. Jason cocked his head to the side. Why did he have to keep watching me? I started to feel uncomfortable.

"You must be mad with someone." He guessed, leaning closer to me on the table.

"Have you ever thought that it might be you?" I didn't give him eye contact, like he wanted.

"It can't be me; I haven't done anything wrong but if I have then I am truly sorry." He held his hand on his chest. I laughed some, without giving a smile. He was good that was for sure. My eyes rolled over to my phone thinking. I did have a crush on him. I smelt his cologne when a warm breeze came through the window, it captivated me into a whole different world. I didn't want to be manipulated by a man with a lot of money. I've seen relationships like this. Not to mention his status, what girl didn't want him? I wasn't his type.

"It was my boyfriend." I lied, blowing it off. His head turned the other way then. The look on his face was unreadable but it wasn't like I wanted to read that story anyway. Jason tapped his pencil on the table glancing back to my phone. His smile vanished as he watched his white paper that had the short lines of a tree outlined on it.

"He must be a real charmer." His voice was not enthused, as he got up from the table going over to sharpen his pencil. Why did he seem so let down? This weird pit formed inside my stomach because I was lying to him. I didn't have a boyfriend. Could he sense that? My eyes went down to the empty white paper, and I saw his backpack lying on the table across from me. I watched his body standing by the wall. His facial expression held a slight look of gloom. The green forest in his eyes was covered over in fog. The pit of regret started opening inside of me. Maybe I should listen to Dave. Hanging my head over the sketch of him; I knew getting involved would be dangerous.

I was walking home reminiscing about what happened only fifteen minutes ago. I wasn't sure what was happening, but I'd always imagined how cool it would be having friends that were famous. I let out a deep breath thinking about the way the conversation went. Was I too harsh with him? I wasn't even sure why I cared because I wasn't meant to get comfortable with anyone. I was worried about having to up and leave again. Complications stood in my way more than I'd like to admit. Always forcing people away that I grew to care about. This time it would be no different, so why did it feel so different?

"Are you crazy?" Dave came in beside me. I sighed watching my feet.

"Dave, I'm not like him." I said, knowing that was part of the problem.

"Like him? Why would he want somebody like him?" Dave sounded mad at me.

"I'm not some princess from Hollywood!" I pulled out my phone checking the time.

"By the way, we never agreed for me to be your boyfriend!" His voice had this odd pitch, moving his fingers between the two of us. A light smile creased his face forcing me to reflect one back. Dave was the closest friend I would ever walk this world with. The thought of us crossing the line to be girlfriend and boyfriend hit this boundary I wasn't comfortable with. If a fight broke out, well I knew I couldn't lose Dave.

"I needed some kind of alibi." I was ready to yell at him. His crystal blue eyes looked deep into mine but left just as fast. The light-hearted smile vanished.

"We've got company." He said, with the sound of a slow car creeping up behind us. Dave vanished as if he was never here. I looked over my shoulder seeing an old Mustang on the road. It was beautiful and candy red. I didn't know much about cars, but the body told me it was classic. Jason sat behind the wheel as he stopped, seeing that I saw him.

"Hey, you need a ride?" He asked as his body curved to the white leather seat he sat on; I laughed a little as I raised my eyebrow at him. His arm dangling carelessly over the steering wheel – was he trying to model for me?

"I'm almost home." I told him not just because I didn't want a ride from him but because I was almost home. My arm fell down after idiotically pointing to my house. Why did I do that? His smile stayed low; the more focusing I did, the more I noticed the small hairs poking out from his structured jawline. The goatee that was formed on his chin that I've only now noticed, I remembered Dave saying he was twenty. That did make me curious as to why he was in high school.

"Okay, just making sure." He smiled at me before taking off down the road. I sighed watching his pretty car drive off into the distance. Right behind him though was another car. This one was silver, and obviously brand new. It had to be right off the lot. The blonde that also happens to be his sister rolled up to the curb. The tinted window came down fast. Fury was in her eyes as she glared at me.

"I don't know what you think you're doing, but Jason is mine; let's get one thing straight here." She gave me that snobby snarl again.

"That's disgusting." I noted, walking down the street.

I took a turn going up to my house and her car took a turn into my driveway almost hitting me. My body tensed jumping backwards.

"Who do you think you are?" She got out of her car.

"I'm not sure who you think you are, but this is private property, now I suggest you get back in your shiny car and hit the road." I blurted out before thinking, not wanting to waste my time with her.

"You are such a cheap piece of trash, Jason is mine and you will not speak with him, get rides from him, or even share the same table with him at school, do you understand me?" She got right into my face. All I had to do was bring one hand up to smack the shit out of her, but I didn't. My hand gripped tight to the strap of my bag. I swallowed hard trying to remain calm even though anger was ramping up inside of my throat.

"And I believe Jason has his own right to be with who he wants, give rides to who he wants to, and even sit wherever he wants to. But if you're into having a crazy gross inbred relationship with your brother, be my guest and go right ahead, but just remember with a name like his, those tabloids will be snatching that story up left and right." I gave her the straight honest truth. With a wink of my eye, I walked away from her heading into my house.

"You might want to get off this property before I call the police." I noted through the crack of the front door. I was not about to let some rich bitch walk all over me. Who were they anyway? Who do they think they are?

The door shutting echoed through the living room from the force of me slamming it with anger. I shook my head sprinting up to my bedroom feeling mad and confused. Once I got through the door Dave sat there on my bed shaking his head. I dropped my bag plopping down beside him. Both of my hands were flat on my stomach while I gazed at the ceiling fan.

"Are you going to become friends with the enemy?" He asked, laying back on the pillows, with a mocking tone to his voice.

"Why would I want to be friends with that thing?" I wasn't following what he was saying.

"She is the sister of the young hot thing in Hollywood, Sweetheart." He smiled handing over a magazine with Jason's picture on it. I sighed, staring into his green eyes. That forest opened up once again. My eyes rolled, feeling something different inside to what I felt on the outside. The inside told me to get to know him while the outside wanted to shove him away. A war of emotions erupted within thirty-six hours of knowing Jason Blackstone.

"Why me? Why does Jason even live in Ohio?" I tossed the magazine down on the floor. I fell back on the bed pushing my hands through my hair.

"Because you're a beautiful, smart, lucky girl. Maybe he lives here to be away from the press." His fingers ran gently across my forehead as he guessed the answers to my questions.

"I am not lucky." I blurted out, knowing what it was I

was running from; the agonizing pain of never being able to settle down. My life felt like I was running through a maze; sometimes we were safe, but it would never last forever. Now I'm catching feelings for someone out of my league, while starting a Trojan war with his disgusting sister. Was I insane? What if he loved his sister in the same way? My stomach turned at the thought.

"Look if he wants to date you, I say you give it a shot, what do you have to lose?" Dave hovered over me and all I saw was his bright blue eyes. Dave's blonde, semi curly hair fell over one eye as he looked down at me.

"The respect for myself and getting caught up in a media rush. What about his sister, she will hate me more because she somehow loves him more?" I said knowing whoever was to date one of the hottest men in Hollywood would have to pay a price. I wasn't sure that life was fitting for someone like me. I remember days when I had wanted that life but right now my life is hell and needs to settle down. I would love to just have my last couple of years at high school spent not living in fear. Not sure if my dad would return to my life or not. I wanted to be alive for my graduation, for my dreams to come true, to get married, to have kids, to be happy. I could not obtain those dreams when everyday my life hung in the balance.

"So, you are stereotyping a famous guy? Also, when did you start caring if another girl hates you?" Dave sat up laughing a little. I narrowed my eyes while trying to figure out so many of the things going through my head.

"I just don't want any more trouble than what I've already got." I crossed my arms walking over to my window. I looked out onto the street of an unfamiliar neighborhood. I wasn't sure I could ever call this home. I just wanted to go back to Miami and stop all this moving. I heard typing over my shoulder, I saw Dave on my laptop. What was he doing? His ocean blue eyes came up to meet mine, smiling even more. He swung the computer around showing me search results. Jason was on the computer screen. I glared at Dave, but he just smiled, almost laughing. Why was he pushing this? I walked over to the bed closing the laptop.

"Oh, c'mon you know you want to know more." His voice was teasing. I grunted not wanting to put up with this. I also knew that journalists liked to embellish things, to make stories sound more appetizing. I never was the fish to grab all the bait that was thrown my way.

"It doesn't matter Dave; he's not going to lower himself to someone like me." This was getting frustrating at this point.

"I don't know he *seemed* worried if you could make it home or not." Dave had this singing tone to his voice. I rolled my eyes once more walking out of my bedroom. I headed down the stairs wondering where my mom was. I entered the kitchen pulling food out of the fridge. Dave flashed in beside me sitting on the counter. He held a plate out for me. I took it putting my food on the plate before heating it.

"And yet his disgusting sister had to follow behind him." I pulled my hair up into a ponytail, continuing this obnoxious conversation. Dave laughed holding a bag of Cheetos.

"Well, I mean being mixed up with an incestuous family sounds like a thrilling ride." Dave laughed eating the Cheetos. My eyebrows came down, watching him before taking the Cheetos out of his hands. He made a sloppy sound sucking each finger that was coated in orange cheesy dust.

"You don't have to eat, so don't waste our food." I told him, closing the bag back up. I knew the dead did not have to eat. I was speechless just knowing he could.

"Hey, I like to be treated as a normal citizen too." He exclaimed, watching as I put the snacks away. Before I could turn back around Dave was on my phone doing something.

"Hey!" I shouted snatching it back from him. I looked down seeing Jason's picture once again on my phone. I sighed glaring at Dave. My hand rested on my hip taking an irritated deep breath.

"Just read it." He begged wanting me to be interested in this. As my eyes scanned the short bio of him, I learnt that he had several awards for his movie roles. I scanned through his personal bio seeing that his old girlfriend was Sarah, a model. His sister was listed on here, her name was Abigail. His dad was listed as his manager alongside a woman named Emma. There was a picture showing young Jason with a woman with short brown hair. It was a very brief bio of his personal life. I scrolled a little more seeing the list of movies he was in, but before I could look any further a text popped up on my screen.

Missy: Hey I saw you walking home, we live really close to each other!

Skylar: What? That's crazy!

Missy: I know I'm coming over!

I paused not texting back. I wasn't sure I was up for company. The doorbell rang and Dave smiled at me fading out of the room. I walked into the living room hating people just showing up at my house. I opened the door seeing Missy standing before me looking rather excited. Her eyes were glowing with happiness. She was holding magazines as she came into the house. Her red hair cascading down over her shoulders and touching the waistline of her white tank top that had a neon purple heart with a neon red arrow darting through it.

"We have to get up on our prom shopping!" She tossed the magazines down on the coffee table. My eyebrows went up, not even thinking about prom. My eyes then lowered, feeling like that wasn't such a good idea. I shook my head not wanting to tell her the bad news that I wouldn't be going to prom. She was just so excited. Why did I always have to be the buzz kill?

"Missy, I don't think it's a good idea for me to go to prom." I played nervously with my nails hoping she would be cool with that. Instead, she gave me a crazy look. She then tilted her head looking suspicious of something. She sat down on the couch, and I swallowed hard not knowing what was going through her head.

"You're eighteen but you're not graduating this year, why is that?" She sounded confused and my palms were becoming sweaty. Why was she asking me these questions? I couldn't be thorough enough to tell her I missed almost a whole year of school because I was running from my dad. She wouldn't want anything to do with me if she knew my horrifying past and why I'm here right now. Then again it might be best if I don't have any friends that he could hurt. I cleared my throat seeing the model on the magazine before us. Her light blue gown was flowing down the front with sparkling jewels popping out. A heavy storm cloud covered my brain, remembering how my sophomore school year went, I was never there because of my dad starting this tyrant of abuse. I went to school one day last year, then three almost four months missed this year. My timeline was so fucked up, I couldn't even explain it.

"You know maybe prom isn't such a bad idea." I confessed, tucking my hair behind one ear picking the magazine up. While my mind shifted through this mess of understanding, my eyes searched over the magazines she had brought over. I had to remain normal.

"Yes, there is a pink gown in here that I am excited about looking at!" She said flipping through to the page she had marked. I laughed watching as she pointed it out.

It was half dress and half sheer fabric trailing down the legs of the model. I tilted my head looking at Missy.

"I don't think the pink dress would fit with your fire red hair." I protested, laughing and pulling her wavy hair up. Missy's eyes narrowed glaring at her own hair. She sighed sitting back on the couch flipping through once more. I was just happy her suspicions of me had eased.

"So, I was thinking we could go together since you're new and I don't like any of the guys in our school." She looked over to me hoping I would be her friend date. I smiled not knowing what to say. I was worried that only bad things would happen. I also had a fear of leaving my mom by herself – what if Dad was to return? My body shook thinking about our past. Why was it becoming so hard for me to make decisions? I just wanted to tell everyone my secret but there was no way I could do that. I glanced back down to a glamorous black gown a girl wore. I would give anything to have a normal life. Missy jumped up from the couch then, swinging her keys around one finger. She laughed pulling me up off the couch too.

"Let's go to the mall!" She was smiling from ear to ear with a spark in her eyes. I never went to the mall on a weekday. Although, I didn't get a say as she dragged me to the door. I grabbed my purse and locked the house up in a hurry. She was thrilled that she had someone to go dress shopping with even though I'd never agreed to this. As she whisked me into her car, I watched our new home. It was no longer soulless. All I could wish for, was it not to end up broken. Licking my lips watching the house leave me in the distance, I stayed hopeful that my mom was alright.

Chapter 3
Who Are They?

Missy and I walked into the lunchroom at the same time. We smiled at each other as I walked over to join her. The line of kids wasn't too long yet, but all you could watch was the obnoxious boys throwing stuff at each other. All the dirty jokes being told, who's going to prom with whom, the party this weekend and so on. My own thoughts drifted back to yesterday. We hadn't found the "it" dress for prom yet.

"How did class go with the stud?" Missy asked, laughing a little. I just smirked not sure where anyone's thoughts on this were going. Dave wants the hook up to happen, and now Missy. I haven't been in this school for a whole week yet and I'm already getting set up with a movie star. Was I the only one who wasn't delusional here?

"Why would it matter?" I grabbed a tray of food moving through the line.

"Um, *hello* do you not know who sits in your class every day?" Missy grabbed an apple out of the tray. Why was everyone so overdramatic about Jason Blackstone?

It was kind of annoying.

"He's overrated." I mumbled, punching in my number code to get my food. We walked out from the line over to the table that we now call 'ours'. We both sat down, and Jason came walking into the cafeteria with his friends. Missy's eyes shot to them like a deer hunter finding her prey. I shook my head trying the mystery food. I believed it was some sort of Mexican pizza.

"That is not overrated." Missy finally turned her attention back to me.

"Why don't you go try to hook up with him?" I was getting tired of this real fast.

"Because I'm not his type." She gave me this look like I was crazy.

"And I am?" I shook my head once more looking back over to their table. I watched his friends laugh. They had that edgy style that would catch any girl's eye. It was mix between Hot Topic edge with an added skater boy style. It was clear that the school idolized them, just from seeing all the popular people who were hanging around their table. My attention was scattered throughout the cafeteria like a deck of cards, I couldn't help but notice that 80% of girls were watching, or at least occasionally glancing at, their table.

"So, who are they?" I questioned her, guessing she would know. She giggled a little while inching her chair closer to me.

"Okay. Well for starters that one across the table from

Jason with the small Mohawk, that would be Mick, then there is the one with the leather jacket, that's Tom, then spiky hair over there is Tim, then there is his best friend with the tattoo's, that's Robby and then there is–" She cut off. I swung back around seeing Jason was no longer at the table. I swung back around in my chair and right then a warm hand came down on my shoulder. Missy gasped with her eyes as big as quarters.

"Hey, Skylar." Jason sat down beside me. His sweet wood-like smell went up my nose. I licked my lips staring down into my food. What was I going to say to him? My heart was racing while my palms turned sweaty. I felt some sort of anxiety kicking in. My stomach started to turn like I was getting ready to do something extreme. I swallowed trying to wrap my head around what was happening. Then again, why was I caring?

"Well, this is awkward!" Missy sipped on her milk. I cleared my throat peering over to her. She gave me that tiny head nudge telling me to talk to him. I watched Jason out of the corner of my eye.

"How are you guys?" Jason asked keeping his focus on me.

"I'm doing great!" Missy was fast to answer. I felt Jason's eyes on me though. I pulled my bottom lip into my mouth not saying a word.

"And you?" His arm came down on the back of my chair. I nodded my head needing to pull myself together.

"Probably better than you." I said, glancing up at

him. His lower lip stuck out slightly. I just watched his beautiful green eyes. Why did I keep losing myself in them? They were so pretty, and his smell was just amazing. His scent, so delightful compared to all these teenage boys who spent way too much time in the gym. The closer I was to him, the more I noticed his maturity. His eyes weren't young with stupidity but were also not too old that he was wise about everything in life. His facial hair was more defined from him shaving more frequently than most of the boys around us. His jawline was more structured along with the rest of his mild, masculine body. His gray shirt was mid-way formed to his body before going into a V-neck with just a hint of hair coming from his chest.

"You're probably right about that." His brows flexed up. I watched his smooth pink lips move. What if I was kissing those right now? *No! What am I thinking?* I looked back over to Missy, and she had the slight look of confusion on her face. She wasn't sure why I was always rejecting him. The thing is, I wasn't sure either. What if this guy was really into me? I can't have him risk his life just for one date.

The sound of clicking shoes on the floor broke my stare from his body. Jason's head snapped away from me and a plunging feeling drifted to my stomach. My butterflies soon turned to terror. I already knew who it was. I saw her pink heels sparkle. Before anything was said my chair was ripped around forcing me to face her.

The whole cafeteria turned silent. The pit in my stomach told me I was in danger. Her blonde hair came tumbling down over her shoulders. She was mad at me, and I knew why but I didn't choose this.

"I told you once, must I really tell you twice?" She got down in my face. I tensed not ready to be whipped around to face this. My heart was beating faster than when Jason sat down.

"Abby." Jason's voice turned stern. I never looked over to him as her light green eyes stayed on me like I was her lunch. She was not about to be the lion though.

"Listen you little tramp, no one is to be with my little brother and when I say no one that means not some trashy little slut without money, without being a model–"

"Abby, shut up!" Jason stood up, backing her away from me. My eyes were wide open, heart still racing. "You do not ever talk to her like that ever again. She is not some piece of trash, and I will continue sitting with her as long as I want to, and you will not have any say in this!" His voice was low yet furious. I gasped at the protection he shielded me with. This warm feeling spiraled in my heart. Intense passion flowed into my stomach. He just stood up for me.

"Is there a problem over here?" The principle cut in making my eyes blink fast. Water coated them like rain. I realized I was staring at Jason, eyes wide open from the sting of tears. My heart was still racing down the rollercoaster tracks as I put my attention back on Jason.

He shook his head making his green eyes escape behind his eyelids.

"No Mr. Blake, everything's just fine." Jason's voice was soft as his green eyes revealed themselves. The principle nodded his head then looked back over to Jason's sister.

"Is everything alright with you Abigale?" He questioned her now. That warm fuzzy feeling left my stomach when she answered him.

"No, Mr. Blake, we are going to need to have a talk in your office." She told him, with her sharp eyes cutting through me like daggers. I swallowed hard, not sure what her intentions with me were. She had it out for me, and I knew why. She was protecting her little brother from any girl that could stand in his way. I knew becoming anything with him was never possible. His family was an army, there to guard his worth.

Jason

"Jason, we need to talk about what happened today in school." Dad's voice made me want to leave. Abby was trying to ruin my life. It was daunting that she was succeeding. My hand ran down over my face not believing that she had the principle call our dad. This was outrageous. I just wanted a normal life, to have normal feelings for someone. I wished for nothing more than to belong but that felt distant.

"Dad, really this is no big deal." I pushed my hand down the back of my hair. I still couldn't stop thinking about her. She was beautiful and her smile made me feel whole. When I watched her brown eyes, it was like I was seeing her for the first time every time I looked into them.

"So, your career is just no big deal anymore?" He was frustrated with me. I rolled my eyes wishing he understood. Somewhere, sometime ago he would have understood me.

"That's not what I am saying, Dad this has nothing to do with my career!" I felt the need to yell at him; to make him understand. He just tossed down the piece of paper he was looking at and shook his head in disapproval.

"Maybe your high school life is too important to you, maybe it was a bad idea ever sending you back to normal school." He couldn't stop shaking his head. I felt like the biggest disappointment there could be even though I have done nothing wrong. Every word he spoke made me feel like the enemy, while I was the innocent one.

"No, the bad idea was letting you play such a big part in my life and my career because I don't need you to stand here and make my choices for me, I'm old enough to move out on my own and I'm realizing what a fool I am for staying here, listening to you. I'm twenty years old I shouldn't even still be in high school, but you always made me take these roles. Now I'm behind in my own normal life because of you!" I walked out of the kitchen feeling guilt form in my stomach but also this rush of love in my heart. I haven't dated a girl since my freshman year, and then I didn't even have a freshmen year. I just wanted a real life again. There was never a thought in my dad's head that I might be embarrassed to be back in school at twenty-years old, there had been other options that would've helped me get my diploma, like home schooling. Now frustration was radiating within me at the mere thought of spending more time with the man who was so strict about everything being nothing more than business.

Skylar

"Skylar, come down here Honey!" Mom yelled from downstairs. Dave and I watched each other. I slid off my bed with a cold hand touching my shoulder.

"It's about what happened today at lunch." He informed me. That crazy warm feeling ran back through my heart. All I was thinking about was Jason now. As much as I didn't want to be with some rich jerk, he just kept giving me this warm feeling in my heart. I nodded my head standing up.

"Be right back." I left the room, already running through everything my mom was about to say to me. I knew the questions that would be asked. Are you dating someone? What's his name? Why did you get in trouble with his sister? Is he cute? The list could go on and on. That annoying, slightly nervous moment of not knowing still hit me though. I got down to the kitchen and saw her leaning on the island. I closed my eyes for a brief moment and walked into the kitchen. She looked up at me from her cell phone. I already knew what happened. She smiled at me waiting until I was on the other side of the island. *Alright, brace for impact*, I thought.

"Your principle just called me, Sweetie; we need to talk." She said, but she didn't seem mad, nor did it seem questioning.

"Is this about what happened earlier?" I was a little confused.

"Yes, you and this Abigale girl, did you almost get into a fight today?" She stood up from her leaning position. My eyes rolled to the side.

"I didn't really get into a fight, she kind of attacked me in a verbal way." I tried to explain, but I wasn't really sure how to. She was just some rich kid trying to protect her brother and I realized that now.

"I see, and she has a brother named Jason which we need to talk about as well." She seemed to get a little unsteady then.

"Mom, Jason is a different story I'm not dating him, and his sister is trying to protect him for god knows what reason." I said, shaking my head. She narrowed her eyes just a tad.

"Well from what I understand you and Jason have something going on and there is a reason she is trying to protect him." Mom now knew more than I did.

"Why does she want to protect him?" That was the mystery I wanted to uncover. His fortune and fame could be the only explanation, couldn't it?

"Honey, we both know Jason isn't like you and me, he's got a big name and big shoes to fulfil, and his father doesn't want him with anyone right now." She colored the picture and I understood it all now. The protecting him was everything I'd already thought. I knew I would never ever be a part of that life just because of that. He was being caged inside a child stars lifestyle. I had nothing more to say because I felt a little sick now. I've seen how childhood stars turn out; Jason didn't seem quite as hell bent though.

"I'm not up to those standards either. I just want to make something clear; Jason is the one who talked to me first." I wanted her to know my side. Mom laughed a little watching me close.

"Sweetie, it is perfectly fine if you have a crush on the actor. That's only normal but I'm not sure being around him is good for publicity reasons." She said, also wanting me to stay away from him. This burning pit of fire came up inside of me. What if he wanted to be with me but his image was holding him back? This sadness washed over me thinking about how I wasn't good enough.

"All that matters is his image then, right?" My lowered voice spoke my emotions as I walked out of the room.

"I never said you weren't beautiful enough because I

know you are!" Mom yelled after me, but I just walked back up to my room. Who was I fooling? I was just an average girl with brown hair who got my clothes from normal stores at the mall. I wasn't the skinniest girl to walk pass in the hall nor did I have handfuls of friends to party with every weekend. I was just me, Skylar Saxton. The girl running with a heart full of fear across states from her mental, aggressive father. I couldn't imagine my face being spread on headlines beside Jason's name. I would do more than tarnish his name, no one would hire him for movies because of him being involved with a girl who has a father that wants her blood on his hands. My stomach turned even more as I collapsed on the bed. My head spun round and round. Jason was in every thought even when a nightmare sparked with the glow of my father's face.

CHAPTER 4
Silence

It was Friday and every class I sat in seemed empty. For the last two days Jason has been gone from school. I have no idea why; I imagined that it has something to do with his famous lifestyle. The more awkward part was Wednesday when he didn't say a single word to me. He didn't even look at me in any of the classes we had together. Then when it came to lunchtime that day it was just Missy and I. He sat at the table with his friends. Everything has already changed in such a short matter of time. All the enthusiasm Dave and Missy had for the hopes of my future with Jason started sinking. Everyone was blunt when telling me to stay away from him. That left the wildest thoughts of what it was he was told to do. What if it was so extreme that he moved schools? It dawned on me then that it was possible, he would just quit school because in all truth, he did not need it. He had enough money to set up the rest of his life. With his family playing such a huge part in his career, that did lead me to believe he wasn't completely in control of his money. I couldn't imagine a life where I was so popular that everyone wanted pictures of me, producers wanted me for a movie or a quick cameo, magazine's wanting to spread my face and body over the front covers, then letting it all crash down for family members to tell you how high you must jump before receiving everything you've worked for. My mind dabbled back to his small bio I'd read yesterday. He was from Dayton, Ohio which made my curiosity peak, and wonder how he became famous.

I twisted my head over my shoulder looking back at the table he sat at. As if I would see him sitting there with his friends laughing. All I saw were his friends then Abby and her friends. My eyes fell away from their table. There was no use wondering where he was or even caring, for the most part of it. Getting my hopes up is a stupid thing to do, I've learned that much over the last year. Trusting people has become a funny action for me. You think you know someone and the next thing you know they are trying to slice your throat open. It doesn't matter how long you know someone because in the end they will always end up leaving, betraying, or hurting you. The ocean became shallower the older I got. It was like standing on one rock watching the water drain away. It made me feel safe, not trusting others, and yet it also made me feel like I was very much alone. The only person I could trust was my mom. Dave is like a knight to me that I still question my own sanity over; I know I'm physically talking to a dead man. Millions of times the thoughts provoked my brain into the scenario of explaining to someone that I see dead people. Even though Dave was just one person. Fact was, even Missy was a person I wasn't sure I could trust. Letting, Jason into my life with his status was a bigger danger than letting Missy walk through my front door.

"Okay, something is up with you and Jason!" Missy's voice broke my thoughts and I blinked away from the floor that I was staring at. I looked back to her shaking my head.

"Nah, not in a lifetime." I felt this awful pain of regret for saying that. It was true though, I wasn't a part of him, and he wasn't about to be a part of me.

"Then how come all week you have been silent and staring at their table like you want to go over there and start making out with the dude?" She lifted her eyebrows, but the bell rang. We both stood up, yet I still had nothing to say. I glanced back to his empty chair one more time. It was true, when we were close that day, I had thought about kissing him. When he stood up for me in this very spot, he made a warmth flood my body but that was nothing more than teenage crush feelings.

"I'm far from wanting to make out with him." That was nothing more than a joke.

"You wanna hang out later?" She laughed swinging her bag over her shoulder.

"Maybe, I'll text you." I said, leaving the cafeteria and walking the other way. I stepped into the hallway, where I knew Dave was waiting for me; his blue aura covered over me like a cape. I smiled to myself as I turned cold. Dave was my safe haven that I could always escape to.

"Good to see a smile again." He winked back, and I watched his crystal blue eyes. A chuckle came out, watching him standing beside me. I walked down to my next class not saying a word. I just sat in art class thinking and wondering what was going to happen next. There would be no more drawings of Jason. Why was I still thinking about him? Why do his beautiful green eyes keep haunting me? Why can't I just let him go? I felt anger rush through my body making me want to scream. My hand curled up into a fist spiraling down hitting the table. Mrs. King looked over to me, but I did not want her attention. She would realize I wasn't doing my work. I didn't want to sketch; I just wanted to stop thinking. I needed a way out from Jason's hold on me. I would not let some rich, cute, handsome man control my thoughts, feelings, and actions. Bitterness fogged my thoughts, noticing that it was too late for that. He was controlling my feelings, thoughts, and actions. Missy was right. I've been the weird, out of place one all week. Not Jason, he was just being Jason. His absence caused this control over me. What kind of sickness was I becoming ill with?

My phone went off on the table snapping my thoughts away. I tilted my head not sure of the number. I unlocked my phone seeing a short and terrifying message. A knot formed in my stomach feeling the panic rise. My heart thumped skipping a beat seeing the jarring message with a haunting cute name from my childhood.

Unknown: Hey pumpkin, your mom won't let me speak with you. I know you're in school right now, but we must talk as soon as possible.

My hand started to shake staring at the text message. It didn't have to have a name for me to know who this was. I had a sick feeling in my stomach right then. How did he get my number? My mind was twisting around and running a hundred miles an hour now. I shook my head feeling scared. My heart and mind hit the tree in the middle of the road throwing Jason right out from my thoughts, replacing him with the man who scarred me with terror. I swallowed hard feeling nauseous. I had to get out of here. Where was my mom? What if he had her?

Skylar: How did you get this number?

Fingers shaking over the keys, I watched as the message sent. I felt sick. I wanted to go home and run for my life. This was the very reason I had to stay disconnected from everyone at all costs. I couldn't put anyone else's life in jeopardy because of me. I had to stop being friends with Missy and by all costs I had to stop talking to Jason which was becoming easier by the day.

School ended and I walked out feeling disoriented. Dave stood there waiting for me, but I said nothing walking right past him. I got a text back, but I have yet to get the courage to open it. It was taking all I had not to be sick right here. The wind blew through my hair, but I felt a million miles away. It was almost like the world wasn't even moving around me anymore. I felt my life slipping through my fingers yet again. My vision slipping with anxiety wrapping me in its tight hold.

"Hey-hey what's wrong, you don't look good?" Dave was at my side in a flash. I just kept looking forward, walking along the sidewalk away from the school. I listened as my phone went off again. I could not answer him. Dave flashed in front of me, and his cold hands rested on my shoulders. I blinked looking into his blue crystal eyes. I started crying, feeling scared. I didn't want to run anymore. I wanted to come out of hiding as much as I could. All the will power inside of me crashed as I emotionally broke down.

"Skylar, I need you to tell me what is happening." Dave gave me an order and I nodded my head. I couldn't speak though. I pulled out my phone opening it up. I stopped walking staring at the unknown name through tear-filled eyes.

Unknown: I have my ways just remember you can't keep hiding from me.

Unknown: I will be there every step you make, every breath you take, and every moment you lie awake.

My whole body shook. I cried harder falling into

Dave. He held me tightly and moved his cold hand down my hair. I felt his cold head resting down on mine. I felt no heartbeat against my body, just coldness. His body was formed into thickness as if he was still in his human shell, yet his fog continued coating me. I didn't care though, I was mortified. I just wanted it to stop. Dave pulled me back staring right into my eyes. I shivered sliding my phone into my pocket. My senses started kicking in realizing he could be right here. He could be watching me at any moment, right now. What if he is watching me crying on Dave's shoulder? My heart started racing as my conscious gave me instincts to be alert to my surroundings. I saw no car, no sign of him. He's good at hiding though.

"Dave, we need to go." I said, running around him. There was no time to walk. I raced down the sidewalk away from the school. I was alone besides the fact Dave was nearby, and I ran as fast as I could in order to get back home. As I turned the corner to my street, I unhooked my keys from my bag; from this distance I could see that mom's white Focus was gone. I was breathing quickly as I rushed to my front door. Once I was inside Dave was waiting for me, as I knew he would be.

"Any given moment would be nice to tell me what is going on!" He said while I locked the door behind me. I turned around and he grabbed hold of me.

"Skylar, take a deep breath and either you let me see what was on that phone or you tell me now!" His blue eyes were wide and impatient. While my mind was going faster than I could even try to speak I took a deep breath in, pushed my hair back and nodded my head. I had to assure myself that as long as Dave was here, I was safe. Dave came to me after the night of my dad beating my mom for the first time. He said he would always protect me, that it was his job as an earthbound spirit. At this point I would not question it. He has always been loyal on his words to me. Dave has helped us escape from my father before by giving us get away plans. Dave saw the world differently now; his brain could navigate us in the right direction.

"He's back Dave!" The thought left my insides shivering. I went over plopping down on the couch. My face went down in both my hands.

"You're not talking about Jason, are you?" His voice was low, thinking. Both my hands pushed back through my hair.

"No! That monster is back, and he won't leave!" I yelled getting back up, feeling tears welling up in my eyes. I had to call my mom. She needs to be safe. *We* need to be safe. I whipped my phone back out of my pocket. Dave left my side right then and I went running to the window to see if my mom was home. There was no car in the drive. The car I heard was just passing down the street. My hand shook as I held my phone up to my ear. *Answer! Answer* was all I could think. My inner voice kept screaming at me to get out, pack my bags.

Dave flashed back to my side nodding his head.

"The house is clear." He confirmed, darting his eyes around us. A small fragment of my attention noticed his glowing blue eyes were different. Darker cracks of blue ran through his irises. It was like mini rivers breaking through the chilled ice. I hung up the phone after my mom didn't answer.

"Dave, she didn't answer, what if he already has her? What if she's locked up somewhere right now? What if he's trying to kill her again?" The more I thought, the more lightheaded I was feeling. Dave sat me back down on the couch shaking his head.

"Listen to me Sky, she is not in danger." He said waving his hand. My eyes went back and forth from the front door to him.

"How would you know that? You have been here with me this whole time." I exclaimed, getting back up from the couch. I called my mom back again planning on leaving a voicemail. I walked over to the window looking for any sign of Richards black car. I had to stop thinking of him as Dad. Even if I said he wasn't my dad aloud my thoughts still autocorrected me.

"Hi, you have reached Kate; sorry I could not get to your call please leave a message and I'll try to get back." After I heard my mom's voicemail, I closed my eyes. I pushed my hand back through my hair again waiting for that annoying beep, Dave came up behind me.

"Hey mom, it's me, you need to come home as soon

as you get this call. I don't care where you are we are in great danger again, please text me when you get this message, I love you, bye." I hung up the phone turning around in his arms, I embraced his coldness. I took in his cool air and his misty scents. I left Dave's arms needing to calm down. I could never calm down, not under this pressure. I thought of something then. I lifted my phone back up calling Joey.

"Hey girly, what's up?" He answered quick and cheerful.

"Joey, I need you to do something very important for me." I said, playing with my necklace.

"Anything, whatcha need?" He sounded very excited to help. Was this the right decision to make? Should I be letting my friend play gofer for me? Joey was my only resource in Florida.

"You remember where I used to live?" I bit down on my lower lip feeling my pulse increase like something bad was about to happen.

"Duh, of course I could never forget." He laughed like this was a joke. If Joey knew he wouldn't be talking with ease.

"Okay, I need you to drive by my old place for me and text me if there is anything left in the drive or anyone living there." I ordered him now. This was not the best thing to be doing – letting my close friend do some dirty work for me but he still lived down there. This was how I'll know if my monster of a father is here watching me or just trying to scare me. He could be searching in the wrong places which would give us time.

"Um, alright yeah sure but can I ask why?" He no longer sounded joyous. Dave tilted his head and then gave me a smile.

"My mom wants to know for some reason to do with selling it or something." I lied; Joey has never known the real story behind why I left. No one does, no one will. The truth was, that house still belonged to Richard.

"Okay, well I'll get back to you after I've been there. I'm moving by the way!" He sounded so excited, but I just felt guilty for making him do this. Just as I was ready to congratulate him on the move and get ready to hang up, I noticed that my mom was calling through on the other line. It was clear that she would be in a panic, but I sighed relieved to know she was okay. So, I told Joey I needed to answer a call on the other line, before answering my mom.

"Hello." I said, and her voice was in my ear in no time.

"Skylar, what do you mean we are in great danger? Is he back?" Her voice was in panic. I swallowed hard, not wanting to believe it. I was more relaxed now, hearing that she was fine.

"He texted me Mom, I'm not sure where he is." I told her, pacing back and forth in front of Dave. He just waited quietly, keeping his eyes on me.

"How did he even get your number? We changed

them!" She almost yelled in fear.

"I don't know, I'm just scared." I admitted, but it was okay, for now.

"I know hun, me too, listen I will be home soon just lock up all the doors and windows, we will call the police once I get there." She gave me the road to walk down. I had answers for a little bit but after that they would all change again.

"I already have Mom!" Dave left my side to go take care of the windows.

"Okay, stay safe, keep your phone on you and I will be home soon, I love you." She said, going to leave me on my own. I felt scared to be on my own. I was shocked she wasn't rushing to get back here. She wanted to stay calm for me, she always acted this way before our lives tilted sideways.

"I love you too." I said, hanging up the phone. Dave was back within seconds. He took my phone from my hand then. My eyes grew bigger as he started going through it. What was he doing? Curious I watched his blue eyes scan the screen fast like it was giving him some kind of guidance.

"Dave, what are you doing?" I was lost. He grinned turning the phone around to face me. I saw Richard's name was blocked but I wasn't following. I lifted my shoulder up clueless. Dave's fingers glided across my phone unlocking something. He faced the phone back to me.

"Don't you see the number?" He pointed to the phone. I looked back at it, but I still wasn't catching on.

"Dave, just explain it." I begged, giving up sooner than normal.

"Sky, look the area code is the same as yours and your mom's!" His blue eyes widened, and my heart stopped beating – dropping to the darkest pit. I sat back down on the couch, understanding it all now. He was here. I had no idea where, but he was watching and now I felt sicker than ever. How were we going to get out of this mess? If we call the cops, then he will just run and hide like he did the last time. He was so good at getting away. His cards were always played best at lying his way out of things and manipulating people to believe his words. God knows he got my mom to believe and trust him. It hasn't even been that long since the nightmare happened. The second time he showed up he almost stabbed my mom, the third time before now, he only broke our window but his face in the cool dusk of the morning was painted in my memories. A cold sweat itched my body like aches, but instead they were fear. The sweat from my palms mixing with the trembling made my phone bounce to the floor, out of my hold.

My phone went off laying below me showing it was Joey, rolling my eyes and feeling bad for wasting his time. I opened up the message and was surprised to read what he had to say.

Joey: Hey girly so yeah there is someone here at

the house, it looks like some lady, did your mom sell the house already?

I Just stared at the message not sure what to think of this one. My hand ran down over my mouth having a good idea what he might be doing though. Dave looked over my shoulder at the message.

“Oh, he’s good.” Dave whispered, making me look up to him.

“You’re thinking what I’m thinking?” I coaxed, knowing he already had the same thoughts.

“He set it up to make it look like someone was still living there.” Dave said the words that were going through my head. Right then the door opened, and Dave was gone. When Mom walked through the door, I was so relieved. Her shoulders slumped down seeing that I was still alright. She let her purse drop to the floor as she came over to me on the couch right away.

“Honey, you must be so scared. I’m glad you are alright.” Her voice was still shaky, while her hand ran down the side of my face. My arms wrapped around her. We hugged each other tightly.

“Mom, when will this end?” I almost cried again, just wanting this madness to be over. I’m afraid it never will be.

“When the right kind of justice gets served.” Her voice had an edge now and we both moved away from each other. I had to get my mind right about this. We had to figure out why there was a lady in our old home. I had to tell Joey to get out of there before something might happen to him. Both my hands went back through my hair taking a deep breath in. I was swift to text Joey back thanking him and letting him know I no longer needed him to investigate. I lied and explained it was a realtor my mom had hired to sell the house. How was I going to explain to Mom a mysterious lady was on our property? She would more than freak out. There was already so much weighing on us, that the conversation about our house might cause more harm. I had to let her know, just not yet.

The bigger question in my own thoughts, my reason for investigating, was why Richard would plant a fake person living there. Did he think it would be too suspicious if we just up and moved leaving the house empty? Was he scared of something leading back to him? Could it be possible this woman was doing more than just living in our home? I should have asked Joey for a description of the woman but that would have led to me needing to explain more. In all the hopes I had, I just wished for Joey not to be watching the house now. He was always into crime dramas, which intrigued him for his own investigations. This was no fictional show, it was real life, and I couldn't live with myself if he became the victim.

Chapter 5
Surprise

It was ten o'clock at night, I sat on the couch. Mom was anxious, rushing to the window to look for Dad every other minute. There was no sign of him. He was off work by now, he always was. Each night it was taking him longer to get home. Mom always worried but I thought it would get to the point that she would realize Dad was having an affair. I didn't know that for sure, but it seemed like the most legitimate thing that could be happening. My mom loved my dad and I believed he loved her back. As time passed, I haven't been so sure though. I walked up to my bedroom getting tired of waiting with her. She was just going to keep waiting, panicking, and worrying. I pulled out my phone to text my dad. He had to tell her he didn't want to be with her anymore. Mom didn't need this kind of pressure. I couldn't watch my mom like this.

Skylar: Dad I know what you are doing but I don't think you realize what you have been doing to Mom, please just tell her the truth.

Moments after I sent the message, I heard the shrillest

scream. Glass was breaking alongside the sounds of my mom's terror. It was like the brilliant sound from the horror movies. I rushed up from my bed running into the hallway. I could feel the power of my mom's scream echoing through my body. I blinked fast, thinking what could be happening. I ran back into my room looking for a blunt object. I found nothing and my mom screamed out again, but this time it was pain instead of fear.

"Get away from me!" She yelled making me turn around, running downstairs. I was unarmed but I didn't care. I went flying into the kitchen and there he was. Dad had Mom pinned to his chest with his arms wrapped around her neck. My mom's face was solid red. My eyes opened wide, having no idea what he was doing. Frozen like a deer in headlights, I couldn't move.

"Da-Da-Dad, stop!" I stammered yelling at him and running over to my mom. She gave me a panicked look. She needed help. Her lips clapped open and closed like a fish out of water. Dad's big hand cuffed over her mouth like a blind going shut.

"Sky, go get my phone!" Mom yelled, out of breath, trying to get past the pressure he was forcing on her throat. Tears were gathering in her eyes. My hands went down to his wrist trying to pull his arm off her throat.

"Dad, what the hell are you doing?" I was freaking out. Mom screamed again, gasping for air.

I came up from the bed fast. My eyes were wide open, my body in a cold sweat. This ringing went from one ear to the next. I haven't had a nightmare about my dad in four months. My legs felt numb, shocked from the nightmare. Tears started streaming down my face and I swallowed in fear. I went down face first into the pillow just wanting out of this horror. I didn't want to remember what he did to my mom, what he did to me. It was horrible and just to think, he's still out there somewhere, watching, waiting. I cried all the more wanting it all just to disappear. The nightmares always relapsed to the second time he hurt my mom, but never the first. When I saw her suffocating in his big hands at our apartment in Colorado, it had scarred me. It replayed in my memories so vividly. I would never forget the first fight, the echoes of his beefy hand slapping her across the face, it made the hair on my arms stand on end. That first hit was what started it all, but the second attack was the most violent.

I got up going into the bathroom. With my brain running in circles, I had to get up and shake the violent past off. I looked at myself in the mirror running my fingertips down my cheek. I felt his hand striking my face all over again. I closed my eyes feeling weak inside. The scarring memories will never leave me, and neither will he. There has to be some type of justice in this world. As my hand fell away from the cheek that once was bruised, Dave floated behind me.

"Sky, you have a surprise waiting for you." His blue eyes sparked with joy.

"Dave!" I yelled pulling my shirt down over my

underwear. He smiled winking at me. He faded away leaving his blue fog behind. It kissed my bare skin leaving more goosebumps than what I already had. The doorbell went off and that was my 'surprise'. I rolled my eyes, hoping it wasn't my unfaithful father that wants to kill his family. Then again if it was, Dave would have given me a different signal besides a wink. I halted then, feeling dazed. I could've sworn it was still nighttime. I shot my eyes over to the curtain at the bathroom window seeing the sun illuminating behind it. What time was it? What day was it? Am I slipping away, turning into a crazy person? My mental status started to tumble in my own head now, leaving me frightened for a whole new reason.

I walked back into my bedroom getting a pair of shorts and pulling them on. The doorbell went off again. I sighed in frustration. *Who could be at my door?* Rushing out of my bedroom and heading down the stairs, I pulled my hair back, quickly twisting it around one shoulder. I got to the door and slipped my key in. Once I opened it my heart raced with shock. My mouth dropped open as a bouquet of mixed flowers was handed to me. The white, pink, and red roses made butterflies swarm in my stomach all over again. The faint smell of his sweet woodsy cologne rolling in from the outside, his green eyes caught a hold of mine.

"Good afternoon, Skylar." His smile made the adrenalin run wild in my veins. Why was he here? How did he know where I lived? Was this creepy or was this sweet? There were so many things running through my head at once.

"Thank you?" I said in a questioning voice. He chuckled narrowing his eyes. I've seen Jason do this before but on a theater screen. He was hoping that this offering would not be awkward.

"You weren't in school today." His voice was soft. My eyes went down to the flowers, trying to hide my panic. *I missed school!?* My mom is going to flip if I've missed school, I hope they didn't call her because I was a no show.

"Yeah, I had other things to do." I said, not sure what to think of all this. I was literally losing my mind now.

"I see, well how would you like to come out with me for a little while?" He turned his head to the side and locked his two hands together in front of himself. He gave me that cute boy smile but all I saw was the scene from that one movie he played in. He stared at me the same way he stared at that girl. They fell in love. Then again that was just a movie.

"Why would I want to do that?" I rested my arm on the side of the door, he smiled even bigger then. Trying to relax was hard while my mind was trying to figure what day it was.

"Because it could be fun, and I feel like we should get to know each other a little more." His white teeth were like the stars in the sky. His black hair shined under the bright sun. His white T-shirt with his black shorts, everything just seemed adorable about him. I couldn't let myself cave into him though. The light breeze of the day brought his sweet woodsy smell into my home. My fingers gripped the mixed roses tighter.

"Shouldn't you be getting home to your daddy and sister?" I asked, knowing that if I did go out with him it would just be trouble. The smile on his face went down a little bit. I could see I'd touched a sensitive subject for him.

"I'm sorry about Abby; look if you come with me then I will explain all of this to you." He offered, and his white teeth were gone, hiding behind his lips. My eyes fell away from him remembering that I couldn't leave the house. It was too much of a risk.

"I'm sorry, I'm not supposed to leave the house right now." I told him the truth. To be honest, Jason didn't seem like the bad guy. He didn't seem like the rich jerk I made him up to be. I did not know all that much about Jason yet; time would tell me what he's made of.

"What, does your mommy not want you to go anywhere?" He left his mouth hanging open a little. He gave it right back to me; the truth was, I would be safer inside my house than I was out there. I pressed my lips together staring back into the roses. I couldn't risk going out there, but I wanted to. My mom would be so upset with me if she came home from work and found out that I wasn't here or in school. She would call the police again saying that I have gone missing. I didn't want to take those chances. I couldn't put her through the hysteria of the possibility of me being kidnapped.

"I guess you'll never know, thanks for the flowers, Jason." I smiled at him, getting ready to close the door. His hand came up stopping the door from shutting. My mouth came open a little and he pushed it back with ease.

"That's it?" His voice was shallow, letting those green eyes come up to mine. What was I to do? He wanted to be with me, and I just kept shoving him away. Deep inside I knew I wanted to give him a chance too, there was just too many things sitting on the table. A piece of me felt this rush of joy as I watched him, while the other half was telling me that this could be dangerous. Jason was showing emotions towards me most strangers never would. He had this sense of passion to him that I couldn't let slip away; my brain was telling me to keep him close, while my heart was already in his hands.

"Do you want to come in then?" I stepped back holding my arm out. A rough chuckle came up his throat. He stepped a few feet in the door then turned to look at me.

"Nice pajamas!" He pointed out, laughing a little more.

"What do you expect when you just come over here so unexpectedly?" I asked taking my flowers to the kitchen. Dave had a vase sitting there waiting for me. I smiled setting the roses down in the vase before filling it with water. The fresh cut roses smelled so sweet. I've received flowers from a boy once before, but it was just a cheesy offering from a middle school dance. The structure along with the vibrant color told me these were high quality. I turned around and Jason was standing there on the other side of the island.

"I expect a beautiful girl named Skylar to come out on the town with me." He smiled, answering my question. I sighed a little shaking my head at him. I smiled at the way he said that, almost as if it was the 70s. Curious, if he was in the classic Mustang, there was a chance he had a whole date set up.

"Say I do come with you, what are we going to do?" I asked him, letting it sink in that he just called me beautiful. He laughed a little sitting down on the island. I would have had to jump to sit on the island, but Jason did it gracefully and with ease.

"Anything your heart desires." His hands lay flat on the countertop. I nodded my head, wanting to go but there was just that pit inside that held me back. I shook my head then with doubt.

"I can't." I almost wanted to kick myself for rejecting him again. It was time to stop doing that, he was welcoming me into his life, I should be doing the same. His green eyes held a look of doubt in them, but I didn't want him to think that he was wasting his time with me. Truth be told he is. I suspected my life to flip in a couple of weeks, maybe even in a couple of hours. There was a clock ticking without any hands to say when.

"Right, your mom!" He breathed out, playing with his keys. I watched his hands and knew this was a bad idea. Once he leaves that would be my last chance with Jason Blackstone.

"I'm sorry Jason." I looked right into his eyes before my phone went off.

"It's okay, I should be leaving." He got up from the island. My heart sank into the bottom of my stomach. I felt sad now; I didn't want him to leave. I walked into the living room with him, following him over to the door. A nauseous ache formed in my stomach. This is what being ten feet deep in regret feels like.

"Thanks for the flowers," I said again, in a low voice while watching the floor. I opened the door as he walked out. His hand came over lifting my chin up.

"Anything to make you smile." His shimmering eyes burned into me like the sun. I did smile then. Chills ran up my body. I just wanted to go with him. He walked down the steps from my door to his candy red vintage Mustang. I waved bye to him as he did the same. I watched as he drove away. He was gone but my heart was in the passenger seat with him. I closed the door thinking about him. I could still smell his scent in here. I could still see his green eyes looking into mine. Was this a dream or was this really happening? Maybe this was part two of the nightmare. The imagination can be just as lucid as drugs.

"You know it's not a school day, right?" Dave was sitting back on the couch. I caught my breath as he filled in the blank of my dreadful question. It wasn't a school day! I had no reason to fear the outcome of that scenario.

"He just asked me out, Dave." I kept staring at the door like he was going to come back. He brought me flowers just to see me smile. My head turned around, looking at the elegant flowers showcased on the island.

"And he also thought it was a weekday!" He mocked Jason once more.

"So, he just wanted a reason to take me out." I said, pushing my hair away from my shoulders. Jason did his mission right; I couldn't stop smiling.

"Or he's an idiot and I just misread him." His blonde eyebrows went up. My mouth fell open, looking back over to him. I slapped his arm, but he made himself fade. My phone started going off again. This time someone was calling me. I got up running back into the kitchen to get my phone. I couldn't stop smiling, just knowing that Jason Blackstone did this for me. I felt all warm and fuzzy inside.

When the phone was in my hand the fuzzy feeling was gone and the sickness returned. My mouth hung open, not sure I wanted to answer this. I know I shouldn't answer this. My phone just rang and rang in my hand. My insides shook forcing the happiness I'd felt to be killed by fear. I swallowed hard hitting the answer button.

"What do you want?" My voice was strong at first,

but my body felt weak. Dave was back at my side in no time listening to the phone call with me.

"A nice man just came to your house, I see." His voice left this hollow darkness inside. My head whipped around looking at the windows. I went running over to the front window. I peeked out the corner seeing no one parked on the street.

"Where are you?" I demanded, scared but feeling the need to not show it. Right then the line went dead. I pulled it away from my ear gazing at the phone shaking violently in my hand. The call was gone. Dave ripped the phone from my hand. He was thinking, I could see it on his face. I left him, going back to the kitchen. I ran over to the door making sure it was locked. Everything in the kitchen was locked, now it was time to check everything else. I turned around and Dave was right behind me making us collide.

"Sky, I will not let anything happen to you or your mom, okay?" His cool hands came down on my arms. I nodded feeling like crying but I had to be stronger than that. Mom would be home any minute; I had to tell her about the phone call. Then again, she would want to call the police and they didn't exactly do much the last time. Cops anywhere seem pretty helpless to my father's threats. There is never a trace of him. They wouldn't just hangout on the street in undercover cruisers awaiting his appearance.

"I know Dave, and I can't thank you enough for it."

I walked around him running back upstairs. I ran into my room and swooped my computer up off my bed. I went back downstairs to get on Facebook. I was about to find some information out. Dave placed his hands on the back of the couch. I typed my dad's name in looking for anything that could give me the information I needed. I clicked on his profile seeing a picture of him and some girl. I didn't know the blonde, but I wasn't going to get distracted by her. I hit the information tab showing brief information. It said he still lived in Miami, Florida. He was a male, but the bells rang to my own dungeon seeing that he was still married. He was a sick man.

"Did he post any statuses about anything that could lead to you?" Dave asked but I couldn't stop staring at the fact that he thought he was still married. He was crazy to think that he still had my mother's trust, I couldn't stare at this anymore. I closed my eyes placing my face in my palms.

"I haven't checked." My voice lowered, not sure that I even wanted to check. This man that I thought I knew so well has become the man I never really knew at all. Someone that was so passionate, caring, and willing to do anything for his daughter, is now trying to kill her. A world I thought was so normal is now just like a movie. Always running, people crying, bone chilling moments that make your heart stop, it's all just a horror movie. A fight that is so unwelcome that you just can't hide from it. I want to stand up to him, right in his face and tell him how I feel. I want to wrap my hands around his neck like he did to my mom, choking him until his final breath. Then slap him across the face with no regret whatsoever. That anger was my strength right now.

My finger went down hitting the back button. Once back on his home page I saw his smiling face. I wanted to rip his eyes out and shove his teeth down his throat. All I wanted was revenge and the bittersweet taste of him crying out. I was not the killer here; I was the victim. I'm not sure I was ready to stand my ground just yet, but one day I would be strong enough and I would be ready. I scrolled away from his face onto his wall. There were no posts made by him since the days before the nightmare began, a year ago. All that remained now were birthday wishes.

"Hey, look at that post." Dave pointed to one of the posts made by that blonde lady. I hit the comments seeing that there were three of them. Her comment was the big one, she wanted to know why he did what he did and where they were going to go next. How was he going to keep running? My eyes drifted up to Dave then, wondering what he was running from. Had he done something else that I didn't know about?

Do not speak of this on here Kristy; if you need to talk, I gave you my number. Everything you have to say about this you say to me not the public. My daughter can see this and I want her no part in this.

I blinked, not understanding what all this was about. I

shook my head reading what she had to say back.

I am sorry Richard I tried calling but you didn't answer, you haven't been home in four days we are starting to worry about you, I wish you would just let us in on everything that you are up to. I just hope we don't find you on the news for all this.

My hand came up over my mouth wanting to understand. Dave and I both just looked at each other. I was confused, as I set my computer aside. I have a lot of research to do. I'm not sure how much I would be able to find on him or whatever it is that this may be. I had to find out though. I need to learn more about this Kristy lady too. I click on her name, taking me to her page. I saw a picture of her, a little boy and my monster father, I swallowed feeling drenched in some kind of pain. Did my father live a double life? Were we just a project to him? I knew for a fact I was his daughter but was my mom's marriage real? Why did he have so much aggression towards us? Sickness formed, curious if this was the woman he cheated on Mom with. He never confirmed the truth to me, but his vengeance almost certainly did.

Chapter 6

Information

I woke up to a knock on the door. My head lifted up from my pillow seeing my mom poke her head in. There was a smile on her face as she came in a little. My head fell back down on the pillow feeling her sit down on the edge of the bed. What on earth did she want? I was up till three this morning searching out every area that could give me any little piece of information. I just wanted to sleep now.

"Honey, wake up there is someone here to see you." Her voice was light, and I shifted over onto my back. Who could be here to see me? The sun was bright and cascading beams into my room which told me it was still morning.

"What time is it?" My hand ran back through my hair. I reached over for my phone.

"Just a little past ten." She answered, leaving my body lifeless to fall back onto the bed.

"Tell whoever it is to go away then!" I groaned, flipping back over. There was a short fuse that went off then; I knew who was here. My mom laughed a little more, getting up off my bed. Before I knew it my body was chilled from her stealing my blankets. I looked at her through one open eye. What did she think she was doing?

"No, you are getting dressed and going down there to meet him, he is waiting." She demanded tossing my blankets back down on the bed. I groaned sitting up. Why was she making me do this? Yes, there was a hot guy waiting for me downstairs, but he can go away if she kicks him out. Sleep was a happy place, at least when it didn't consist of my father haunting me.

"Mom, he's not my type." I whined, not wanting to get up.

"Honey, when a boy comes to your door twice with flowers and chocolate, I say you give him a chance." She rubbed my leg sitting back down. My eyebrows came back down, *he brought me flowers, again?* Shaking my head and getting up off my bed, my mom wasn't going to give up until I went down there. She smiled, following with me.

"Tell him I will be down in a minute." Rolling my eyes, I saw the biggest smile light my mom's face. She hugged me walking back over to my door. I'd never had a boyfriend throughout my high school years. She left and I ran over pulling on some clothes, then brushed my hair. It wasn't a big deal to get dressed, he had already seen me in my pajamas once, what harm is a second time? I brushed my hair quickly and Dave showed up behind me. He took my hand twirling me around. I laughed a little landing in his arms, against his icy cold chest.

"Someone's finally excited about going out with a movie star." Dave sang, and we both laughed.

"Going out, no, but I will go out with him." I said, going over to the door.

"Isn't that the same thing?" He laughed some more making me shake my head.

"Nope." I left the room, skimming through my thoughts for what to say to Jason. My thoughts didn't move as fast as my feet did. I was at the stairs looking down. I saw him in the living room laughing with my mom. I sighed not sure why he wouldn't just leave me alone. When I placed my hand on the railing it hit me, my mom wanted me to stay away from him. All of a sudden, she'd changed her mind because he brought me flowers and chocolate? This did not add up. I tried wrapping my head around why she was so eager about this too, being that this could end badly with Richard. I walked down into the room and they both looked at me. His green eyes came up meeting mine, his bright shining smile taking over my heart. My lips fell apart listening to two things. My heart said to kiss him, then my mind said to shut up and kick him out. His smile made me feel warm inside which made me smile back.

"Hey." His voice was low mixed with roughness. Chills ran up my body just wanting to lunge into his arms. That would just make me look crazy.

"Hi." I sheepishly responded, pushing my hair back.

Mom smiled at me.

"Well, I will leave you two alone now." She said heading back into the kitchen.

"Nice meeting you, Mrs. Saxton." Jason told her, nodding his head. Mom chuckled a little, blushing behind her hair. Everyone was always so overwhelmed by being around him, I wasn't though.

"Okay, what are you doing here?" I whispered looking up to him. He laughed a little lifting his shoulders up.

"I'm taking you out today." He said tapping his finger on my nose. My eyebrows came down, not okay with this.

"Oh, are you?" I crossed my arms not liking this. He laughed a little lifting his eyebrows. I smacked his hand away from my face.

"Yes, and your mom is just fine with it, now go get what you need." He took a seat on the couch. My mouth fell open looking down at him. I wasn't even sure what to say to him, I didn't want him to think he could push me around; it was not sitting well with me. Those green eyes came up to mine; *I will not let them control me,* I thought to myself. My heart was telling me to listen to him, and yet my brain was telling me to stand my ground, and it was then I realized what I needed to do. I held up my finger and went back up the stairs, rushing into my bedroom where Dave was waiting for me.

"Who does he think he is?" My voice snarled out. Dave smiled at me, crossing his leg under himself.

"A rich kid that can have what he wants!" His blonde eyebrows raised, and I wanted to scream in anger. A part of me wanted to give him a chance. The other part wanted to rip his head off for doing this. We already had one man controlling our lives we sure as hell did not need another one.

"Obviously, he even asked my mom!" I was freaking out. Dave got up, pressing his cold hands on my shoulders.

"Sky, this is simple, do you want to go with him or not?" His blue eyes froze right through mine. My eyes drifted away then. I didn't want to, but my heart said otherwise. Then I thought of yesterday when he came here. I blew him off, I always blow him off and he still doesn't give up. That could mean one of two things. He was a rich kid trying to get what he wants and won't give up until he gets it, or he is eager to date me and see me for who I am. There was such a huge mix of emotions running through my body right now.

"Skylar, go!" Dave encouraged me, making our eyes meet. His ocean blue eyes were cold like a frozen lake but underneath ran wild with warmth. I nodded my head going to give Jason the chance he wanted. I hugged Dave's icy cold body then rushed to slip on my flip-flops. I left my room with purse in hand, heading back down the hallway. I sucked in air, feeling a little nervous now. Once I was back down there Jason stood up. I looked at what he was wearing – jeans, black V-neck with some odd design on it, and Converse shoes.

"Ready?" He asked, raising his black eyebrows. I nodded my head, yes, sucking my lips back into my mouth.

"Have fun and take care of my baby!" Mom yelled to us from the kitchen. He laughed turning around as we reached the door.

"No worries, your daughter will always be safe with me; I won't let anything happen to her." When he assured my mom, it left a warm tingle in my heart. I smiled to myself, walking out the door. Maybe he did care for me, more than I'd like to admit. I still think it's too soon for that but maybe that was just a part of the show. Does his heart hold good intentions or is this just a play of an embellished life?

Jason walked in front of me opening the passenger door. My smile grew as I slipped into the seat of the classic Mustang. He closed the door jolting around to his side. He was out to impress me. I watched him, remaining silent as we backed out of the drive. He was calm and didn't seem to mind my staring. Then again, he is always being stared at by other girls. I looked away from him and out my window, when I saw an unfamiliar car driving slowly and passing us, I narrowed my eyes a little watching the black car. It was going slow, almost like it was looking for a house. I turned around in my seat watching as it stopped in front of my house. My eyes widened, wondering what was going on. *Who was that*, was the main train of thought? My eyes were darting back and forth, and I just hoped it wasn't him. I knew I should've stayed home. It wasn't too late to turn back, but I didn't want to ditch Jason now that I've got in the car and left with him; but I still needed to see the man in the black car close up.

"Is there a problem?" Jason's voice snapped my attention away from the car, my head didn't move though. What was I going to say to him? I didn't want him to know that I'm on the run from my violent father who'd tried to kill my mom. I sat back around in my seat. The area on my cheek stung with pain, at being flooded with memories of my past. He could not hurt my mom again, how would I live without her?

"No." I replied, feeling worried now. I didn't want anything to happen to my mom while I was gone. I couldn't live with myself if it did. I was the one who left even though she'd encouraged me. I was so stupid.

"Are you sure you really wanted to come on this date with me?" He gave me a crooked smile as we came to the end of the street, where he stopped. My eyes were still watching the mirror for any sign of movement from the black car. The formation of the car was just a black chunk on the road from this distance.

"Are you sure you really wanted to take me on this date?" I shoved it back in his corner as we left the street, vanishing from the mysterious black car.

"What happened to don't answer my questions with other questions?" He laughed a little, shifting his green eyes over to me. I gave him a little smile, still thinking back to who that might be.

"So, why did you want to take me on this date anyway?" I asked him, watching the road move by us. His smile widened as he took one hand from the wheel. What if Jason was involved? My eyes grew wide with curiosity as to what Richard's play might be. There are a couple of days where Jason hadn't been at school this week; that would have given him the perfect opportunity to set a plan in motion.

"Maybe I just want to get to know you." He said, taking a turn around the bend where we came to a stop light. What were his reasons for wanting to know me? What if he was acting, that's his job? I shifted my thoughts back to the flowers and chocolates he brought me, where were they? I never saw them. The sound of a girl whistling grabbed my attention. Two girls in the car next to us flirting with Jason, I already knew how this was going to go. I sighed letting the attention sink in. I watched the blonde girl wink at him and the one driving blew him a kiss. Jason smiled lifting his hand up and we left them in the dust.

"You're disgusting!" I complained crossing my arms. He sighed shaking his head. Seeing the smile wipe off his face, I might have said something wrong, but it was true. So many women drooled over him.

"Why do you say that?" He pulled into the parking lot of this breakfast café.

"Because you have so many women coming after you and god knows how many you had to be with in movies." I said, getting out of the Mustang. He got out as well, walking up to the door with me. No words were exchanged as we walked in. You could smell the bacon and eggs. The coffee was the strongest smell of them all, it made my mouth water. A lady walked towards us smiling. Her eyes went straight to Jason. My eyes drifted away after she said, 'right this way'. We sat down in the booth across from each other with menus in front of us. I gazed at the downtown area of my new home. We sat in the middle of the road as traffic zipped by on each side. This was such an odd hole-in-the-wall café tucked into the middle of this smaller concrete jungle. It was a very small city compared to Miami and no tourists were around snapping pictures while cluttering the beaches.

"Would you like coffee, milk, or orange juice?" The waitress smiled over at him then glanced at me. She was an older lady, so I think she was trying not to make it so obvious. We both ordered coffee making her descend back behind the counter. We didn't say anything to each other, just watched the coffee get sat down in front of us. She asked what we wanted, and we ordered. I felt awkward sitting here without a conversation.

"You know just because a lot of women look at me and blow kisses and whatnot at me doesn't mean I hook up with them all." He was gloomy watching his coffee. The corner of my mouth slanted, maybe I am a bitch. My heartstrings pulled in the same directions as before. Trust him, don't trust him.

"Them all?" Sitting my coffee back down, quoting his words. I heard air come rushing out of his nose.

"I don't hook up with any of them, okay?" His eyebrows lifted as he pushed the words back. I jumped a little, averting eye contact. A little hesitant but a flash of anger hit me.

"And you just want me to believe you? A man that is so good at acting which is really lying about who you are?" I questioned, deciphering everything he had to say. His hand ran down the side of his face shaking his head. His eyelids hid the forest from me.

"So, what I'm getting here is that everything I will try and say to you, you are just going to think I'm lying?" There was no hope in his eyes once they reopened.

"No, it's just I know how people like you are." I said shyly, watching the few other older people sitting in here.

"You think you do; but see the people that really can't be trusted are the ones who write those shitty stories about us." He said, pointing his finger at me. I smiled a little, knowing where he was coming from.

"How would I know that?" Sitting back against the booth, the lady came back setting our food down in front of us. Jason thanked her but placed all his attention on me.

"You don't unless you trust us." His green eyes sparked, a tiny light in them. I smiled tilting my head. I felt as if he missed the whole acting his life out part. He didn't understand that I was trying to see the real Jason vs the fake Jason. At this moment I had to believe he was being the real Jason. If he had a reason to act, he would. In this case it could be just to impress me, to win me over. For some reason Jason had taken an interest in me.

"And by us, you mean you?" I pointed my fork at him. A half smile formed on his face, creating a lighter tone. His fork chopped through the omelet letting cheese ooze out onto the plate.

"But you see I'm not like all the rest of Hollywood!" He told me giving that flirty stare. I've seen that expression from him too many times, even though we only met a week ago.

"Is that so?" I felt like that was a blow off just to get my attention.

"Yes, just like how you're not like all the rest of the girls out there." His head came up as I set my fork down. I felt my cheeks blush with this intense warmth spiraling inside of me. I've never felt this feeling before and something odd told me that he never has either. The look in his eyes could tell so many stories. I wondered what it would be like if I ever took a run down that forest. How trapped I'd be or how easily I could walk out. Things were changing between me and this random stranger, who's way more popular than I'll ever be. I felt like this was bad with good sprinkled all around. His hand reached over the table gently resting over mine. The warmth of his hand made mine vibrate. My eyes locked back with his taking in this cozy feeling he gave me. It was odd but comforting.

His phone started ringing then. Our eyes slipped away from each other, and he pulled his phone out. Seeing the shiny screen, there was a picture of Abby on it. She was calling him, I looked over to the windows. Within seconds everything turned a lot more awkward. The sound of the ringing went away, and he put his phone down. He didn't take the call but now I felt that it would only be moments before she would find us. Her heels clicking on the floor with her boney hands choking my neck. That was the last thing I wanted. Every tarnished moment she had caused, stuck with me.

"Is everything alright?" Jason asked but his phone went off again but this time it was a different noise. He picked his phone back up gliding his fingers across the keyboard.

"I'm fine but we better leave, sounds like someone else needs you." I said, realizing how awkward this could get, really fast. His eyes shot back to me.

"No-no, Skylar listen this is what I really wanted to talk to you about." His hand came back over mine. I tilted my head wondering what he was doing.

"There's nothing to explain Jason, no matter how much you want to date me, they will always stand in the way." The truth came out and we both knew the hurdles we'd have to jump to be able to be together. I wasn't sure

I was up for playing a game of Romeo and Juliet.

"No, they won't, I know you don't believe that, but I will try as hard as I can for that not to happen." His voice was so promising, yet I felt that it wasn't the truth.

"So, what about school, she watches everything we do and is always there?" I wondered, knowing that would be the biggest obstacle to get over. His lips retreated back into his mouth as he gazed down into his breakfast. He knew I was right just as much as I did. I shook my head feeling ready to leave. My heart wanted to be open to him, but my mind said just leave it. It was just something to leave in a book as heartbreak if we continue down this path.

"Let's just keep it on the down low." He said, raising his eyes back up.

"But we're not even dating yet." I was feeling a little rushed into things. He smiled at me nodding his head.

"We don't have to be, but even as friends, it needs to be a secret." He told me, and I knew that was for the best. Whether anything escalated between us or not, it still needed to be hush, hush. I agreed to these ridiculous terms before we both got up to leave. I feel like my whole life is turning into secrets now. No one knows about the man I am running from, and I have a dead best friend that no one can know about because I'll look crazy, and now add on to that I might be dating a famous Hollywood star. More and more kept being added to my list of secrets. How many more things am I going to have to hide from the people that I care about? I always hated lying even when it was the best way out of things. I felt like I was always hiding inside my own bottle, sinking down into the ocean. It's never made me feel great. I always felt like people knew when I avoided telling them the truth, then they would think I'm some sort of freak. I didn't want things to turn out that way between Jason and I. Even if we didn't turn into anything, I still didn't want that. At this point he seems more than willing to try. He did not want to push me into a relationship, which shows he wasn't just trying to get me because it's what he wanted. This whole date was to assure me he would try and protect whatever we had from his family. He cared; one thing I've never .felt from a guy before. Jason was handsome on the outside but inside there was a war with his own family. The one's who should bring him peace only brought him misery. A sad tick hit my heart, realizing Jason and I aren't all that different when it comes to family life. He is being abused in a different way than me; his was for name's sake. I ran in terror from physical abuse. Did Jason have the ability to see the story I hid without reading it? I couldn't help but feel connected to him in a way I never thought possible.

We arrived back in front of the house. We pulled into the driveway as he shifted into parked. Why did he park? Was this the scary heart pounding moment that every girl waits for? What was he doing? My mind was going insane, and he turned his head to me. He moved a strand of hair back onto my shoulder. We watched each other until a light sigh broke our stare.

"I told you stuff today and yet I still haven't found out much about you." He said, letting his hand fall away from my shoulder.

"Well, that's because you're the one that wanted to tell things." I reminded him, remembering what he'd said. He chuckled a little, watching my hands.

"True but I also said I wanted to get to know you." His green eyes returned. The forest opened back up, making my heart pound.

"There's really nothing to know about me." I lied and told the truth at the same time. I wasn't an exciting person. He tilted his head giving me this disbelieving look.

"There is always something to know about somebody, everyone has a story to tell." His voice was so sincere. I felt his words; he has been through stuff like this before. It wasn't just some sort of act he was putting on to impress me, he meant that. I felt his words run through me and I knew he was right. I just couldn't tell the true story, not yet.

"I'm just a boring, simple, ordinary girl." I shrugged my shoulders, wanting to get away from my thoughts.

"Why did you move here in the middle of the semester then? I mean it's almost Summer break." He tilted his head with wondrous eyes. My heart was racing for all the wrong reasons now. My eyes drifted away knowing

I had to give the mom story again. I knew people didn't believe it, but it was all I had to hold onto. A quick thought jogged my memory back to the black car from earlier. No one got in touch with me. Relief crushed over me knowing it was just a normal car.

"My mom got a better job offer." Pushing my hair back looking up at the garage, knowing there would be questions. The short silence between us, I shifted my eyes over to him. He was thinking, I felt like I knew that look.

"Hmmm… I see." He said in a gentle voice, full of wonder. His eyes watched me from an angle. He was thinking about what I said. I could see the questions still running through his eyes. It was almost like he could feel my lie bubbling up.

"Why are you a junior in high school at the age of twenty?" My head tilted as far as it could tossing the ball back in his court. If I wanted to protect Jason, I had to steer him in the opposite direction. It never hurt to understand him either by doing this. His eyes narrowed like he was caught off guard. One of his hands slipped from the steering wheel while his body shifted sideways in the seat. He licked his lips, bringing his beautiful eyes to meet mine. The sun left a flare tracing across his jawline, the black stubble fields of hair were emerging from where he shaved last.

"To make it simple, I've been way too busy to finish. I thought it would be easier to get my G.E.D and be finished but my dad persuaded me differently," he chuckled, playing with a strained of my hair, "I'm kind of glad he did, I wouldn't have met you." His smile became whole from the underlining truth of his past. A smile rose quickly to my face, blushing once more. My teeth came down on my knuckles, feeling butterflies swarming around my stomach. I took a deep breath in, glowing back. He saw that his words played out just as he wished.

"I hate to break it to you, but Florida is still better than Ohio." I teased, raising my eyebrows, debating my next words. Jason's hand went up as if I had a good point that he could not argue with. "But there is one thing about Florida that did suck., I admitted, before exiting his car.

"What, the heat? You haven't lived here long enough." He joked back, and I popped my head back into the car. I laughed a little, glancing down at his body sitting ever so casually on the driver's side.

"Florida didn't have a Jason!" I winked at him before closing the door. I watched his cheerful face all the way up to the door. My hand rested on the doorknob seeing his hand running down over his face. The forest was glowing with so much sunlight I could feel it radiating. He licked his lips backing out of the driveway. His two fingers came off the wheel in a wave goodbye. With a blurting horn screaming, his Mustang came to a jerking halt. The glow inside of me was swallowed by darkness as I watched a black SUV swerve around Jason's car. Two shadowy figures were hidden behind tinted windows. The car went on down the road allowing Jason to make his escape. With my hand rattling the doorknob I rushed inside the house. All I could wish for was that they wouldn't follow Jason.

Chapter 7

Inconspicuous

Later that night I sat in my bedroom on my laptop. It was still where I'd left it, on my dad's profile. Nothing new has been uploaded, however, the random blonde girl named Kristy had. She made a random status saying, 'I can't stop wondering'. I'm not sure what that is supposed to mean but I felt like it had something to do with him. There was a part of me that wanted to get involved with this random lady, although I knew it was better if I didn't. I wondered if Mom knew anything about them. My eyes went over to my door continuing to hit Kristy's name taking me back to her profile. I hit her pictures to do a little more snooping. I saw a picture of her and a little blonde boy. They looked just like each other which told me they were mother and son. The next picture was of some party, then her and a bunch of girls in dresses. I wasn't digging into anything good yet. I got out of the picture file I was in and went to the one that stated: My New Life. The first picture was her lying in a hospital bed, surrounded by congratulation balloons and other ones saying it's a boy! I saw nothing more and I flipped to the next picture. Shock took over my body making my hand fly to my mouth. My heart raced in crazy turbulence. My dad stood beside the hospital bed next to her and the baby. Do I dare turn to the next picture? As soon as I did, I saw all I needed. My dad was kissing the forehead of the baby and the picture was entitled, Daddy and Me. I have a half-brother.

Dave's cold body came in beside me forcing the blankets on the bed to go stiff. I closed my eyes resting my fist up to my forehead. I didn't know what to say. Was there anything to say? Should I tell my mom? Does she know already? There were just so many untold things. I sucked in a shaky breath moving my head back. Dave's icy body never left, even as I wanted to move.

"Dave, what am I supposed to do?" I felt tears coming to my eyes, just knowing this was getting worse. My mom and I are in danger but then what about these people? They could be in the same place as us some day, or maybe they already are.

"You need to go tell your mom and talk to her." He advised, moving his hands up and down my shoulders. I wasn't sure I could tell her though.

"But how? I'm so shell shocked!" My voice was quiet, shaking my head in disbelief. My eyes started to burn and blur from the tears as I stared at the computer screen relentlessly.

"You just go down there with your computer, sit it in front of her and show her, trust me she should start the talking." His voice came up from the calmness. This thorn spiked through my heart. I know I shouldn't care about a man that wanted to kill my mom and had the heartless feelings to hit me, but I still did. The saddest part was this poor family has no idea.

I didn't say a word as I got up from my bed, taking my computer with me. I could not grapple the right words to say. I felt weak inside, but my mom needed to know this most. I went down the stairs to find her standing by the window looking out. She was focused on something, and that worried me.

"Mom?" My voice spiked higher than intended as I stood there holding onto my laptop. She didn't respond to me though. What was she so focused on? I sat the computer down and walked up beside her. She jumped at my appearance. She looked frightened, backing away from the window. I wasn't sure what she looked so scared of. Should I peek out the window to see?

"Are you okay?" This was starting to freak me out.

"There is a black car sitting in front of our house." She murmured, causing my visions from earlier to return. The black car that drove slowly past us. I went over to the window peeking out. Sure enough, it was the same black car. It was gone when Jason brought me back home, which means it left for a little while. This was starting to get creepy. A short fuse went off in my head wondering if this random car was a lookout for Richard. If he had hired a spy, was he going to new lengths?

"I saw that car earlier, it passed us." I told her, moving away from the window quickly. I imagine they know that we know. My mom got a frightened stare in her eyes. She went over picking up her cell phone.

"I'm calling the police!" Her voice cracked with urgency, dialing the number. I listened to the buttons being clicked and right then the front door was busted inward. We both screamed shuffling towards each other. The bone-chilling sound of wood cracking away from the door hinge made me gasp. A huge chunk of wood soared across the living room as the door swung open. All I saw was a black shadow standing in the doorway with a crowbar. My eyes were big, and my heart was beating out of my body. I felt my whole world spinning out of control.

"Leave us alone!" My mom yelled, holding me close to her. He swung the crowbar up, but it fell back onto the palm of his other hand. He had white hair and a big round body. He was dressed in all black. I didn't know this man. His hand came out trying to rip me away.

"Don't touch me! Help!" I yelled out, hoping someone around would hear. *Dave, where was Dave?* He gave me an angry stare as I kept yelling. He shook his head releasing this growling sigh. Why did this man not speak? He tried once more to take me from my mom, but she refused to let go, shuffling our feet backwards. There were about two steps between us and the white-haired beast with the crowbar.

"You touch my baby one more time, so help me God!" She threatened in a vicious tone. Anger washed over in his eyes. I didn't feel good about this random person. He pulled out a knife, it glistened under the light when it switched up. My eyes widened and Mom staggered our bodies back away from him once more. He just followed us back into the kitchen until we hit the island. He got close up into our faces. The long knife went down slicing across my mom's hand. Her hold on me fell away and he whipped me around into his hold. I screamed bloody murder, wanting to be set free. His head came down next to my ear and all I felt was his rough breathing echoing static. I closed my eyes trying to get loose. The cool crowbar came up pressing against my neck. This man was not a spy, he was an assassin. Richard paid to have us murdered which means our blood wouldn't be on his hands. The cool iron of the crowbar sank into my neck as pressure began forcing harder on my windpipe. The curve of the bar choked close to my vital signs allowing the rapid pace of my heart to howl through my entire body.

"Your father won't be very proud of you." The man huffed, making his voice tickle my ear. My shoulders jerked back and forth trying to free myself. One of my hands twisted up in an attempt to pull the crowbar away from my throat. The big man's arm grew stronger to any force I fought with. Something busted over my head out of nowhere and he lost his grip. The crowbar went clanging to the floor.

"I told you not to touch my baby!" Mom stood there with a rolling pin. The heavyset man got back up swinging around with the crowbar taking my mom to the ground. His body mass covered her with little for me to see. She wrestled against the crowbar he had pinned her with.

"Mom!" I screamed leaping forward for the knife sticking out of his holster. The burly man felt my presence. His heavy arm swung back hurling me across the kitchen floor like a bowling ball. I crashed into a cabinet seeing Jason's shadow in the doorway. My eyes widened, having no idea what was happening now. My fingers rubbed my head blinking several times to reassure myself he was really here. His eyes were bigger than I've ever seen them before. I didn't want the man that broke into our house to get his eyes on Jason. I looked back at him gripping the knife tightly in my hand. I successfully *had* the knife! The heavy man lifted the crowbar back up. The rapid pounding of my heart stopped, seeing the crowbar aiming to crush my mom's head in.

"Hey, asshole!" Jason yelled swiping his attention away from my mom. My heart throbbed again, not wanting him to be seen. I shook my head as the heavyset man walked over to Jason. Right before he got there, Jason was pushed to his knees allowing my father to appear in the doorway. My mouth dropped open as I breathed hard. My horror story would end tonight, I could feel it.

"I'll take it from here!" Richard commanded the man in his deep voice. My whole body was shaking. I pulled myself up feeling the aches of hitting the floor while my head throbbed from the impact. My father's eyes locked with mine in milliseconds.

"You won't take anything from here." I told him through clenched teeth. Gripping the knife ever so tightly, I got right up in front of him. I had no control over my body, my instincts went into overdrive. The knife trembled in my grip from fear, but now vengeance was the target.

"You won't stab me!" His voice was confident as he kept steady eye contact with me. Jason got up from the ground and Dad turned whipping a gun out. There were sirens getting closer, speeding down the street. Who called them? I watched my dad's finger on the trigger.

"No!" I yelled rushing in front of him grabbing my dad's arm and swinging it away from Jason. The last thing I heard was a loud ringing noise. A metal sound clinging on the floor as if someone dropped a penny.

I was running down this burning forest. Mud was under my feet squishing between my toes. Flames blew up on both sides of my body. I stopped, looking around myself. I was breathing hard and choking on the smoke. I bent over coughing on dry air. There was an awful pain in my side. I realized a white dress blanketed my body. I analyzed the beautiful gown I was in. A wedding dress? I was lost and confused. I lifted my hand up seeing blood on it. My body felt weak, pain was throbbing from my torso. Blood colored the white dress like it was a marble floor with blood spilling out. I started breathing harder now, scared of what had happened.

There was a gun shot that rang out in the distance. I heard this man yell in agonizing pain. I looked around but all I could see was trees engulfed in flames. Smoke was covering everything like a steamy blanket. Then I saw blue fog gathering around my body. There was just a short kiss of coolness. Dave's blue aura appeared in front of me. I couldn't touch him though. His face was see-through. I reached out but his body evaporated into the smoky air.

Different colors flew over my head and around my body. It was like a rainbow crossing with the fire. Bright red, purple, orange, yellow, blue, pink, gold, there were so many. Where was I? What kind of twisted world was this? Then I wondered if I was in Hell. Everything was on fire including the painful bloody spot on my side. I felt like this was a world of destruction. Someone did this and I felt as though it was all for revenge. I was here but I'm not sure why, I just knew I was a part of this. I feel like I created this Hell. I started running again just to find myself tumbling to the ground. I yelled in pain, sitting next to a tree that had fallen. I glanced toward where the man was yelling from. He wasn't far from me.

"Sky, honey wake up." My eyes fluttered open from the

sound of my mom's light voice. Everything was blurry, I was freezing. I blinked my eyes a few more times and realized I wasn't at home. Dad was no longer standing near me trying to shoot Jason. My eyes moved around me seeing cords hanging down the bed connecting to me.

"Why am I in a hospital?" My throat was dry and sore. Looking at the IV's hooked up to me, I saw my heart moving up and down on a monitor. The sound of a low beeping in a perfect rhythm came from the machines I was hooked up to.

"Honey, I'm not sure if you remember but–"

"He came back, Mom." I said, finishing her sentence. She nodded her head as worried as could be. Then I noticed the big knot on the side of her head. The dry blood that was in the roots of her hair and also her lips. She was bruised all over. She moved the hair away from my face as tears welled in her eyes. My lips came apart, not sure why she was crying. I looked down at myself making sure I still had every limb. I felt no pain, so I was confused.

"Sweetie your father, he-he-he shot you." She stumbled over her words, breaking down into full blown crying. My eyes widened as I lowered my head. I remembered now; I moved his arm away so he wouldn't shoot Jason. My hand lay over my chest as I closed my eyes. She came down kissing my forehead. The blood from the dream, the tender pain of my torso. It all made sense.

"I'm just so happy you're still alive," her voice was faint, and I saw she was holding a tissue. The door to my room came open revealing Jason. Why was he here? He brought a glass of water over to me. Just the first glance of the water shifting up the cup made my desert dry mouth water. He had a small smile on his face. Mom moved away, going over to the window sniffling. We didn't say anything to each other as I took the water. When the moisture hit my taste buds a simple joy lit inside me. Water has never tasted so good. The cup was light and empty before I knew it. Setting it down beside me, Jason took it back. When his knuckles skimmed mine, we both looked at each other. The soft apologetic gaze in his eyes showed the guilt. He had no reason to be guilty though. This was all my fault. I caved; I allowed him access into my world.

"Would you like more?" He asked, letting his sorrow filled gaze leave me. I shook my head, no. I wasn't sure what to say to him as he sat the cup down behind himself. My bottom lip sucked back into my mouth. It was all dry with sharp edges of skin. I wondered how long I'd been unconscious. I rubbed my eyes feeling the IV's move with me. Jason and I both watched each other, and I saw a look in his eyes that I haven't seen before. I wasn't even sure how to explain what he might be thinking. All I did know was that his eyes were passionate. I saw that heartfelt gleam in his eyes, there was more to him then just his fame and money – he cared. The forest in his eyes touched me with softness. A voice told me he would always be here for me. The look of guilt evaporated, turning into a gaze of devotion.

"Why are you here?" I decided to ask, allowing my hideous sleeping voice to come out. He was here because he had to witness what happen.

"Skylar." Mom's voice came up fast. I didn't move my eyes off Jason though. His hands came down on the bed railing.

"You saved my life." His voice was low, taking my free hand into his. I couldn't force my eyes from the forest looking back at me. I saw the affection, the passion, the lie that he was telling me. He wasn't here just because I saved his life; he was here because he cared about me. I felt captured as he made time stand still.

"Well, you're welcome." I said, going to play his game even though I wanted to tell him he was a bad liar. A tiny smirked creased his face.

"Thank you." His head went down a little, but his eyes stayed right on mine. Mom came up beside him resting her hand down on his shoulder. That's when our eyes left each other. There was this funny feeling of warmth in my heart. The same one that has been there for days, every time I was around him. What if Jason was the one?

"Jason, hun, I think you better get home, your dads probably worried." She told him, making the warm feeling leave. I remembered the demons that hid in the shadows. He nodded his head, averting his eyes back to me.

"I'll be back tomorrow." He assured me; I tilted my head on the pillow. A small smile took over my face and heart. He was coming back. A thrill of hope shined inside of me. Amongst all the darkness devouring us tonight, he gave me a moment to look forward to.

"You don't need to." I said, seeing my mom give me this look like I've said something wrong once again. There were a few times my mom rolled her eyes at me like a best friend being defeated, this was another one of them.

"I know!" He winked at me, walking away from us. I watched as he left the room leaving Mom and me together. I wish he wouldn't have left. His cologne still lingered in the air around me making me feel calm. I wish Mom hadn't sent him away. Everything was about to turn awkward now. My head went down, then I realized my necklace wasn't around my neck. Panic engulfed me.

"Where is it?" I said searching around. I felt the strong threatening pain in my side. I stopped, crippling over from the strong burning sensation.

"Honey be careful, what's wrong?" She asked, putting her hands down on my shoulders and laying me back in bed.

"My necklace, where is it?" My voice was frantic.

"It's right here in this cup with your earrings." She said picking it up. My heart stopped racing then. It was safe and sound. The stone in the middle was cold black showing that it wasn't on my body and Dave wasn't around. That left a slight feeling of concern in me. Where could Dave be? Maybe he's looking into what my dad is up to. I was not hopeful that he got arrested. Richard always made his escape before the police came with guns drawn.

"Where did I get shot?" I sort of already had a clue.

"Luckily it went right through your side and crazy enough it went right through the opening between your ribs." She explained, taking a seat on the edge of the bed. I nodded my head looking down at my hospital gown. This thing was hideous. My mind drifted to something else then. Glancing at my mom, seeing that she was watching my heart monitor. I wonder if she knew about Kristy. I felt the need to ask her. Then again, her mind was on me and worrying that I would be okay. I didn't want to break her heart or cause some sort of other commotion.

"Does this mean I avoided surgery?" I cut through my thoughts, staying on topic of my own well-being.

"Thankfully yes, you have twelve stitches. Six in the front and six in the back." She informed me, with so much suffering filling those eyes. Her appearance and attitude were the things that set the mood my whole life. When Mom was happy, I was happy. When she was sad, I reflected that emotion. Now her grief gave me doubts.

"Where is he?" A question that made me feel sick, had to be ask. Her eyes glanced from me to the TV I never realized was on. A news reporter stood at the front of our house showing the splintered wood of the door frame. Mom sighed placing her cold hand over mine.

"He took off moments before the cops arrived. Jason tried to stop him, but I begged him not to. I can't imagine another innocent person being hurt by him." Her eyes focused on the huge window in my room. Lights from a different room in another wing of the hospital shined back under the night sky. I rolled my head, feeling completely perplexed by tonight's events. There was a huge question I had that just did not connect. Why was Jason at my house? We went out earlier that day. There was a reason he'd returned, but why?

Chapter 8

Obligation

I heard a light ticking sound forcing my eyes to open. Color was moving from the TV screen on to the wall. Through my blurry eyes I saw Jason's figure. He was back. My vision became clearer. blinking several times showing me he was doing something on his phone but then I saw my phone beside his. Why did he have my phone?

"What are you doing?" My voice was hoarse making his head fly up fast. A crooked smile lifted on his face as he sat both phones aside.

"Hey, how are you feeling?" He got up from the chair.

"A lot better if you would tell me what you were doing with my phone!" I cleared my throat, scanning the room for my mom. She wasn't here. I could only wonder where she was.

"I feel that we need each other's numbers." He gazed down into my eyes. The sun came through my window making his eyes turn light green. They shimmered along with his beautiful white teeth. What was I supposed to say to him? I saved his life and now he's here because he feels that he owes me. That feeling didn't sit well with me.

"And why is that?" I watched him wanting to see if I could pick up lies like I did last night. He didn't say anything at first just averted his gaze. His eyes were focused on the window. Just as I thought, it was more about the guilty feeling than the truth. Maybe that was the truth though. It saddened me inside because I thought he did care, when will I ever stop fooling myself? I watched him walk over to the window and I gathered my words. He still might be the man I felt he was, then again, he might not be. One date proves nothing and now that my dad had got involved by almost shooting him, that just makes the thin string between us thinner. Jason was one bullet away from losing everything.

"I understand that you feel you need to repay me somehow, but you really don't, so please don't feel in any way that you are obligated to protect me or stand in front of moving traffic for me because what happen last night, I-I-I-"

"I didn't do this because I felt pity for not repaying you, is that what you think this is?" He turned away from the window cutting my stammering words off. The expression on his face was half offended and half guilty.

"No, I just thought that you would feel obligated in some stupid way to–" I stopped, wondering how bad this was sounding. He came walking back over to the bed right beside me. He shook his head with this look on his face that was anger and something else. His eyebrows came down forming wrinkles between his eyes.

"Obligated? Skylar you saved me from a moving bullet, if it wasn't for you then I would be exactly where you are right now but I'm not. Yeah, I feel like there is some way to repay you, but deep down in the bottom of my heart I know there is no way on this earth until the day I die that I would ever be able to repay you. No one can pay back such a thankful debt like that one, not anyone, but me putting my number in your phone has nothing to do with wanting to pay you back for saving me. Maybe-maybe I thought I had feelings for a real girl that isn't afraid to be herself when she's around me, but I guess it's just all about me being obligated to you for saving my life." He shook his head, taking a deep breath in. My eyes opened wide, feeling upset for even saying that. What is wrong with me? Jason turned away walking over to the door. I didn't want him to leave, I didn't want to be alone. Most of all I didn't want him to be angry with me. At this point I just want to protect him.

"Jason!" I couldn't let him slip through my hands with that much ease. He stopped before leaving the room. His head came back over his shoulder looking at me. I shook my head not sure how to bring him back. "I'm sorry." I apologized; it seemed like the right thing to do. He sighed, letting his head fall forward onto the door. His hand slid down the inner part of the door before falling back to his side.

"No, don't be sorry." His eyes never made contact

with mine, they just stayed focused on the wooden door. I felt bad inside, wanting to take back what I said.

"You're mad with me." I felt the hatred and rejection. The one he had to give to so many girls. I was now printed in the same lineup.

"No, I'm not." His green eyes were frustrated. All I wanted was to take back the stupid words that just floated out of my mouth. He does care, he just said it himself. Then it hit me, he said he thought he actually had feelings for me. Everything seemed to stop then, all I could hear was my own heartbeat. Nervousness was kicking in and I felt my palms get sweaty. He really did want to be with me.

"Jason?" I whispered, feeling this glee inside that painted a million pieces of my heart. Shifting my eyes back up to his eyes still filled with sorrow and anger.

"I need to go Skylar." His head went back down, heading back out the door.

"Jason, no wait!" I lifted up and felt the pain ripple up my whole body. I bent back over holding my side. A tiny cry of pain came out of my mouth. Jason was back at my side within seconds.

"Careful, you're bleeding again." He noted, realizing my side was leaking some blood. I sighed as he laid me back in bed. Feeling his hands under my back reminded me of my dad when he cared. When he used to carry me to bed at night, through the store, even when we would walk out of late-night movies. Jason's hand ran down my hair. Dad used to do the same every night before kissing my forehead and after telling me some stupid story he'd pull out of his ass. I felt my eyes line with water and a phone went off. Jason pulled his phone out, then a tear came sliding down my face.

"Hey, hey why are you crying?" He slid his phone back into his pocket. I shook my head, not wanting him to watch me cry. Both my hands covered my eyes wiping the tears away.

"My life is hell." I breathed through my weak tears. His hand ran down my arm.

"Well, if it makes you feel any better your mom will be coming back soon." His voice was unsure of what he should be saying. I felt so awkward right now. I continued wiping the tears from my eyes once more. So many emotions were consuming me at once. My heart was laced with a new love, but my brain was stained with memories of the man who was supposed to love and cherish me. Jason didn't really have any idea about my fucked-up life. I listened as he sat back in the chair; his actions made my thoughts stop, even as the tears continued to rage.

"Jason, how are you not wondering what all that was about last night?" My quivering voice even gave myself chills. I wasn't ready to talk about last night nor was I ready to talk about the past few months. Jason was going to end up finding out if he wanted any kind of relationship with me. I wasn't ready to spill the truth, but it wasn't good holding it all in either. These questions would be asked. There was no way in hell I could keep it from him, it wouldn't be right. If we end up in a serious relationship at some point down the line, he needs to know what he is signing up for.

"You mean you know why all that happened last night?" His voice confused, like some shocking story had just come out. It was a shocking story to be told though. I didn't make any movements, still unsure if I should tell him or not. I felt the tears threatening to escape; I didn't want to leave behind or lose anyone else in my life. By not telling him, I felt as though I would be protecting him. I already saved his life and now I had to do him a favor by not telling him the truth. He needed to get away from me; I was the danger zone.

"Jason, I think you should go!" I said, trying my hardest not to let my tears fall. His fingers ran down through the side of my hair.

"Skylar, are you in some kind of danger?" He was asking questions and I felt stupid for even crying because he cares enough to come back. I was in more danger than imaginable, but I didn't want him to be the knot hanging onto that danger with me. I let a slow breath come out through the crack in my lips trying to collect myself.

"No Jason, someone just broke into our house and shot me for no reason! Please just leave I don't need you here right now asking me questions!" I snapped at him wanting him to leave me alone. To run away and never try to be a piece of my life again. His mouth hung open a little as he got up from the chair. His expression was conflicted and I knew I had caused it. Begging him to stay, then requesting him to leave. He was forcing himself on this rollercoaster by not leaving.

"Skylar, I didn't mean to hurt you." He pleaded, and I could see the sorrow fill his eyes once more. I was on this emotional rollercoaster and I didn't want him on this ride with me.

"You didn't hurt me, I just need some time alone, please just leave." My voice trembled feeling sorrow in my own heart. His lips separated like I hurt him in some kind of way, but he would be fine. He wasn't in the same kind of hell as I was in. He wasn't a helpless victim.

"If that's really what you want." His voice was low as he watched me sob, as if it was my defense. Nodding my head and wiping my eyes, once more taking a gasping breath in like a fish out of water.

"It's for the best." Sniffling back the pain, I had to let go. Letting go before anything started was the best way to go. I had enough hope that it wasn't too late already.

"Okay, are you sure you're going to be okay?" He handed me a tissue as I thought about what he said. I couldn't say I was going to be okay. I was so far from fine it wasn't even funny.

"I'm a strong woman, Jason." Reminding him of that reminded me I didn't need to sit here and cry. I was strong, so why mope around thinking I'm a delicate doll?

I was by far not made from porcelain. Each hit Richard took gave me the will power to continue forth with my life. This bullet coated me with the armor I needed.

"Alright, well I'm here whenever you need me." His voice was low with roughness. He walked away from me then. I had a lot of thinking to do. I didn't want to be by myself with the killer out there on the thin skin between us. The monster that shared my blood had to go down and I would make the rest of his life a living hell if he ever did anything to hurt Jason or my mom. My thoughts paused then, did I just care if Jason got hurt or not?

"Were you really about to tell him the truth?" Dave's cool body made the whole room change temperature. I looked at the wooden door thinking about Jason. I was about to tell him the truth but the guilt of saving his life overpowered it.

"I feel like he should know, Dave." Wiping the last of the tears off my cheeks feeling the need to catch up with him in the hall. I knew I was in no shape to run to him.

"I feel like that is a horrible mistake." He sat down on the bed, forcing my eyes to him.

"Not like I haven't made enough of those." I whispered to myself, thinking about what he had to say to me. Jason had feelings for me, and I might have just blown them all away. Jason is not the bad guy I know that much; I can feel it.

"Sky, I know he might become your boyfriend or whatever but if you tell him about your extreme life with the man that tried to kill him, he won't even want to look at you." He shook his head. keeping those frozen eyes on mine. Dave might be right; however, I feel that keeping him sheltered from the truth might push him even further away. Jason wants to know so much about me, but I can't just open my doors and tell my story like he can. Of course, he hasn't opened his doors all the way either.

My hand pushed up through my hair. Maybe he wasn't the one that was obligated to give back to me. Maybe this whole time it was my obligation to protect him. That's why I didn't want any involvement with him, or anyone. It's just too much on one person's plate. I just wanted to wrap up this life of running in horror before meeting anyone. Turns out life had a different path for me.

"Dave, I have to keep Jason safe now." I nodded my head, more or less telling myself that since my dad saw him, Jason was now a part of the list. Family or not, Jason was a small part of me which gave him room on my dad's killing list. Yet another puzzle piece being jostled in the mix.

"Skylar, please, don't do this!" Dave begged me, before he faded away leaving his fog. My door came open, seeing Mom walk in with a bag of food. To my surprise Missy came in behind her with a smile on her face.

"Hi Sky!" Missy's voice was excited to see me. I smiled at her but looked over to my mom. What did she think she was doing letting Missy come here? The more people we welcomed in, the more threats and throat slashing is going to happen. I don't know about my mom, but I was not about to let these innocent people get hurt, killed, or taken because of me.

"I thought it would make you happy if your friend could come and see you." She said, giving off the biggest fake smile I've seen. She pushed the table over to me opening my food up. How did my mom know Missy? Now a flush of frustration washed over me. Would this have been more awkward or less awkward if Jason was still here? With either outcome, I wish he was still sitting beside me. Just the slightest thought made me realize I could still smell his cologne lingering in the room. I briefly shut my eyes feeling serene.

"Well, it is definitely a surprise!" Lifting my eyebrows up and smiling at Missy.

"You don't expect me to leave you in a hospital bed while a hot celebrity takes care of you, do you?" Missy sat down in the chair Jason had been occupying. I tilted my head looking back over to my mom as she ate.

"You told her?" The last thing I wanted Missy to hear was that Jason was here with me. She would be all over that and want like a year's worth of scoop.

"I didn't really think it was necessary keeping it from your best friend sweetie." Mom laughed a little, eating her soup. I rolled my eyes to myself looking back to Missy. My life escalated so fast that I wasn't sure I wanted to see anyone's face.

"So, are you two dating now or what?" Missy ate fruit and I didn't know what to say; besides I knew this would happen.

"Right, he is such a kind young man for having all he has." Mom pointed her spoon over to Missy. This room had exploded into a girl's lunch within seconds.

"And his looks are just killer!" Missy was getting all excited about him. My mom wasn't exactly helping matters either. All I could do was shake my head wishing that none of this had happened; it was entirely my fault. This was terrible and I just wanted them to shut up; all I cared about was keeping people out of my mess and preventing them from any harm. I knew my mom was only looking out for me, but this was not a good idea at all. Besides, I've never really been one for a girl's lunch where all you do is gossip about boys and personal relationships. I just wanted them to realize Jason and I were nothing more than two people who were held at gunpoint. Was lying to myself about my feelings for Jason going to help though? He admitted his feelings to me, and I sunk like a rock, because the truth is – I want to be with him too.

"What if they go to prom together?" Missy exclaimed in a peppy voice.

"That would be wonderful, I bet she would get the works!" Mom's eyes grew big. I sighed, putting my hand over half my face. This has got to stop.

Jason

I came to a slow stop watching all the cars surround me. I had no idea what happened last night. Why wasn't I the one to be shot? Why were those two men even in Skylar's house? I knew something strange was happening, I also felt like she lied to me. Something told me that she knew what was happening or why it was happening, she was never very open with me. That was one thing that I had to figure out – why.

A man pulled up beside me, his eyes squinted like he was driving right into the sun. What was he looking at? He wore all black, even his car was black. The traffic at the light moved just a little but he didn't stay in sync with it. He was watching me. When my light turned green, I started to take off, but he followed along at the same pace as me. I had no idea what he was doing or why he was doing this. He merged into the turn lane and right as he did so he held two fingers up making a gun. His hand went back as if he was going to shoot me, then he left my sight within seconds. What the hell was going on?

A car blew its horn, I swerved back into my lane. Blinking my eyes a few times thinking about all of this, I curved my fingers around the steering wheel. I didn't see the other man that was with the guy that held the gun to me. But it made no sense why a random man wanted to shoot me. I decided to take another way home. I crossed over a few streets leading me back to Skylar's house. I had to see some stuff for myself. Once I approached the house, I could see that the front door still had yellow police tape guarding it. The front door was still busted open and sharp pieces of wood splintering out of the sides. I pulled over to the curb turning off my car. Jumping out and having no idea what I was looking for, but anything would be good at this point. I ducked under the yellow tape entering the house. Glass was spread out everywhere on the floor, one little numbered sign sat up where the bullet shell had been. There was still blood on the floor. This place was a mess. I didn't even know where to look for a start. If I touched anything the wrong way, I could be the gun man. Best idea was to not touch anything down here on the lower level. I went sprinting up the stairs seeing pictures hanging on the wall. They were simple, Skylar and her mom, a few pets here and there, I opened the first door to my right. Seeing a nice made bed and a clean room, this wasn't Skylar's room. It didn't look like anything she would live in. I walked on down the hall a little more, opening the door to the next room. Darker shades of colors filled it and I walked in. Seeing the bed wasn't made and a black canopy hung from the ceiling over the bed. I hadn't imagined her to have one of those.

I went over to the dresser seeing a couple of pictures of her then there was this blonde guy with her. His arm wrapped around her shoulders as they embraced each other. They both looked so happy. I picked up the next picture seeing the same guy in the picture with her; this time they were on the beach. I felt like I understood why she was pushing me away now. She already had someone, whether he was here or not. He could still be wherever she came from. I closed my eyes setting it back down. Sighing to myself realizing that I was the fool here. Who was I fooling? She had a normal life with some guy that wasn't always being attacked by crazy women. She told me she had a boyfriend that day in art class. I was naïve to calculate that was a lie. My wishful thoughts lingered about having a normal life.

I walked back over to the bed seeing her computer sitting there. It was open but not on. I hit the power button watching as the screen lit up. To my surprise there was no password needed. That was just luck. Facebook popped up but it wasn't on her profile it was on this lady named Kristy. I clicked her internet tab to the bottom of the screen seeing the background on her computer. Her and this blonde guy I keep seeing everywhere. His eyes were so blue, who is he? I went over hitting her files bringing up the pictures. Scrolling through them seeing the same people over and over, then I saw something. Skylar was in between her mom and this guy. Flashbacks took me back to the other night. This man was the guy that was going to shoot me. An ache formed in my throat sensing that man was her father or a family member. Skylar was in danger; she was persistent about pushing me away. It all made sense now.

I was careful, placing the laptop back in its original spot, before I stood up. I caught a glimpse of my own reflection in her mirror. What was I doing here? Glancing around the room at the emptiness, realizing I just broke a boundary. Skylar would never trust me again if she knew I was here in her home uninvited, let alone in her room. Why did I bring myself here? I've never done this before. In that moment I snapped, not understanding why I wasn't in control of myself. I paced over to the hallway leaving her room behind. One last look at the picture hanging on the wall, feeling my heart skip a beat. She was so beautiful, and yet she had no idea.

Skylar

Listening to Missy and Mom go on about me going to prom with Jason was getting annoying at this point. They laughed and joked, all I wanted to do was choke the both of them.

"I'm not going to prom with Jason!" I yelled over them, making the giggles stop. They both looked at me with utter shock. It was no big deal I just needed to make them stop this nonsense gossip. I had to stay away from Jason and that was that.

"Are you crazy?" Missy yelled back at me, throwing her arms out.

"Honey, I really don't see what you have against Jason." Mom shook her head in disbelief. I groaned, only wishing they could understand me. Yes, Jason was a good guy, I could see that, but he was not about to get caught up in my life drama. Mom should be smart enough to keep all these people around me, away from me. This left anger in my veins.

"No one said I had anything against him." This seemed to be turning into an argument now. My phone went off bringing their attention to me.

Dave: Jason has decided to do some looking up on you.

My mind was racing now. What was Jason looking up about me? How was he searching anything up about me? Then it hit me. It must have been because of my dad. He wanted to shoot Jason, now he wants to cover his tracks. Smart guy.

Skylar: What is he doing?

I couldn't even begin to understand but I wanted out of this hospital bed. I wanted to go after him. He needs to know all this stuff so he will stop searching. I didn't want him to know that I had a demented father that wanted to kill his family. It was the most messed up thing ever. No one will ever want to date me or ever be around me under those circumstances.

Dave: He was on your laptop searching, I don't trust this guy anymore Sky.

Even though Dave didn't trust him, I did. That might sound crazy, but it was true. The more I pushed Jason away the more he came back which made me fall harder for him. The more I wanted to be with him and the more I knew I was supposed to be. A fire continued to glow inside me even with all the warning signs. I wasn't angry that Jason went back to my house. I couldn't be upset with him for trying to search for answers; it's what I would have done. Jason's energy matched mine, and that in itself ignited a fire within me. As I thought more about it, the chatter from Missy and Mom faded away more and more.

Lying my phone upon my chest, I closed my eyes. A smile painted my face, imagining Jason's forest green eyes capturing me. His black choppy mid length hair was soft, cascading over one eye. The happy glow revealing his white teeth, left sensations of bliss blooming inside of me, feeling a connection that once was misguided. This feeling was new. I've never felt this way in my entire life. I might be crazy for going head-over-heals for this movie star, but my intuition told me otherwise. She was eager for this next step in my life. I had to grasp my own courage and stop being afraid.

Chapter 9
Waking Up

I heard a bunch of conversations around me. My eyes opened fast, seeing no one in my room. What was I hearing? Rolling my eyes around the room seeing the sun peeking through the big window, my mom stood there staring down. What was she looking at? The door to my room opened and to my surprise cameras flashed all over. My mouth fell open and Mom turned around fast. Jason came in the room shutting the door behind him making the camera flashes disappear. Mom walked over to him quickly. She whispered something in his ear, and he nodded his head in agreement.

"What's going on?" Listening to my groggy voice was awful, but Jason glanced over to me. Mom's eyes followed suit picking up on us watching each other. Orange, yellow, and white flowers hung by Jason's side loose in his hand. A smile crept onto my face; this was the third bouquet of flowers he had brought me. I smiled, unsure why he always brought flowers.

"Well, that out there is what I like to call a pain in my ass." He hitched his thumb over his shoulder towards the door. Mom laughed a little with him, but I was still taking in what it was. Chatter arose outside the door of my room; I saw shadows of footsteps beneath the wooden door.

"That's the fame, isn't it?" I took the flowers smelling them, but the door came open again. Seeing the doctor walk in with some papers, he flipped them over his board scanning each one. Flashes of light pivot through the door like a portal. Jason closed it behind the doctor fast.

"Good morning Miss. Saxton, how are you feeling?" The doctor's eyes came down to look at me. I looked at his pepper hair then his eyes that told his age. I feel like I haven't ever met this man before but then if my mom was taking care of it, that's why. This was the first time I was meeting the doctor; I've spoken with three different nurses but never this man.

"Fine." I said, thinking about where the bullet went through me.

"Good fine or bad fine?" He asked, walking around the other side of the bed. I didn't know how to answer that question.

"I'm not really sure." I admitted, and he glanced at my body over his glasses pulling my gown apart on the side. I flinched when he opened my gown darting my eyes over to Jason, his attention was occupied with his phone. A whimper seeped out of my lips, feeling pressure on my lower rib as the doctor's big hand pressed inward. His fingers moved around the big white bandage causing the pain to increase. I bit down on my lip feeling tears threaten my eyes once more.

"Does this hurt?" He asked, pressing a little harder. My hand went down tossing him off me.

"No, it feels like a magical land over the rainbow, what do you think?" I snickered, yelling at him. Mom came walking up and I heard Jason laughing to himself. Jason's thumb and index finger tugged his lower lip out spectating me from across the room.

"Now, Honey, he just wants to make sure you're well before going home." Mom told me, resting her hand on my shoulder. I was going home, a little bit of excitement hit me then. I was going to get out of this hospital bed.

"I would say that after three days of being in here you are healing quite well, Skylar." The doctor spoke with wisdom in his eyes while writing something down on paper.

"So, I'm going home?" All I wanted was to get out of this hospital. Everything seemed like it was falling away from me in here. Then again, it did give me a lot of time to think.

"Yes, I think we can discharge you today." The doctor said, walking on over to the door. Flashing lights started to creep in. My smile left my face. All the commotion commenced again. I heard people asking the doctor questions before the door shut it off. Jason's head went down a little as he sighed. I already knew why they were here, but I was nobody important.

"They're here for you." I said, knowing who they were, just not sure why. His green eyes came back up to mine.

"I'm sorry you have to put up with a piece of my hell." He apologized, not seeming thrilled with the idea of having them here.

"It's okay, it's kind of exciting." I admitted shrugging my shoulders. He gave me a crooked smile and a nurse came in the room. She had gauze in her hand. Flashing lights followed behind her as she stared at Jason with a smile. Things always got awkward when people knew him. I haven't been out with him much, but I could tell. A reporter snuck in the door, but Jason was quick to whip her around escorting her back out.

"Are you going to wrap her up?" Mom broke the stare, and the nurse had a warm smile on her face.

"Yes, I need to change the bandages and then she will be ready to go." Her voice was cheery. I watched her shiny black hair pulled back in a ponytail. Her eyes were sharp and squinted with her smile; they felt warm and were giving me confidence – it said to me that she was happy with her job. She came over taking the bandages off and I saw the dried blood. The wound was sore and still vibrant red with purple and blue bruises around it like a halo. I sighed resting my head back on my pillow. The door to my room come opened briskly allowing the flashing lights to flush through the room and to my surprise an older man was standing here. The door behind him shutting with a thud, my bed trembled from the force he left behind and the nurse stopped holding my used gauze.

"What do you think you're doing?" He went straight up to Jason coming face to face with him. Mom's eyes were wide open as she watched. The nurse let go of me rushing over to them.

"Excuse me, who are you?" She asked, her voice a little frantic. The older man, that I imagined was Jason's dad, held his hand up to her in an act of silencing her.

"Do you have any idea what you are doing to yourself?" He scolded Jason, shaking his finger in his face like he was a bad dog.

"Well, that's good parenting." Mom whispered in a sarcastic voice, crossing her arms. She left my side walking over to them too.

"I'm sorry but I am going to have to ask you to leave, sir." The nurse told him, and the fire that burned in his eyes lit up. My mouth fell open a little bit and Jason's eyes were huge, watching his outraged father.

"Excuse you but I am talking to my son who does not involve you in any way, shape or form." His voice was so thick, like hateful acid. I didn't understand, but then again, I never did. I haven't dated Jason; Jason comes after me. Do I like Jason? Yes. However, I feel as though this changed everything once again. Jason wanted to keep everything we do private, so no one knows. Now everyone knows. I soon understood his reasoning behind keeping our potential relationship on the down low. Outside my door, the press stood flooding the area with lights, inside my room Jason's dad stood ramping up a hurricane.

"Whoa, whoa, whoa, I'm sorry but you don't talk to her like that and furthermore you don't just bust into a hospital room when a patient is being treated." My mom told him, getting an intense look in her eyes. The snarl on her face was the same one she gave my father when she was trying to protect me a few nights ago.

"And you want me to listen to you? A woman that doesn't watch her daughter enough to make sure she doesn't get shot by some psychopath?" He got close to my mom's face and her mouth dropped open. The anger has reached the boiling point and before my mom said anything Jason stepped in between them. His hands backed my mom up before she took action to his words. This man had a lot of audacity.

"Don't tell her how to take care of her daughter, Dad, and don't sit here giving me a lecture on some bullshit that doesn't even matter at this point. This isn't about the press being here getting the pictures they want; this isn't about my job nor is it about me at all!" His green eyes grew bigger, while my mom stepped further away. His dad's head moved back some, seeming a little confused.

"I'm sorry but if you need to talk can you please take it somewhere else?" The nurse asked them, still trying to get her piece of mind in. Jason's dad gave her a dirty look, but Jason got the chance to speak before he ever did.

"Yes, we can leave, and I am so sorry about my dad." His apology to the nurse was sympathetic. Jason took his dad escorting him to the door. He pulled his sunglasses down over his eyes to hide from the cameras. He didn't wait for his dad to say anything as he opened the door and let lights consume the room. Heavy waves of voices came washing in and I saw the slight hints of recorders being put in his face. Jason's dad looked over to us and then eyed my mom. With the press flashing cameras and vigorous questions, he said not one word but left with a warning glare.

"This is entirely your fault." His finger came up asserting his words to me before leaving us behind. My eyes traveled, looking up to my mom. Her eyes showed hurt, but she just shook her head. I felt mad inside knowing that I saved his son's life, and it was our fault. Jason's dad was not wrong to accuse me of that. I broke my own vow to myself to keep Jason safe by shoving him away. My heart caved weakening. Guilt stricken; I watched the spiky edges of the white flowers Jason brought. I knew we weren't so different. I was just on level eighty while he was running courses on level ten.

Jason

Once outside Dad swung around giving me that unbelievable face, he was mad with me for being here. He was just making an ass out of himself, but he never saw it when he did such things. I waited for him to talk, but then the press came following behind. He said nothing as we went to his car. Jumping in the passenger seat quickly just wanting to get out of here now, the doors locked when Dad looked over, the death glare in his eyes was the very reason I wished to escape my life. I despised being controlled, I've been on his leash for way too long.

"Please tell me you know you're making a mistake!" His glare never faded.

"The only person making a mistake is you for coming in there like you did." I told him, not amused by any of what he was up to. If the press never showed he would never have found out about my own whereabouts.

"You know that could be you lying in that bed." He said, giving me those hateful eyes. How did he know? It was not to my benefit that the news kept this story running. I knew Abby informed him, Skylar wasn't in school the last two days, which left connections he pieced together on his own.

"And I'm not because Skylar jumped in front of me, Dad!" I wanted him to understand this. I wanted him to see that I cared about her. He didn't understand that she wasn't some obsessed fan that just wanted to touch me. Hell, she doesn't even want anything to do with me. She gets easily annoyed by me but then she gets this wild look in her eyes that tells me she likes me. A look that makes my heart race faster than my car can go. The feeling of losing her that night almost left me in a shambles. How was it possible to fall so fast and almost lose it just as quickly? Life has no timeline, no way to adjust the split-second outcomes that we never see coming. Just like that she could have died, I could have died.

"Look I don't care if you dodged a bullet, but this will not happen again, do you understand me?" His voice was harsh, and I just wanted out of this car. I didn't want to sit here and get lectured about this girl that saved my life. He didn't care about anything besides keeping me safe, and my job. Making sure I'm safe is one thing but caring about my job is another. That's my responsibility not his. He was way too involved in my work life. I could never have a normal Dad anymore, not after Mom left. He was half of my management team, a job he drowned himself in to shun a broken heart.

"You know, instead of throwing up walls you could have just thanked her for saving my life." I told him, ready to get out at the next stop light. I didn't need this, and I didn't need him being my assistant manager. It was time for my independence.

My phone started going off and it was my real manager. I rolled my eyes letting the call go to the wayside. I didn't need to take any more of this. Emma would be questioning me left and right, meanwhile my job obsessed father continues to lecture me. I rolled my head over against the seat, wishing to be back at the hospital. I wanted nothing more than to help take Skylar home. She wouldn't want to see me after my dad's absurd outburst at them. My eyes closed tightly, hearing him accusing Skylar of it all being her fault. She already had so much on her plate; she did not need to feel culpability. My hand rested against my forehead knowing I had to get my car back from the parking garage. Dad wouldn't take me back; he'd be afraid I would go to see Skylar. Truth was, I would. I feel peace with her, a happiness glowing from within. She was sarcastic, moody, shy, secretive, most of all she didn't allow anyone to control her.

Skylar

We pulled into our driveway and the house was untouched besides the busted in door along with the wood filling in the window. Yellow crime tape quivered in the wind, with our front door halfway shut. Mom stopped the car, looking down in her lap. I wasn't sure what she was thinking about, but she had a worried look on her face. She was in deep thought; she always was when she started biting on her lip. Either she was thinking about the shooting, me, or Jason's dad bursting in the room telling her she wasn't a good parent. When her eyes came back over to me there was tears in her eyes.

"I'm so happy I didn't lose you." She broke the silence, smiling at me. My heart felt a little warmth and I smiled back but that still didn't fix the bad feeling that sat in the pit of my stomach.

"I'm a fighter I guess." Giving back the positive, but

I knew the negative would come soon.

"Of course, you are, all your family were fighters." She said, patting my hand. We got out of the car walking up to the broken house. Looking at it made me feel sick inside and I wasn't sure I was ready to reenter the place where I had almost died. Walking in, my eyes went straight to the place where there was a stain on the floor. My blood was like ink tattooing the carpet with faded red. Just thinking about it gave me chills. I wouldn't be able to sleep at night and that was more than an understatement.

"They cleaned it up as best as they could, and I could only do so much." She told me, I snapped away from staring at the floor. I nodded my head, wanting to go get close to someone. Something told me I had every reason to get out of here. This house was traumatized now.

"This place is a wasteland." My voice was grave, knowing this new home was now just a broken home. Scars that scraped into my skin that will always remain. Mom wrapped her arms around my shoulders.

"It will be okay; I will make plans." She told me, and I wasn't sure what she was talking about. There was a piece of me that wasn't ready to ask yet either. She kissed the side of my head releasing me. She walked away and I went over to the stairs staring up them, like I was looking into a whole different world. The dark hall with just a few pictures hanging, everything still new and fresh. It has been broken in the worst way. All I could do was close my eyes as I walked up the stairs. I passed the few pictures of us that hung on the wall, remembering what it felt like to smile. The only genuine smile I wore as of late was when Jason was around. Time has come to wash that away from me as well. All good things come to an end. I only wished that for once, I wished to be able to set the ending myself instead of destiny doing it for me.

Dave sat on the bed waiting for me, he had a small smile on his face, but I couldn't bring myself to return it. I felt as though there would be a line to cross soon, and it would just be too late; someone would lose their life because of some unfaithful man who couldn't be trusted. There would be nothing left to fix after all this.

"Don't worry, I'm here." Dave wrapped me up in his cold body. I felt the coldness seeping into the wound. I winced moving back a little. His blue eyes washed into mine.

"I don't want to be here Dave." I chose honesty, resting my head down on his shoulder.

"I know, but I don't think you will be for long." He said, running his hand down through my hair. I lifted my head up from his shoulder then.

"What do you mean?" I felt that Dave knew something that he needed to share. His blue eyes went down from mine alongside his arms.

"Think about it Sky, she's not going to let her daughter stay here where she can just get hurt again." Dave said, making a good point. I was so tired of moving, running, and living in fear. There had to be an end to all this.

Maybe my death would have been the end.

My phone went off startling the both of us. Pulling it out from my pocket I saw that Missy was calling me. What could she possibly want right now? Hitting the answer button, Dave moved in closer.

"Hello." I breathed, feeling kind of awkward when Dave got this close.

"Sky, turn to H! right now, you won't believe this!" Her voice excited and Dave flashed away from me. Watching the TV pop on as he flipped through the channels. My mind went back to the hospital with all the cameras.

"Missy, am I on there?" Feeling the nervous pit opening up, she said nothing as the H! News people started talking. The tall caramel haired lady was covering the story while pictures floated behind them of Jason leaving the hospital followed by me soon after.

"Looks like we have a new couple alert, isn't that right Tyrese?" She turned to the younger guy, who wore a pleasing smile.

"Absolutely Gigi, it seems to look as if Jason Blackstone might have his very own mistress." His eyebrows lifted, and my stomach plunged down even deeper.

"We have the footage to make you believe he has a new girl right here." She said, and they flipped over to a video of him leaving the hospital. He was leaving my room and questions were being blasted at him left and right. He didn't say a single word and neither did his father as they left. The clip changed to me leaving with Mom. My eyes widened; I had not even realized they were videotaping me. My hair looked horrid. I reached up knowing that was taken just moments ago.

"Sky this is great!" Missy was so happy to see me on the entertainment news. I had nothing to say. I just pulled the phone away from my head and hung up. I watched the TV as they went back to the newsroom.

"That was the latest footage of Jason and this mystery girl, no reps have confirmed a dating couple, but they did tell us that Jason was visiting this young girl in the hospital and he was there the last three days. Tyrese what do you think?" She looked back over to her co-host. He smiled once more holding his hands out.

"Gigi, I think this could be a very huge possibility, I mean he spent three days in the hospital with this girl, there's got to be something." He said, shaking his head.

"Now on to J-Lo–" The woman cut off as Dave turned the TV off. My stomach was so twisted, making me feel nauseous. What was happening? I almost died a couple days ago, I live in the hospital for three days, Jason is there because he cares about me or maybe he just felt obligated to do so, even though he poured his heart out to me and made it clear that wasn't the case. Then today there are cameras everywhere, his dad burst into the room like a volcano exploding, and now I'm on this entertainment news show. My life has been flipped upside down. I feel like I've just lived through the biggest wake-up call of my life.

Chapter 10
The Truth

"Skylar get down here!" My mom called from downstairs, I sat up in bed quickly. My side ached making me gasp for a moment. I rubbed my eyes just waking up. I didn't want to get yelled at for some unknown reason. She does realize I have twelve stitches under my rib cage, right? I realized her voice was urgent, I flew out of bed. This time I grabbed a blunt heavy flashlight wobbling out of the room. Dave stopped me fast with surprised eyes. His cold hands lay against my bare skin. He shook his head taking the flashlight from my hand.

"It's not good, but it's not that bad." He assured me, as he walked away. I looked back over my shoulder to him, going to ask what it was.

"Sky! Are you up? Get down here now!" Mom yelled at me again, so instead, I turned back around heading down into the living room. Mom stood staring out the window. What was she staring at? My heart raced in my chest, scared that the black car might be sitting back out on the street. Dave said it wasn't that bad though. I walked up to her luring her eyes from outside.

"These people are crazy; do you know anything about this?" She held her hand out to the window. I peeked around the curtain seeing all the paparazzi out there. Cameras were flashing and there were people standing out there with microphones. They all wanted to see me, and I knew why. That sick feeling kicked back in, making me walk away from the window. My wound started to throb as the pressure was kicking in and building because of everything.

"Sky, why are these people here?" She was freaking out over them, and I just wanted out of this crazy life. It was like a whirlwind of torture. I glanced at the barely hinged front door.

"You really can't figure it out?" I said looking back at her. She folded her arms as I watched her answer her own question. She knew why these people were here.

"You need to call Jason and tell him to get these people out of here!" She hissed coming closer to me. I squinted my eyes not going to do that. Jason was the Novocain to the pain for them. I was not about to feed them what they want.

"No Mom, that's the last thing he's going to want." I didn't have to know Jason to know he didn't want this. No famous person wants to always be in the spotlight.

"Well, I can't get them out of here!" She was freaking out, but I really didn't care.

"Just don't walk out the door and everything will be fine." I walked away heading back up the stairs. I could feel the stitches tearing at my skin. I lifted the side of my shirt up seeing the gauze still in tack with the medical tape.

"Sky, you can't just walk away from this." She said sounding defeated. I could just walk away from it though; it was no big deal. They just wanted to make a story that wasn't true. The news would report about a simpleton; my havoc filled life would be publicized to millions of people. No one would care about me, just him. Although, one thing could lead to another and before we knew it, my mom and I could wake up to a crime drama team pounding on our busted door.

"Just don't answer the door, Mom." I told her heading back down the hall. Once in the room Dave was on my bed looking through my phone. My mouth dropped open as I went over to snatch it out of his ghostly hands.

"Why are you going through my stuff?" I felt like Dave had crossed the line of being my close friend. Everyone loved taking my phone away.

"Because I care about you." He said smiling.

"If you cared about me, you wouldn't just go through my personal stuff!" I almost yelled at him, but I knew that if I did, I would end up looking like the crazy one – yelling at a dead person only I could see. My mom would think I was tripping out on pain meds.

"Someone's moody today!" He flipped over onto his back.

"Yeah, I don't like thinking that I can trust someone and

then finding them snooping through my things." Holding my hands down on my hips realizing that I was just in my underwear and shirt again, my eyes grew bigger, and Dave laughed a little. The pain started growing more intense in my side. I was stupid for rushing out of my bed the way I did.

"You're yelling at me because I read a text and now you realize you're half naked and want me out, awesome!" He gave me a big smile and left my room before I could hurt him. I was so mad, but I can't hurt a dead man. No one can. I looked down to my phone then, seeing that Jason texted me.

Jason: Hey thought I would stop by is that okay?

I sighed in frustration thinking about the press. He would not be happy to come over here to this mess.

Skylar: I don't think it's a good time right now.

Tossing my phone back onto the bed I went over slipping myself into my pajama pants. I peeked out my window seeing all the people down there. Then I saw the neighbors gawking out their windows too. Great the whole neighborhood knows about something. My phone went off again, why can't he just respect my decision for once?

Jason: Sorry we're already on our way…

My eyes widened wondering who *we* were. He was with somebody this time? I hope it isn't his sister, my life really would be ruined then. I climbed back onto my bed resting my sore body. I was on bed rest, and yet I'm jumping around causing myself more harm.

Skylar: Jason that's really not a good idea.

I didn't want him and whoever it was here. I was trying to save him, but something told me that wasn't going to work out too well. Before any other message could return, the doorbell went off. My heart started pounding with my lips slipping apart. My body rolled out of bed feeling the pressure on my side again. I really shouldn't be moving. I waddled down the hallway to the stairs. Mom was already at the window peeking out. *Please just let it be the press.* She came back from the window and unlocked the door. That was enough to tell me that it wasn't. I backed up the stairs before she could see me peeking from around the corner. Jason and his dad walked in the door with flashing lights following behind. They got here really fast. Jason did not lie about being on the way. Mom carefully shut the half-unhinged door making it screech.

"Hey, did Skylar call you?" She asked Jason as she attempted to lock the door.

"No, I told her I was going to come over to see if she was doing alright." I heard him say and then I heard something else. Someone that gave me chills, and I peeked around the corner again to see Abby standing there, dressed like some Barbie. *Oh god, the whole family was here?*

"Oh, well do you want me to go get her?" I heard my mom ask and I swallowed not wanting to go down there to face my enemy standing with the guy that cared for me.

"Not so fast there, Jason only wanted to stop by to see if she was alright, I'm sure you can tell us." I heard his dad say, and it made me angry. Why did he have to talk for Jason?

"Oh, uh-well she's doing just fine, you know we never really got to properly meet each other yesterday." Mom told his dad with a genuine smile. I could feel the mood of the room change to displeasure.

"Yes, well there was no need because Jason isn't allowed to see your daughter anymore." He said sternly to my mom, and my mouth fell open. Peering around the corner again seeing my mom's expression; she looked floored that he would even say that to her. Abby's smile told me how amused she was, but Jason's face was solid darkness because of what he just said.

"Don't listen to him, look can I go see Sky?" Jason asked and my eyes widened again. Did he just give me a nickname? Butterflies took off zooming inside of me like a cage. Everyone called me Sky but the way he said it, it was different.

"Hey, you heard what Dad said." Abby had to get her two cents in on this. I rolled my eyes watching what Mom had to say.

"Do you think I really care?" Jason was still mad, but he was trying to cool it down.

"Jason this is not the kind of behavior you show

me while we are in someone else's presence." His dad pointed his finger down at the floor showing his true side. Jason squinted his eyes becoming more furious.

"I don't want to cut in here, but Mr. Blackstone I think that Jason can make his own choices." My mom told him, and I had mixed feelings about that. My mom was about to get a mouthful of something she wouldn't want.

"And who are you to talk for my son?" His dad was getting pissed off. I had to go do something before all this would turn to hell.

"I'm the woman that owns the house you are standing in." She threw it back in his corner making a valid point. His dad's lips pressed together.

"Come on Jason it's time to get out of here." His dad turned back around going to the door.

"I'm not going anywhere." Jason shoved his hands down into his pockets protesting his dad's authority.

"Jason, you listen to me, and you listen to me now, I will not tolerate this behavior out of you, she is not the kind of girl you want to be involved with!" His dad yelled at him, making my eyes shut. My fingers gripped the edge of the wall thinking about what I needed to do. The butterflies continued to swarm but a thickening pain steered the bliss away.

"You can't sit here and tell me who the right person to be involved with is, Skylar is not a bad person, and neither is her mother. You don't know the first thing about these people and all I have to say is they treat me a lot better than you do right now." Jason told him making something warm creep into my heart. He cared about me and that was obvious. I walked around the corner wobbling down the stairs. Everyone looked at me as I reached the last step. Without saying any words, I went over to Jason wrapping my arms around him. The grim look on his face turned into complete happiness. The sweet woodsy smell engulfed my nostrils sending me to cloud nine. The purest form of love rained from his mouth in the defense of my family. Jason's arms felt odd, like home, as he embraced my body. He was so tender, noticing how I stood from my healing wound. His big warm hands ran down my back. With my head nestled on his chest, I felt his masculine body. Yet another manly thing setting him aside from the average high school boy. The thickness of his heartbeat was the most soothing part. Blood flowed vigorously like a waterfall.

"Oh, this is great." Abby smiled pulling her phone out. I shifted my head as she acted coy taking pictures.

"No, no, get your hands off my son, we need to go." His dad grabbed Jason's wrist unlatching him from my body.

"Stop, you can't make Jason go with you, if he wants to be here, he can." I said, looking up into his green eyes. His black eyebrows raised and the smile on his face made me feel warm inside. Everything Jason has been begging for has finally been given. I was ready to accept him. I was ready to date him. Hearing his heartfelt words, feeling the most enjoyable hug I've ever had, I knew it was time to call him, mine.

"You people think this is a good idea but it's not." His dad folded his arms.

"Then I guess Jason being my boyfriend isn't a good idea either, is it?" I spoke with courage feeling my heart race out of control. Jason wasn't my boyfriend, but I think I just confirmed a lie that was believable to everyone in this room. Abby's mouth dropped open as her phone went down, and Jason's dads arm fell away from his chest. Shock took over everyone, even Jason. My mom had surprised eyes and a little smile too. She shipped us together just as hard as Missy did.

"That's right so I'm staying here to help take care of her." Jason put his arm around me going with it.

"Now since Jason has made his choice, I would really love it if you could take your rude ass out of my house." Mom walked around Jason and me, and over next to Abby. Her eyes grew big as she flipped her blonde hair back.

"Excuse us?" She gave my mom the snotty voice.

"Let's just go Abby, Jason we are having a long talk later." His dad stared him in the eyes with that deep daring gaze. It almost scared me. They opened the loose door letting all the lights come in. When the door slammed shut everything was soon gone again. Mom turned back around looking at us. Her eyebrows lifted showing an especially pleased smile on her face.

"Your father and sister are welcoming." She told Jason, patting his arm. Jason's smile faded and his eyes dropped to the floor.

"Sorry about that Mrs. Saxton." He apologized to my mom, and I took his hand pulling him along with me.

"It's not your fault, where are you guys going?" She asked tilting her head.

"Jason and I need to talk Mom." I told her sprinting up the steps with Jason's hand still holding onto mine. I gasp feeling low on air, with the sting of my wound threatening me again. I wasn't sure where I was going with this, all I knew was I needed to talk to him and figure out the truth. He needed to know the truth about me too. Going into my room and letting go of his hand, I closed the door taking a seat on my bed. He just watched a little unsure of everything. I was amused at his green eyes, filled with joy, yet still cautious.

"So, I'm your boyfriend?" He rested his hand on his chest smiling. I sighed not wanting to start with that awkward question.

"Let's not start with that." Shaking my head; feeling my side throb with pain, Jason's head went down then. Those green eyes had caught my look of pain.

"So, what do we start with then?" His voice lowered and I moved back on my bed. I motioned for him to sit down. The black shorts he wore rode up his legs as he pretzel crossed them on my bed. I had the oddest instinct to run my finger through his leg hair, but I refrained.

"I need to tell you the truth." I sighed, not sure how to explain my secret.

"The truth about what?" His eyes full of questions now. I didn't have the guts to tell him in the hospital. I still wasn't sure I had the courage to tell him now, but I was going to anyway.

"Remember in the hospital when I didn't understand how you weren't questioning what had happened to me?" It was time to expose myself with what I knew. This could end badly, and I could lose Jason. It was going to be safer for him though.

"Right, look I know that you knew why all that happened to you, I just don't understand why you didn't tell me." His voice was full of honesty. He'd read my eyes so clearly that day, like a bright sky-blue day. I knew he did, I also knew it hurt him knowing that I couldn't just be truthful with him.

"Because Jason, the man that was going to shoot you, he's the reason why we moved here." Pulling my legs up close to myself, and then feeling the pressure of the wound and letting my legs go back down. Jason's eyebrows lifted, watching me.

"This man has been after you and your mom all this time?" He tilted his head.

"Not all this time, it wasn't too long ago he took his first strike at hurting us." I couldn't look at Jason. I felt a pain plunging into my heart.

"What did he do before?" His voice was full of

concern. My head fell down not sure this was a good idea. Jason had a short fuse of fear in him now.

"He wants to kill my mom." My hand flew to my mouth; the thought ripped me to pieces. He was a monster that couldn't be broken.

"Oh, my god," he paused in silence, "Sky I don't know what to say." He shook his head moving his hand through his hair. There wasn't anything for him to say. I knew this had to be said otherwise I would always be lying to the man that cares about me.

"You don't have to say anything, the man is a monster." I said, feeling ready to cry but I wasn't going to let myself break down over him again.

"Do you know this man?" His legs were pulled up to his chest. His eyes were in awe, as though some kind of forbidden story was being told. I shook my head at first, but I did know the man. The hard part was saying who he was.

"He's a cold-hearted bloodthirsty demon that I thought I knew so well, someone that I could trust and a man that would always protect me no matter what. My whole life with him was a lie and he made that all so visible in just a few months." Shaking my head reliving every memory he left. The cold hard pain of the past and present will always remain in my heart. Not as love but as a regret.

"So, he was somebody important then?" His voice low, like he was connecting the pieces.

"He was my dad." My voice turned to a whisper;

chills rushed across my skin. Jason's green eyes were huge. His mouth fell open a little, and that made me look away. I couldn't stand to see the amazement on his face. It made me feel sick all over again. My new life was turning into my old life. A story that a million people have tried to force into movies was my reality.

"What are you guys doing about it?" His voice was low, and the amazement was washed away with an unfortunate gaze. We both stared at each other like we were waiting for the next move. It was my turn I just didn't know how to go.

"Back when it all first happened, we got a restraining order against him, but it didn't do anything." I glanced up to my ceiling thinking about how my life would be if this had never happened.

"They have never caught him?" He laid back on my bed propping himself up on his elbows.

"No, he is very good at staying out of the public eye, and the police don't care to look that far into it." I said, feeling depressed that my life is like this.

"Wow, what about that other man that was with him?" He left his mouth open a little, leaving me to stare at his soft lips.

"I couldn't tell you, someone that works for him I would imagine." The truth was I didn't care who that random man was. I just wanted justice to be served and to watch him fall to his knees. I wanted to see the cuffs latch around his wrist. It would be one of the happiest days of my life.

"And I thought I was bringing a crazy life to you." His voice mesmerized by everything I had told him. I laid down on my side next to him staring down into his eyes.

"You know my secret now, welcome to my crazy life Jason." I whispered, just hoping no one else would learn about this. He nodded his head raising his hand to the side of my head. Watching his eyes turn back into the forest and opening up to me. He wanted me to take his hand and enter this new story with him.

"It's okay, your secret is safe with me." He came up from the lying position and his hand ran down the side of my face. We watched each other closely yet carefully. The warmth from his hand vibrated the cells in my blood. My heart thumped out of its normal pattern. He laid me back down against the pillows and then he was like this strong lion lying over me. His eyes watched every single movement I made. He breathed with every breath I took. His hand came over me, his fingers were gentle running up the palm of my hand and straightening it out. His face came closer to mine. His warm breath resting upon my lips. The tingle that ran across them and the chills that rushed up my skin. Within seconds his warm breath was escaping down my throat. My heart was a wild storm with lightning striking in every direction. My hands plunged up into his hair and his strong arms wrapped around my body. I got lifted up from the bed nestled in his lap.

This icy cold air wrapped around my body. I pulled away from the kiss fast. I gasp seeing Dave's blue fog around me. My necklace glowing with that blue aura, I looked back to Jason and his eyes were jolted with shock. Confusion was on his face as I backed off of his lap. What was I doing? I just realized that I was kissing Jason Blackstone. My hand ran back through my hair, Dave was gone. The room turned warm again and my necklace stone turned black. Why did Dave have to come and ruin this?

"Sky, what's wrong?" Jason's hand came back over, resting on the side of my cheek. I shook my head making his hand fall away. I got up from my bed quickly knowing this wasn't who I was. Jason turned me into something else. My hand rested over my heart feeling this aliveness inside. It felt wild. A rush of heat I've never felt.

"I can't do this." I blurted out, rushing over to my window. I peeked out seeing the press still there, all lined up. Waiting for the chance of something they won't get. The hot news line they awaited just played out on my bed.

"I'm not following." He said, but I couldn't turn away from all of them. I just opened up and gave my whole entire story to him. I was just kissing him on my bed. The last thing I should be doing is making him want to get into my pants. I was so stupid. Jason wants to be with me, and I just let him have what he wants. I was never the person to just give in. What was happening to me? Jason turned me around and we both looked at each other. He took me away from the window matching his gaze to mine wanting me to know that everything was going to be alright. Truth is told it wasn't. It might be for him but wherever I go the past will always follow.

"Skylar, I'm sorry I should have never kissed you." His hand slipped away from me realizing he did something that was way off from what I was ready for. He knew what he had done wrong, but I was the one that did it all wrong.

"No, Jason, I'm sorry. I should have never led you on like this." I moved away from him once again. I wanted to be close to him, but I knew I couldn't. It would be a huge mistake and he could end up getting more hurt than me.

"What are you talking about, you never led me on?" He got that confused look in his eyes. I could never tell him what I felt for him. I also wasn't sure I could tell him that we couldn't be together just because of all this. If I was being honest, it wasn't his life I was scared of, it was mine.

"I led you on in every way, including telling your dad that you were my boyfriend." Suddenly I felt myself becoming sad. I was once again pushing him away after letting him get close. I was such a bitch to him, it was crazy. He didn't deserve this and neither did I. I knew there were only two ways this could go, either I give in and date him like we both want, or I tell him to get out of my life forever and have to live with the pain. The last one was the best option but the first one felt right. Jason came back over to me tilting my head back up. His eyes filled with hurt like he knew what was coming. He tilted his head and brought his lips to mine.

Chapter 11

Time to Move On

Mom dropped me off at school the following Monday. She didn't want me walking anymore since Dad had shot me. Everyone in school knew about what happened, which meant my name was in everyone's mouths. I just ignored them all like I had on the first day of school. The worst ones though, were the teachers asking if I was alright. Everyone also knew that Jason was at my house when all this happened. I was not the only talk in school but now I was feeling like an awkward popular kid, everyone watched me in class. This was the first time a lot of them had even tried to make friends with me; I just pushed them away. The more friends I made the more at risk everyone was. The gawking eyes from students, teachers, and even a random call to the nurse's office for my wound to be checked made me feel like a weirdo instead of a cool kid. The last thing I wanted anyone to do was coddle me for this. I wanted far away from the fake friends who sought out to make me feel welcome, but in the end, it is just to get the dirt on me. I knew a great percentage of girls that tried speaking with me just because of Jason. Questions splurged from their mouths all day long. Only a few of them actually asked if I was alright. Occasionally a guy would ask if the gun wound hurt, I even got the 'can I see the hole' question. I was the center of attention making me the most interesting person in school. There was no doubt that Jason was the *most* interesting person in school, but I might have topped him.

I sat in art class just staring at my empty paper. A new project with little detail to prosper. Jason sat across from me staring at his pencil. Why was everything so awkward now? I never told Jason to stay away from me nor did I have it in me to say I didn't want to be with him. The moral of my life just keeps changing repeatedly. Jason's pencil came rolling over hitting my paper. It rolled up on the edge and I looked up at him. He gave me a crooked smile taking his pencil back. Without words his smile left like he had read everything that was wrong with me.

"Nothing on your mind to draw?" He asked lifting his eyebrows up. I said nothing, letting my eyes fall back to my paper. I couldn't draw, I was in too much deep thought. I just shook my head and he continued watching me.

"Hey guys what's up?" Mrs. King came over to our table. I rolled my eyes to myself not wanting her to come over here. I didn't say a word and neither did Jason. "So, you know what the project is, do you need to go to the nurse's office?" Her hand rested on my back; her voice sincere. I just looked in the other direction. Staring at the white Mac computer that was waiting for someone to log in, I just wanted out of here.

"I bet she does need a nurses help." Hearing this boy laughing at another table I looked over my shoulder at him. I squinted my eyes not sure why I have to be the target of choice. Was it wrong that I wished it was Jason instead of me? I glanced down to my side feeling the light sweat my huge bandage caused.

"Shut up or you will be the one heading to the nurse!" Jason spoke up and my eyes went back to him. The whole class was silent. The screeching of the stool the big kid sat on raised the hairs on my arms.

"Hey now, settle down and get back to your table Dallas." Mrs. King held her hands up in front of herself. I didn't realize how big this kid was until he was standing up. I chuckled to myself hearing Jason calling him out. My eyes darted up to Jason who also was standing up, not afraid of this random guy at all.

"He just threatened me!" The Dallas kid pointed over to Jason. Mrs. King closed her eyes nodding her head. She walked him back to the table saying something quietly to him. Jason and I both watched each other. I smiled at him, and he gave a smile back taking his seat. Before I could say anything to him Mrs. King came walking back over. She looked down to Jason with her hands on the table leaning inward.

"You know you can't threaten people." She told him

in a low voice.

"Tell him to keep his comments to himself." Jason had an annoyed look on his face. The same expression he got when he fought with his dad. Truth be told, Jason was just exhausted of being told what to do on command. He was worn out from being handled like a puppet.

"And I will make sure he does but you still can't just tell people that." She patted his shoulder walking away. I sighed as the bell rang. Kids got up quickly racing for the door. Jason followed behind me exiting the room. He reached for my hand, but I pulled it away. I couldn't lead him on anymore. As much as my heart wanted to be chained to his, it couldn't. We headed down the stairs brushing by Abby. She swung around giving me her evil eyes. I just walked past her choosing not to worry. I reached my locker fiddling with the combination.

"There's something wrong and you can't deny that." His voice was a whisper, trying to keep it away from everyone. I closed my eyes hearing a group of guys laughing close to us.

"Hey, look its Romeo and Juliet!" The guys laughed, seeing his friends standing there. I smiled at them backing away from Jason. His green eyes widened and I saw what they said, *please don't leave.* I grabbed the algebra book slamming the locker closed.

"Yeah, how's the new couple doing?" The guy named Robby with the tattoos, wrapped his arm around Jason's shoulders. I've yet to meet his friends.

"I don't know who you're thinking is in a relationship but it's not us." I told them, seeing a world of pain crash over Jason's face. I knew I had broken his heart, but it was the one thing I could do to protect him. Shaking my head walking down the hallway grasping at the strap of my purse. After all, Jason wanted to keep us a secret. I dove into his wishes while shoving him away for his protection.

I stood outside of school waiting for my mom to come pick me up. My eyes were alert to everyone around me. My thoughts were still with Jason though. I couldn't stop seeing that painful expression on his face. It was over before it even began. I felt like finding him, running into his arms and kissing him all over again. I couldn't though. My heart felt broken for giving up this crazy love I felt. One that I always wanted out of, but I gave into. The wind blew and this smell went up my nose. I knew it so well and it smelt so good. Looking up to Jason as he stood beside me, his green eyes fixed right on me. One masculine hand was holding the strap of his backpack, while his free arm dangled beside him. I saw two veins that made hills on his arm trailing down to his wrist. Why was he so attractive? *Please come home with me*, I thought followed by me kicking my shoe in the ground holding myself back from what I craved.

"Look I understand if you don't want people to know about us because it's what we discussed but you don't need to cut me down in front of my friends like that."

He wasn't looking at me any longer and I was searching for the right words to say. I felt like crying but it wasn't going to happen.

"Jason, there can't be a you and me." I fought to keep the tears hidden behind the curtain. His eyes shifted back to me. He nodded his head with an awkward expression on his face.

"There can be anything you want but, this; I don't think you really want." He moved his finger between him and I. I closed my eyes knowing that wasn't true. Why couldn't he just understand why I was pushing him away? I swallowed feeling the tears burning my eyes.

"Jason." I whispered, feeling horrible inside. He pushed my hair to the side leaving a kiss behind.

"I won't make you do something you don't want to." His voice was a low rough whisper. My heart broke into so many pieces. He walked away from me. Watching as he escaped into the school parking lot. A tear ran down my face as Mom pulled up blocking my view of Jason. I swallowed feeling the sore threat the tears gave. I think I just let him go.

Falling down into the car not saying a word, we pulled up to the stop sign and Jason of course pulled up behind us. I saw Abby in the passenger seat with her sunglasses on and her lips shining under the sunlight. Shifting my eyes over to Jason seeing his thinking face, his eyes staring out the window like he wasn't even in the car. He was miles away somewhere else and that somewhere involved me. I was the first girl he cared about because I was different from all the rest. I wasn't crazy for being around a famous person; I didn't treat him differently from the person he wanted to be treated as. He was just another normal person to me. No one spectacular like all the rest of the girls thought he was. Maybe that's also why I was falling for him. I was his great escape even if it did only last for a couple days. Maybe Jason needed me more than I wanted him. He needs normal to survive because his life is anything but normal. We were matches to be stitched together, it was just that the material was different.

"Hello? Honey is everything alright?" Mom's voice snapped me out of my thoughts realizing that we were long gone from the school. I blinked a couple times looking over to her.

"What? Yeah, I'm fine." Wrapping my fingers around my bag as we pulled into the driveway, she gave me her disbelieving stare. I was going to have to come up with some lie.

"You are so not fine; did everything go well in school today? How is your side?" She asked question after question opening the door.

"You mean besides the part where everyone knows what happened? Yeah, it was great!" I said in a sarcastic voice while getting out of the car. I limped around the car to find my mom opening the trunk. What was she getting out? I went around next to her seeing a for sale sign in the trunk. My eyes widened, looking up to her.

"Honey we need to have a talk about the decision I have made." She told me, pulling it out of the car. I knew what was about to happen, something that seemed to never stop happening. She closed the trunk and I followed her inside the house.

"Where are we going now?" I wasn't hurt over leaving here, I was more or less just feeling lost in all this. I don't have many friends here; I haven't even been here long enough to get to know the area. The only path I was getting to know was Jason.

"Well, I talked to our lawyer, and he suggested that we go back down to Florida." She told me, laying the sign up against the wall.

"Are you crazy?" That did not sound like a good plan.

"No, listen he is getting a house set up for us right now and we should be out of here by the end of the week if not sooner, so you should be getting your things packed." She rested her hand on my shoulder. I shook my head, not believing this. How could she think this was the right idea? We were going back to the same trap we escaped from. We were moving in circles of the same rotation. Our tracks could be followed by a squirrel.

"Why back to Florida? You know that's right where we came from." I fought the idea that we would just set ourselves back up for trouble again.

"I know, but it will be a different part and a much smaller place, we have to go undercover." She moved her hands in front of her like somehow that would explain more.

"This is stupid!" I exclaimed going up the stairs. I had to talk to Dave; I needed to get my head straight. I closed my bedroom door throwing my bag across the room into a chair. Dave was nowhere to be seen. He hasn't been with me all day, which made me wonder where he might be. I sat down on my bed taking out my phone. Seeing I had a message waiting for me, but it wasn't from Dave. Jason's name popped up and I pinched the bridge of my nose turning my screen black. I couldn't talk to him. Getting him out of my life was the right and safe thing to do. Which told me erasing everything I have from him is the best option. I opened my phone back up going to my contacts. I saw his name and my thumb shook over the option button. My heart pounded knowing how close I was to closing a set of doors that wasn't even half-way open.

A cold hand came down on mine making chills running up my spine. Dave took my phone out of my hands, and I looked up into his icy eyes. Not saying a word to him my body collapsed into his. A blanket of coldness captured my body. So cold it felt like my body was drowning in ice water in the middle of December. Tears were running down my face and I felt so far away from the life I wanted. His cold hand ran down the back of my head, I sat back up wiping my face off. Dave's eyebrows were raised from seeing the pain I felt. My heart felt broken, and I didn't know why. I was an emotional disaster. When my body heaved from the crying, my rib cage began to ache. The bandage was tugging at my skin. Dave's coolness made the soreness dissipate. A loud ragged gasp came from my mouth as I cried harder.

"Shhh, it's alright." He told me, pushing my hair out of my face. I shook my head looking through my blurry eyes.

"It's not alright." I said, looking over to my window. Just yesterday Jason was here on my bed and the press were willing to do anything to get what they wanted. Today it's all just peace and quiet. I felt like something was missing now.

"Is this because you're moving again or because of Jason?" His eyes were full of wonder.

"He gave me every chance and still I can't do anything besides push him away." My voice was breaking, and my heart was falling to my stomach. Nausea grumbling along with the tears from everything I had to set free.

"So, it's Jason then, and why are you pushing him away?" Dave was more confused than ever.

"Because it's what's going to keep him safe and when I care about someone all that matters is keeping them safe, it doesn't matter how close I am to them or how much I love them it's just–" I stopped realizing what I had just said. Dave and I both looked at each other and my eyes grew bigger. *I love him*. I couldn't stop hearing my own voice saying that. Dave's mouth dropped open a little, sitting back from me. Shock filled his face, and it also filled my body. Bumps rose on my skin knowing now why I felt so bad.

"Did you just?" He gave me this weird look.

"I think I just did." Rolling my eyes to the side seeing my phone laying there, what was I thinking?

"You have feelings for him. Finally, you're admitting it!" His blue eyes widened with excitement. I smiled a little, feeling a warmth inside. It was full of color; I knew this was right. A heavy weight replaced itself with joy.

"I'm not sure what this feeling is Dave." I laughed a little, thinking about his charming smile. I saw it almost every day and each day I got this same feeling. The thing was he wasn't here right now to even show it to me. This feeling seemed to have set its place now that I had said it. Jason has captured this huge part of me, I just never wanted to admit it.

"And yet you want nothing to do with him." He folded his arms in front of me. I bit down on my lip still knowing what the better choice was. I closed my eyes feeling hurt all over again.

"Why do you think I was crying Dave? It's still better without him." My voice started to go downhill again, feeling the pain of his absence. A person can't be hurt over someone they've known for a couple weeks. Dave looked confused again, picking up my phone.

"So that's it, you were just going to give Jason up that easily?" Dave still didn't seem convinced. I sighed and my phone went off. We both looked, revealing Missy's name. He smiled handing the phone over to me.

Missy: Hey girl wanna go dress shopping today?

My mind reeled remembering her and mom talking about prom. They both had this glowing enthusiasm for Jason and me to go together. At the time it seemed foolish, now not so much. How was I ever going to tell Missy I was leaving? I wouldn't even be here for prom.

Skylar: Sorry I'm not really into the whole prom thing.

I sent the message and Dave's blue eyes were solid on me. He looked like something bad had just happen and I'm not sure what.

"What did you tell her?" He sat back down on the bed.

"That prom wasn't my thing." I shrugged my shoulders still thinking about Jason. I knew what I felt for him. I also knew that I could never tell him. This was such a terrible battlefield. I just had to let him go. That didn't sit well with me though.

My mom screamed downstairs, and Dave and I both snapped our eyes back to each other, frightened. My heart pounded again like the nightmare was back. It was all happening again. I reached down by my bed grabbing my heavy flashlight. I went sprinting down the stairs into the kitchen where she stood. She was curled over like something had happened. I went racing over to her swinging her around. She looked shocked to see me by her side.

"Why are you screaming?" I saw that there was no one here. My heart stopped its racing, but that plunging felling in my stomach was still increasing.

"There was a huge bug over by the fridge, Sky." She told me, pointing over in its direction. I rolled my eyes crossing my arms.

"Did you have to scream and scare me?" I set the flashlight aside seeing Dave had brought my phone down here. Mom gave me a sorry stare. I grabbed my phone to answer Missy's text but quickly realized it wasn't Missy at all. I swallowed hard, scared.

Chapter 12 Choices

There was exactly twenty-four hours until prom. Mom deliberately pushed back moving by two weeks just to force me to go to the prom. She said it was part of the high school experience and that these were the memories that I needed to make. I suppose this was her attempt at keeping my life normal, although in my opinion this was the worst thing on earth to me besides my father, I just stood and stared at the red dress with the glimmering neckline; I hated dressing up and making myself look like some kind of doll. Rolling my eyes to the side where my phone was. The message I got two weeks ago from an unknown number still remained as an unseen message. The pulse of my heart was unsteady at the thought of accepting the message. I wasn't sure who it was, but they told me that they could help me. Shifting my eyes away from the phone, curious of who knew about our situation. I was leery, wishing this wasn't a trap. Another part of me couldn't help but believe Richard was a wanted man for another reason. The person that was willing to help may well be a victim of my father as well. Maybe they wanted some sort of peace. I chewed my lower lip mulling over all the ideas of how this person could help me. Truth was I didn't believe anyone could help us, unless we hired an assassin. There was not one single piece of me that even knew how to look into that. My thumbs hovered over the keyboard of my phone. I didn't know what to say. Red flags flew on the account of it being an unknown number just like dads, yet if it was someone who flew under the radar this could be their cover. It was possible this offer had expired, after all I had never responded to the message in the past two weeks; blowing a huff of air out I decided to put my phone down and try and get some sleep.

I was running back through the woods. My feet were bare, digging into the mud. Smoke flew around me like a flock of angry birds. Flames raging on both sides of me, I coughed feeling the smoke threatening my lungs. I bent over feeling the pain kicking in. I had to get out of here but how? Looking around and seeing just smoke and fire, how do I keep ending up here? I ran fast feeling the heat melting into my skin. Sweat was rushing down my body and I noticed the white dress I was in. Where did this come from? It almost looked like a wedding dress but now it was dirty, covered in mud and soot. Everything was burnt. Raising my eyes up to the sky seeing all these colors flying overhead, my mouth fell open. What was happening? Fear took over my body again, like I was trapped.

A scream came from further in front of me. My eyes

grew wider hearing this man scream. He was in pain and begging to be set free. I ran faster to the voice following the haunting fire that caged me in. It was like a tunnel of survival. Running faster and taking the bend I went flying to the ground. Tumbling a few times and rolling to a stop. I felt like I was knocked out, but I looked behind myself to see a huge tree lying in the middle of the path. I coughed some more hearing the man scream again. It was so close now. The agony that was in his voice was awful. Getting to my feet fast just to fall back to the ground, blood flowing from both knees, how did this not hurt? I couldn't stand up though. I limped my way forward falling into the opening. There was a big fire raging in a pit. I was surprised to look up and see Jason tied to stakes above the fire, struggling to get loose.

"Hey Sky, wake up!" My mom's voice was spinning around me, and my eyes opened. I blinked away the blurriness seeing Mom waiting on the edge of my bed. My body was stunned from the dream. My hand ran back through my hair feeling the sweat that was there. My body was tense with heat as if the fire had warmed me in real life.

"Hey girl, it's time to get up, we have a lot to do." Missy came walking into my room with bags in her hands. My eyes widened knowing all these plans were hitting me in the face now. I sat up not ready to have makeup put on and my hair done. I felt like everything was happening so fast. I heard the dress bags being laid out on the chair. I felt like my head was spinning. My hot hands ran down my legs under the covers. I remembered the fire I was just caged in and the tree I fell over. Then at the end there was Jason hanging over a pit of fire. What the hell was this dream about? Jason wasn't in the first dream, what would cause him to be in it this time? I just wanted to understand what all this meant.

"Sky, we need to get our hair done and everything, let's go!" Missy grabbed my wrist pulling me up out of the bed. Mom laughed and soon my body felt cool to the air. Mom pulled my curtains back letting the sunlight shine through. I squinted my eyes, yawning. I wasn't ready for all this.

"This better be the best night of my life." I said, seeing myself in my mirror. I looked like a sweaty train wreck. After the nightmare I just ran through, I suppose it made sense.

"Well duh, of course it is we may not be seniors, but we will be living like them." Missy came over holding my hair up. I laughed a little rolling my eyes. *I should be a senior*, was all I could think. I had a chance to finish the grades I missed but once we moved to Ohio their school rules were different. I was held back, just like my life that kept trying to move forward.

"I believe that is called living the dream for you." I smiled, turning back around. She giggled and my mom unzipped our dress bags. I saw Missy's purple dress come flowing out of the bag. Then I realized it was just the train of it. I tilted my head noticing her dress cut up in the front and flowed down the back. I smiled a little hearing my phone go off. It grabbed all of our attention. Mom picked it up, holding it out for me to take.

"Is that our movie star?" Mom smiled and Missy laughed coming over behind me. I hated the fact that everyone was watching me like I was uncovering some kind of clue to a murder. Opening my phone seeing Jason's name pop up, I sighed.

"What did he say?" Missy's voice was full of excitement. Mom's eyes were filled with anticipation.

Jason: Hey I need you and Missy to be ready by 6.

I smiled turning my phone away from all of them. I didn't even know that I was going with Jason. Things had changed since the last time we had talked. It was like his popularity was overwhelming and he was more committed to that. We talked here and there but it felt like Abby was keeping him on some sort of leash. He had to play into his reputation card after I was shot, and then the paparazzi made their headlines of us dating.

"I guess we're getting picked up at six." I told her, swinging around. Missy's blue eyes were ready to pop out of her head. She screamed grabbing my arms making us both jump! My mom started laughing and so did I. I feel like this was more amusing for them than it was for me, but I should be excited too. Something inside me just didn't feel right.

Skylar: Ok we will be ready.

I sent the message back to him and before I knew it, I was being turned into some kind of Barbie of my own. My mom covered my face in makeup and Missy did my hair. They were transforming me into something I'm not. Once everything was done, I stood up wanting to see myself. Missy was next in line for her makeover. I let my mom take care of her since I had no idea what I was doing with all that makeup.

I walked out of my room to go find Dave, I knew that escaping to the bathroom would be the best way to do so. His cold body was wrapping around me within seconds, and he smiled as he took both of my hands. He shook his head as he spun me around; I started giggling, seeing my reflection in the mirror. His chilled hands landed right on my shoulders. I watched his crystal blue eyes glowing back at me. My eyelids shimmered with silver and a haze of ruby red eyeshadow. My lips glossed over in cherry red lipstick. A line of black scooping under my eyes forming a short cat eye at the edges. Blush coated my cheeks in a light rosy pink. My hair in a curled high ponytail with two independent strains of curled hair framing my face. All I had left was the red dress.

"Jason is one lucky man." Dave said, stepping back. I smiled turning around to face him.

"You think this is the right thing to do?" I squinted my eyes not feeling right about this.

"Of course, you're a teenage girl, what else do teenage girls dream of doing at this age?" He leaned back crossing his arms. His blue eyes roaming up and down me like I was being judged. I was still in my pajamas.

"I mean because of all the tabloids watching us and everything." My nails clicked with each other.

"Sky, let me ask you one important question." Dave held up one ice cold finger.

"Yes?" Worried of what this might be he stepped closer.

"How bad do you want this relationship to last between you and Jason?" His head tilted making his blonde hair drift to the right. I rolled my eyes knowing where this was going.

"Dave, I know I have to get used to this if I want to be with him but when you watch other celebrities, they are all so coy about their relationships." I said, lifting my shoulders up.

"True but he obviously doesn't mind it if he is picking you up in about a couple of minutes." He said, looking up at the clock. My eyes opened wide. Dave gave me a hug and let me go. How on earth had that many hours passed already? I sprinted from the bathroom back to the bedroom. Mom held my red dress up already unzipped. I wiggled my body inside pushing my hands down the front as the zipper pulled everything together. My fingers straightened the thick shoulder straps. I swiveled to the right and left checking myself out, the jewels glistening under the light jumping from the reflection in the mirror. Missy giggled again, stepping into her heels, I did the same before grabbing our clutches. We smiled at each other and locked our arms together. We laughed a little as we tried walking down the stairs in our heels. This may not be the best attempt at something but if we break our necks at least we did it together as friends. By the time we got downstairs Mom was standing there ready with camera in hand.

"You girls look so beautiful together." She held her hand over her chest. Missy and I both laughed like young teenage girls gossiping about boys. My mom was ready to take picture perfect moments but for just a second, I saw a beautiful moment of just her. She was blissful taking in this moment of her daughter growing up living an average life. The life I was supposed to be living. I had come to realize going to prom wasn't just for my youth, but it was for my mom too. She felt like she was doing the right thing as a mother by dolling me up just for her own happiness. My mom was amazing. I thought she was so stupid for sticking around here longer but in all honesty, she just wanted me to have the best life I could.

Right when the camera clicked a fist banged on the door taking all our attention away. My heart started pounding faster. All of a sudden, I realized Jason has never seen me like this, but I have seen him a million times like that. My head started spinning and Mom opened the door. I heard his light voice and Missy and I looked at each other. Her smile was a million times brighter than mine. I was so nervous for some reason. Either it was because I have never walked in heels for a long period of time or it's because Jason was steps away from me. Mom welcomed him in, and I saw another guy following behind. His friend waited with him. To our surprise it was Robby. Tonight, I would get to know his friends.

Jason's smile lit the room taking over everything I saw. I no longer saw my mom, Missy, or Robby. I went walking up to Jason slowly and his green eyes welcomed me in just like it was any other day where I might have seen him. We both smiled at each other, and he took my hand with ease. I felt the small shake in his hand, he was nervous too. I swallowed blinking away from the dreaming moment and snapping back into reality.

"You look flawless." His voice was smooth as he spun me around just like Dave had. Only this time my heel caught on the carpet. Jason caught me fast before we both erupted into laughter. My hair swung back as he rebalanced us both. I took my hand running it down his tux sleeve.

"Maybe not a good idea." I continued, nervously laughing. He nodded his head and all I could stare at was his green eyes. So beautifully passionate. Robby bumped into the back of Jason nudging his head. Jason blinked away from me looking to Missy.

"Right, Missy I heard you didn't have a date, so my friend here wanted to take you." Jason stepped out of the way of Robby. He smiled waving his hand. Missy smiled waving back at him. The unexpected glare in Missy's eyes was the most excited I have ever seen her. Robby walked around us holding the corsage out. Missy's eyes came over to me.

"That is, if you want to go with me." Robby's voice was nervous and shy, and Missy was blushing. Everything was like a romantic moment in a movie. Both of us were happy and of course Mom was ready to take a billion pictures. My eyes went to Jason after he put the flowers around my wrist. Seeing the black tux, white shirt, and a silky red tie, then the white rose pinned on his jacket. The wonderful smell of forest with a hint of bourbon drifted up my nose. He was in fancy attire but not as rich as when he's on the red carpet. His light laughter brought me away from my staring.

"Never seen a man in a tux before?" He held his arms out laughing some more. I glanced back over to Missy and Robby. They were smiling at each other.

"No, it's just you look just like you would on TV." I became shy, looking back up into his green eyes. He chuckled turning me back around. A camera went off to my surprise. Mom laughed urging us to leave. We walked out of the house to see the Hummer limo waiting for us. Missy and I both looked at each other with our mouths open. We laughed not believing it. It was no surprise Jason had a limo hookup, but I've never been in one.

"Our chariot awaits ladies." Robby went up to the

door. Missy and I were so excited to just be in a limo for once. Before Robby could open the door, it came open so fast it almost hit him. His eyes were big, and we all stepped back.

"Hey!" Jason shouted but soon everything inside of me fell. Abby was there holding the door open with her snobby attitude written across her face. She folded her arms and all I saw was her glossy pink lips with curly flowing blonde hair.

"You've got to be kidding me." Missy said in a low voice. I looked up to Jason hearing Abby clear her throat.

"We have no time to waste, you know I have to be the first to arrive at prom." Her voice was just as fake as the rest of her. In that moment I wasn't sure I wanted to join Jason on this night. My hand fell away from his. I could feel his attention locked on me with a hesitation that grew thicker.

"No one said the evil queen was going to be joining us on this chariot." Missy turned to Robby. Abby laughed a little stepping out.

"Well thank you ever so much for referring to me as your queen." Abby held her made up hand over her chest that was showing way too much cleavage. Her plunging neck was revealing more of her than I ever want to see.

"You as my queen? Sweetheart that will be the day we're all dead and gone." Missy squinted her eyes getting just as close.

"Guys stop!" Robby moved in between them.

"They will only be dead because a freak like you will kill everyone." Abby had that disgusted look on her face again. This was awful, I didn't want to sit in a limo for half the night with some snobby bitch that had to be here. I looked over to Jason and he looked down to me. He had those apologetic eyes. I shook my head walking away from him. I had to make some sort of choice, or our night would end in disaster. We didn't just get ready and all dolled up for someone else to take us down. Hell, if I was about to let it happen.

"Missy, come on we don't have to go with them." I said, placing my hand on her arm. She gazed over to me lifting her eyebrows.

"Oh, thank god the traveling freak shows don't have to come with us now." Abby smiled taking a few steps back. I said nothing as I walked away from her pulling Missy along.

"Sky, wait." Jason came over to us; I winced at the tone of his voice.

"No Jason you wait, you could have told me that she was going to be with us. You didn't have to lie to me." I was frustrated feeling like there were so many things left out again. He knows better than to bring his sister into my life. Nothing good ever happens, because his dad sets the whole thing up every time. This whole relationship is a game of hide and seek. I couldn't stand secrets like that. I'm either with someone or I'm not.

"I never lied to you, but I knew if I told you then

you wouldn't want to go with me." His green eyes were apologetic but that still wasn't changing how I felt. He sighed letting his shoulders sag. I glanced back to Missy, but she was watching Robby. This tied my hands behind my back. These choices I have been faced with are so complicated.

Suddenly, black cars came rolling up with people jumping out with cameras. My mouth came open and Missy's eyes grew big. The press came running up to Jason snapping pictures of us left and right. Questions bombarding out of their mouths. They wanted so much personal information. Jason took me by the arm turning us away from them.

"Either you get in that limo now or we keep getting pounded by questions, I know this isn't what you want to do but we need to get out of here now!" Jason's voice was just a whisper, but he was right. As much as I didn't want to set foot in that limo, I had to.

"We have to go." I told Missy walking quickly over to the limo. Without any hesitation Jason lifted me up, and Missy came next. The door closed making everything go dark. The windows were tinted in the darkest of black. I sat down on the long row of bench seats. Missy came down next to me. We all sat together in solitude. Abby sat on the other side with her group of Barbies. This whole place smelt like rich perfume that neither Missy nor I could afford. The limo pulled out of my drive quickly while the cameras were still going off.

"Did you have to jump in?" Abby tilted her head at us.

"No, but we can throw you out!" Missy smiled at her. I laughed a little watching Jason sit down beside me. He didn't look happy; in fact, he looked a little sad. Robby came down beside Missy right when Jason's arm came down around my bare shoulders.

"I know this isn't what you want." He whispered into my ear. I placed my hand on his leg assuring him it was alright.

"Whatever made you think this was going to be okay?" I whispered back trying to keep our words away from Abby. He shook his head closing his eyes.

"This is all your fault, now we are going to be late." Abby shoved a hard glare at me along with a couple of her friends letting that sassy sigh out. The other one rolled her eyes. I wanted to get out of this limo as fast as I could.

"Well, if you didn't have to be here there would be no issue now would there?" I said already having had enough of her attitude. I wanted to leave her somewhere else so badly.

"I believe there still would be." Her friend held up her finger like she was making some kind of point.

"And who the hell are you?" I asked already knowing she was just a follower. I would take my nightmares over this hell any day. Jason ran his hand down over his face like he wanted it all to stop. He realized his mistake, but it was too late now; it was already made and has been served. I couldn't understand why he would let his dad control his life like this. I'm so unsure that this relationship will ever be able to work.

We arrived at the fancy restaurant where the chauffeur opened the door to let us out. Of course, Abby and her clique were the first to leave the limo. I laughed when Missy acted to kick them out with her heeled foot. Jason smiled along with us as did Robby. We left the limo and Jason took my hand helping me out. Once we reached the door Jason didn't follow his sister.

"Just so you guys know we're not sitting at the same table." He held his hands up.

"Thank god." Missy's head went back like she was thanking the gods. I laughed a little more taking Jason's hand. I'm not sure what made him make the fast decision, but it was a good one. We were supposed to stay in our group, but we told the hostess to seat us somewhere else. She was happy to do so, escorting us to the other side of the elegant restaurant. Abby, with her posse, sat at a round table far-far away. As we sat down and read over the menu my phone went off. I waited the few minutes it took for the waiter to come back, and we ordered our food. I was cautious, sliding my phone out seeing it was the unknown number. Who was this person?

Unknown: I can help you with your father.

My heart dropped every time I read a message from this person. I felt the need to know who it was and what they knew about my dad.

Skylar: Who are you?

Laying my phone back down, watching as Missy was gradually picking some bread from the big bread hill that they gave us. Jason and Robby were talking and making Missy laugh. I had no idea what was happening all I know is someone else knows about my father. My phone went off again.

Unknown: We will talk later when you are alone.

I swallowed looking around me. Who was this? How did they know I wasn't alone? Someone else was watching me and I had a feeling this was not for a good reason. I was scared, once again wondering what was going to happen. Who was this unknown person? The thought of a spy grew to be a bigger possibility. What if this was the man with the crowbar? It could be someone very different. Richard knew plenty of people. My eyes took a tour around the room we were sat in. A man in a work suit sat across from a redhead. Over at the bar sat two men half dressed in work attire as their sports jackets hung on the tall chairs. No one around seemed to be watching.

The chatter of our table tuned back in once the food was set before us. My thoughts trailed off wishing I knew what Robby was saying so I was in the loop. I wanted to know Jason's friends, yet a bigger void stood in my way. Whomever this was, they knew I was busy, and therefore were leaving me with my freedom for now. I took my fork slicing into the delicate salmon. The salty tingle of garlic sprung up my nose. On queue with Missy's laugh, I chuckled along to seem engaged. Jason's arm came over my shoulders like a shawl. My cheeks rose smiling at his closeness. My night was far from over, I could feel it.

Chapter 13
Horror

We walked into prom and Jason's arm was locked with mine. Missy and Robby were before us with their arms locked together as well, they showed their tickets, and we were next. Mrs. King was sitting at the table taking the tickets. She smiled when we came in together.

"You two look beautiful together." She sang, writing down our ticket numbers. Jason smiled thanking her. A new expression was added to Jason's face that I've never seen before, he was blushing. Once inside the dining hall I saw everybody close together, their eyes drew to us like we were the couple everyone was waiting for. My hands turned sweaty, and my heart jumped. For some reason I imagined this to be what it would feel like when I get married. No one said a word, they just watched. We followed Missy and Robby over to the table. Jason's other friends were there waiting for us. They smiled raising their glasses.

"Hey look who finally arrived." The one that I thought was Tom stood up. Jason and Robby laughed leaving both of our sides.

"Well, I guess that wasn't supposed to last forever." Missy laughed, looking over to me. She reached past her empty plate picking up a plastic seashell. They were scattered around the table for center pieces. *How cheesy*, I thought.

"Guess not." I replied, noticing my handbag felt heavy. The only weight in there was my phone. All I wanted to know was who messaged me, but all the answers I wanted remain uncovered. That one person could know so much. They could also be very dangerous. I couldn't help but wonder if they could end all this madness though.

All of a sudden, the whole room of people stood up with a roar of excitement. Girls went running to the dance floor with their guys in hand. Some girls even held their long flowing dresses up just to get to the dance floor. It almost made me laugh how these girls reacted to the music. Missy grabbed my wrist whipping me away from my chair.

"C'mon we are not going to be a couple of bums!" Missy yelled over the loud techno music. Before I knew anything we were under rainbow lights. I looked around the floor beyond all the people bobbing up and down. I saw the hokey décor they dressed this place in. There were fake popup birds hanging from the ceiling as the lights beamed right through them. The DJ's set up was supposed to be all covered in sand tailored with drinks with umbrellas in them. I'm not much of a designer but I could do better than this. The idea of a beach themed prom was overrated. Kids in Florida would be disgusted by this cliché idea.

"I see you made it to the dance floor without me." Jason twirled me around letting me see up into his eyes. I laughed holding onto both of his hands.

"Well, you were having too much fun with your friends." I giggled, swaying my hips back and forth. I couldn't dance to save my life so swaying was the best I could give. His white smile turned into pink under the neon lights. I laughed shaking my head at him.

"So, you just ditch me?" He held his hands up laughing with me.

"Maybe you were the one that ditched me?" I threw it back into his boat. His eyebrows lifted right when the fast beat cut, leaving us to a slow piano tune. John Legends voice took over the room, half the people on the dance floor left. Jason's arms wrapped around my back pulling me closer to his body, he was so warm. His head came down next to my ear. Chills rushed up my back wondering what he was doing.

"I will never ditch you." He whispered in my ear moving my hair away. I swayed my head slightly to take a glance at his expression, it might be dark, but I could see all the compassion in what he was telling me. I felt like no one else was in the room and I just wanted to live in this moment forever. It was just me and him. Not even the music was breaking through our stare. I didn't even realize our bodies were swaying back and forth.

My heart was pounding inside my chest so hard I could feel it knocking on my ribs. The cage that held my wild heart from being set free, almost like it wanted to plunge into his hands. I felt some sort of trust with him, and it was incredible. I have never felt this way in my entire life. The only person I have ever trusted to keep me safe was Dave, and Jason made me feel safer than that. That sounded so crazy to me. My nightmares sent me to a forest, the only thing I ever saw when peering into his eyes. These forests were different even if they looked so similar. His was a safe haven, the other a hell-bent rollercoaster. My hips swayed when his hand ran down my back reaching my butt. My arm came up resting on his heavier clothed chest. His arms gently luring for a comforting embrace. Jason tilted his head with his two fingers nudging my chin up. My eyes opened wide watching as his lips came out to meet mine. I started to close my eyes but before anything touched, I hit the ground. My eyes flew back open seeing Abby standing there. My mouth fell open as I sat up. Jason's face turned into a mask of madness.

"What the hell do you think you're doing?" Jason's arms flew out in front of him.

"Getting a little tramp away from my brother." She hissed, crossing her arms.

Missy came over behind me helping me up off the ground. I realized everyone's eyes were watching us. Teachers came to the dance floor lining the entrance ways. I was not about to get in trouble for something I didn't start. I tugged my thick strap back up on my shoulder realizing that's what she used to pull me down.

"Hey now girls let's stop this before the whole night gets ruined." One of the teachers was between us.

The music stopped abruptly with the lights flickering in a panic motion on the dance floor. Just a second later you could hear a spark as all the neon lights fizzed out. We all looked around us, there was conversation going through the whole place. Missy let her hand drop away from me as we all stood in a group. I looked up to the ceiling, suddenly people started screaming following the sharp shrill sound of a gun being fired. Everyone was ducking and running out of the room we were in. Someone grabbed my hand leading us away from the crowd. We went running back onto the carpeted floor, I ran into someone. This room was just as dark as the dance floor. Squinting my eyes and realizing it was Missy. We dashed in the opposite way from the huge crowd rushing for the exit.

"Sky? Is that you?" Missy's hands came out in front of her reaching around. I grabbed her wrist and Jason held his hand on my lower back.

"Yeah, are you okay?" I asked her hearing everyone's frantic voices.

"We need to go!" Jason yelled over all the screaming. We went running for the exit just like everyone else, but we took the one to the right instead of the front doors.

Right as we reached the door a part of the ceiling came crumbling down hitting us. My arms went up covering my head. Missy screamed and we were both jerked away from the door. Dust flew all around us. Hearing Jason cough we moved back some more. Crumbled ceiling parts made a small hill blocking the door. The silver handle was bent sideways locking us inside.

"What do we do now?" Missy's voice was right beside me in panic. We couldn't see each other it was like being underground.

"Follow me." Jason coached, taking hold of my hand again. I grabbed Missy so she wouldn't get lost. Running in heels was the worst thing I have ever done. I felt like I was going to tumble over at any given moment. Jason stopped abruptly in front of me making us all run into each other. My eyes searched through the darkness while the thick air went rolling up my nose. Jason coughed some more forcing me to peek over his shoulder seeing what he could see. The last exit door was engulfed in flames. Our chances to get out were lost. Jason turned around to face us. With the glow of the fire, we could see each other once again.

"How do we get out of here?" I shuddered in fear watching him but already knowing he didn't have a clue either. The place was being taken over by the smoke. Within seconds my world spun back into my dream. However, this place was nothing like a forest. Mesmerized by the bright flames torching the whole wall in front of us, I couldn't move. The white curtains being eaten by the vicious fire consumed me, like a trance.

"I don't know, both the exits are blocked there is no other way." He shook his head bringing my long stare away from the fire and back to him. My heart dropped into my stomach. This could not be happening. There was no way I could escape death from a bullet, and now escape death from being trapped in a burning building with both exits barricaded.

"Wait a sec." Missy bent her leg up slipping her heels off. I watched as she sprinted over to the big glass windows. She picked up a chair smashing it into the block like windows. My mouth gaped open as one of the small blocks of glass got a crack in it.

"Missy, stop that isn't going to work." I told her, running over to her side. Her pinned up hair fell down the back of her neck. Sweat beads were slipping away from the roots of our skin within minutes.

"We have to get out of here Sky, before this whole place burns to the ground!" Her voice was freaking out and she hit the blocks of glass once more. I shook my head looking back to Jason. He looked to be thinking of something. His hand ran down his face looking up to the ceiling. I watched as his eyes squinted as if he'd figured something out.

"Jason, what is it?" I yelled back over to him, and Missy stopped.

"The ceiling, it fell out by the door where we were

trying to get out, but that side of the building caught fire." His voice was perplexed as he turned back to the main entrance. I walked over to him following his gaze. He had a point. Why did the ceiling just give way? There had to be something to make it crash down. Then I thought back to the gun fire. Who shot the gun? Who were they aiming to hit? Was this all because of me?

"It makes no sense why that would fall." I said, finishing his thoughts. He looked down at me. His sweaty hair hanging over his eyes and his chest moving rapidly up and down. Water seeped from my eyes feeling the sting from the smog. Jason coughed hard from the smoke inhalation.

"Exactly, there's no other way out which means we have to make one." He went walking past me over to the ceiling lying against the door. I could see the flashing lights outside as all the emergency people arrived. We might not have to find a way out. I tossed my head over my shoulder hearing the violent flames raging closer. I knew if it hit the kitchen this building would explode.

My chest grew colder, and my necklace was lighting up. Dave was here. I swirled around searching for his blue aura. There was nothing though. My hand went down touching my necklace but something odd happened. The cool blue was starting to turn warm. Dave was never any kind of warm. Everything physical about Dave was ice cold. Besides his heart, he tries to make me believe that is made of ice now as well, but it's not. I wasn't sure what this meant.

Feeling my phone inside my handbag I unzipped it; I'd forgot all about it. Dave text me telling me that someone bad was still trapped in here with us. I swallowed hard looking around myself. Missy was still over by the window trying to break the tiny blocks of glass. Jason remained by the door searching for something to lead us to our escape. Then there was me standing in the main part of the dining area. Who else could be here? My fingers moved fast texting Dave back but as I did so a shrill scream made my phone drop to the ground. Missy stopped what she was doing. We looked at each other in unison.

"Help!" The girl's voice was loud and frightened. It was a voice I have come to know. Looking back over my shoulder to Jason as he peeked his head around to us. Missy dropped the chair running into the dance floor. I followed behind her fast. We stopped when no one was in here. The loud sound of a sobbing girl was so close though. We glanced all around not finding anyone.

"Is someone here!?" Missy yelled out wiping the sweat away from her face.

"Oh, please help me!" The girl cried out for help once more. Missy looked over to me and we walked forward with more caution.

"Where are you?" I yelled out looking over the DJ section. Once again there was no one. Rattling came from the ceiling grabbing our attention. The chandelier was vibrating above us. My eyes grew big with my body spinning away. It came crashing down to the floor. We all screamed. My tense body hit into Jason's. His hand held over my head and Missy hugged us tight. The sound of the glass bulbs crashing was like bells ringing in my ears. Jason winced holding us together. POP! CLANG! CHING! POP! A thousand pieces of glass and light bulbs shattered leaving a million puzzle pieces of glass.

"Are you still there?" The crying girl's voice brought us back. We moved away from each other running on once more. I shook in fear scared of what was happening. My life has seemed so non-stop since I got shot. I stopped. The return of my father then this, nothing seems right.

"We're coming!" Missy yelled out to the girl we were trying to find. We heard a loud bang and we looked back to the entrance.

"They're trying to break down the doors, you keep looking I have to tell them there are people in here." Jason told me running back to the doors. We all had jobs to do but my mind was reeling with so much more. I saw the fierce flames darting out as Jason flew past them in a flash. A cracking sound from the ceiling took my focus. I saw burning scars unleashing pain to the wood above us. I gulped.

"Sky, she's in here!" Missy called for me and I ran to the sound of her voice. I entered the only room that was still lit. The kitchen, but it has been taken over by blood. My hand wrapped around my mouth, seeing the girl lying on the ground. She had bullet wounds in her stomach and a knife sticking out of the chest. I closed my eyes turning away. What had happened? This was like a horror scene from Clue.

"Do you care to help?" Hearing the girl's voice again, I realized the girl on the floor was not crying for help, I looked back around. Abby was stuck under a metal stand. Lifting one of my eyebrows up looking back down to the girl on the floor noticing no movement. She was dead. I remembered her then; she was the girl in the limo across from me. I closed my eyes once more walking around all the blood. I bent down helping lift it from her.

"Who did this?" I asked as Missy helped Abby to her feet. She brushed her dress off glaring down to her friend. The puddle of blood was growing bigger.

"You think I would know?" She barked over to me with that ugly snobby reaction.

"You were in here with her." I protested, following as she left the kitchen.

"No, I wasn't, I came in here trying to get out because someone grabbed me." She turned around giving me the look of death. I squinted my eyes at her, and Missy stepped around me.

"Do you remember who grabbed you?" Missy's head tilted like she was onto something.

"Look, for all I know it could have been one of you that killed Stacy." Abby said, pointing two fingers in between us. My mouth fell open not believing this.

Missy's eyes were huge as we reentered the dance room. The dark room was being taken over by smoke. We all started coughing and flames burned their way onto the wall.

Someone grabbed me from behind holding their gloved hand over my mouth. My eyes got bigger as I was jerked back behind the DJ stage. A flashlight shined into my eyes blinding me from seeing the man standing before me. I tilted my head having no idea who he was. I breathed hard seeing his muscles jump from each arm. His hair a brownish orange. My necklace was burning my chest. I looked down seeing the stone in the middle had turned from icy cold blue to flaming hot orange. Something was off. I peered back up to him as he placed one finger over my lips.

"Who are you?" I choked from the smoke, watching him unsure why he had grabbed me. He was a part of something that wasn't human. I could tell. He was a ghost.

"I am the man that can help you." He told me, pulling out his phone showing me the messages that he sent me. My mouth dropped open.

"You did this." My voice hesitant, realizing he had shot the gun. He made this entire riot happen so he could talk to me. Why would he do this though? A scared feeling crept into my body wondering if he was also the one who'd killed Abby's friend in the kitchen.

"Whatever are you talking about?" His smile was

coy, that was enough to tell me that he knew everything. I've never seen such an evil bliss on someone's face. My mouth came open as I moved back from him. The stone on my neck was burning like the fire that was creeping closer. Dave appeared behind this mystery man. He ripped him away from me and the necklace turned into a mix of hot and cold.

"Sky, get out of here, now!" Dave's eyes were intense. I went running from behind the DJ stand, around the broken chandelier. The glass sparkled as the fire came up the right side of the wall. I ran out of the dance room seeing Jason through the smoke. He saw me and we ran up to each other, but the weird thing was he whipped me up off my feet. My eyes were watering from all the smoke. Soon, I was outside where the cool air took over my body. I was rushed over to an ambulance where he sat me down. I gasped the fresh cool air of the night into my lungs before heaving forward into a coughing fit.

"Oh, my baby thank god!" My mom was in front of me pushing my hair out of my face. I choked and cleared my eyes. There was ash all over me. I looked away from my mom realizing the person that carried me out wasn't Jason. It was just a firefighter. The smoke had made me imagine something that wasn't there.

"Miss, look here please." The ambulance guy turned my head to face him. He shined this bright light into my eyes. Water was streaming down my cheeks. The light left my eyes, and he flipped some papers. I looked over my shoulder seeing all these people standing around. Students gathered wearing torn elegant clothes. Conversation rattled my body. I saw a couple of people speaking with a police officer about the stampede of people. I saw a guy laying on a gurney with blood dripping from his scalp. I saw Missy gathered together with her mom and dad. She was at another ambulance being treated. Running my eyes threw the heavy crowd I failed to see the one person I worried about the most, Jason.

My head was tilted back as a medic dropped liquid into my eyes. It burned yet felt soothing at the same time. He coached me to blink several times. I was worried about being admitted into hospital again. The medic behind me brought over a breathing mask. He positioned it on, and I felt this compressed air entering my lungs. With my eyes continuing to sting I heard them speaking with my mom. I overheard them say that I would be okay, but resting was necessary.

Through the tears I watched the hoses spraying the historical building. Firefighters continued courageously to put it to rest. Several more tried mapping out the building in search of anymore victims. Awe took over me seeing blue and orange streaks coiling through the smoky sky. What was that? It zipped behind clouds of thick smoke. My attention shifted back to my necklace still seeing Dave's blue mixing with the orange from the dead stranger. If that man wanted to help me, he would not have attempted to threaten my life. My thoughts were spinning in my head before I snapped out of it when the medic took the oxygen away. He started asking a few questions, leaving my wondering thoughts to one side for now.

Chapter 14
The Enemy

I was sitting on the couch thinking about everything that had just happened. Who was that man that said he could help me? He wasn't going to help me by any means and for whatever reason he killed that girl tonight. Not one thing was right about what had happened. How did he even manage to get into our prom? And why did my necklace change color? He wasn't human, I knew that. He might not confess but he didn't need to. It was evident he was bad from the fact that Dave told me to run. The solid urgency in Dave's eyes unleashed the realization that there was a new fear. His face was concerned for many more reasons than just the fire engulfing the historic building. The ocean that protects me now showed a shadow of a dauntless storm brewing.

My teeth stopped chipping my nails as the TV came on. Mom was standing behind the couch watching the breaking news. All I kept staring at was the place my soul stood in. I could have been dead. The fire was out but the place was demolished. Just witnessing the charred building forced me to wince away from the horrible aftermath. I was in there, most of all Jason was in there. All I wanted was to be in his arms. To feel the comfort of his tight hug that made my madness wash away. With my heart still adrenalin filled, I knew that if I surrendered to the fear, it would consume me into a panic attack.

"I am happy to say that the fire is now out, and the mystery still remains of what has happened here tonight, Bryan. We have talked to a few students as well as teachers that have made it out of this fire just fine." The news woman cut off to a different scene where someone from the senior class was talking.

"I honestly don't remember much of what happened besides a lot of screaming and my girlfriend pulling me along with her." He had a slight smile on his face. There was nothing to smile about. The screen cut to Mr. Timbale our science teacher.

"I remember hearing gun fire and then I know a couple of our students got trapped in the building, but we did get word that they were alright." Mr. Timbale spoke with fearful eyes. The news woman was back on and I shifted away.

"As you can see Bryan this place is getting cleaned up and everyone is still shaken up over this prom that took a horrifying curve ball tonight." They went back to the newsroom where they talked more about the causes that could have led to tonight's events. They still have no one to blame for this. They started talking about the girl that was dead. She was murdered in my eyes, though. I knew the man that was behind this. He came just to find me, but God only knows why he killed that girl. He had no reason to shoot that gun.

"Do you remember anything that happen?" Mom sat down beside me turning off the TV.

"I saw a lot tonight that I wish I could erase/" I confessed, seeing Stacy's bloody body all over again. Not even the fact that I could have died tonight haunted me as badly as seeing her body did.

"You saw that dead girl, didn't you?" Mom rested her hand on my leg.

"Was Jason alright?" I switched subjects not wanting to think about her lying there anymore. It was bad enough knowing I was going to relive it in my dreams tonight.

"I saw him come out like you, but they took him to another ambulance." She explained to me, shaking her head. She had no clue where he went then. I found it funny how he wasn't talking to me. No messages, no calls, nothing. I knew Missy was just fine she let me know before we left. Jason was long gone by then.

"I think you should go take a shower and get cleaned up." Mom told me, but I saw something working in her mind. Not sure what it was I just stood up. I didn't want to talk with her anymore. Even though I knew I should tell her that the girl was murdered not just dead. I couldn't see what she was thinking about, but I felt it wasn't good. That look was the same look she had when we left Florida because of Dad.

When I arrived in my room there was a man sitting on my bed. My eyes opened wide seeing him sitting there with one leg over the other and hands perched on his knee. The stone in my necklace turned fire hot once again. My hand never came off my door as he stood up. The smile on his face was like the sweet taste of revenge. I squinted my eyes walking closer to him. I felt the fear creeping up inside my stomach and up to my neck, but I kept approaching him. I felt scared inside, but fearless on the outside.

"What the hell do you want from me?" My voice was angry as the door shut behind me. His evil smile told me he was no good.

"I want to help you." His hand came out skimming across my ash filled hair. I flinched away shaking my head.

"You're one of them." With fear creeping closer in on me and the necklace burning my skin, before turning cool again.

"Hell, if he's one of us." Dave stood on the other side of the room. The mystery man snapped his head over to Dave. The evil smile turned into a grin.

"I see you have made it safely, Dave." He swung around to face him full on. I had no idea what was happening and who this man was. Dave didn't trust him though which told me to get so far away from him it wasn't funny. This man was dangerous.

"And the way you will be leaving won't be so safe."

Dave flashed over to him wrapping his hands around his neck. My eyes were huge seeing him lifted off the ground. The evil poison was draining down into Dave's eyes now. He wanted to kill this man.

"Dave, wait!" I pleaded wanting to talk with him a little longer.

"Sky, you have no idea who this man is." Dave's voice was violent like he was cutting through his skin to rip his heart out. I tilted my head taking a deep breath in.

"Now, now don't you think we should let the poor girl say what she wants?" His hand came out to me away from Dave. My mouth dropped open not sure what that was supposed to mean. Dave shook his head setting him back to the floor.

"You have three minutes with him!" Dave called over to me like I was being handed some kind of permission. I didn't understand the line limits here. Why did Dave hate him? Why did this guy want to help me? And most of all why did he kill Abby's friend?

"Why did you do all of those things tonight?" I stepped closer to him. That evil smile came back.

"Let's just say it was a distraction from what was about to happen." He held a finger up.

"Sky, please don't listen to him, he wants you to believe–" Dave was cut off as the mystery man swung around and his orange aura came flying out of his hand. My mouth dropped, seeing it wrap around Dave's neck. He struggled to get free and before I could yell to let him go, they were gone. All that was left was warm smoke and cold fog. What had just happened? Was he going to kill Dave? How can you kill someone who is already dead? I remember Dave telling me he can be trapped on the other side for the rest of his existence. They called that side of the bridge Heaven or Hell. All depending on what you did to get stuck over there.

I had to remain calm and know that Dave was able to protect himself. There wasn't much I knew about this other guy. I didn't even know his name; all I know is he's not like Dave. He was dead, yes, and he was a ghost. One that wasn't here to look over you like an angel, more like a curse maybe. He was the devil of the angels. I haven't seen or met any other ghosts but what I was seeing showed me that there had to be more out there. I could not be the only one with a ghost protecting me.

Wiping the water away from my eyes and stepping out of the shower, I looked at myself in the mirror seeing nothing but an innocent girl staring back through the muggy glass. I ran one finger down it feeling the residue left behind. I closed my eyes feeling the chill creep up my back. Wrapping the towel snug around me I saw Dave's aura in the reflection. I looked down seeing my phone lying there. Dave had retrieved it from downstairs. One missed call from Jason. He was alright. I turned around hugging Dave's crisp coolness. My head rested against the thick air that posed as his shoulder. I felt his cold fingers run through my wet hair making me shiver. He stepped away listening to my teeth chatter. His white teeth shined through the blue and I shook my head smiling back.

"You're okay." I was glad to see he wasn't gone forever.

"Damn right, although we do have some serious things to talk about." He ran his hand down over his mouth. I nodded my head hoping he could tell me all I wanted to know.

"Dave who was he?" I didn't care about anything else right now besides who that man was.

"A very dangerous man that was locked in Hell for a very long time." His eyes were tense like he had bad memories of this man.

"How did he escape?" Folding my arms; wanting answers to everything, Dave lifted his shoulders up.

"I'm not sure, not friends with the guy." He told me, not seeming to even like the fact he was talking about him.

"But he wasn't like you; he was warm, hot – almost like fire." I said to him, wondering if that was from him being trapped in Hell. Then I wondered what he did to get there. I wanted to talk to this so-called dangerous man. I believed every word Dave was saying about him, I just needed to know more.

"That's because there are some things that I have never told you about our kind." His hand rested against his chest. I squinted my eyes hearing my phone go off.

"What haven't you told me, Dave?" This made me a little weary.

"There are two kinds of ghosts." His head tilted and I heard the doorbell go off. Who was at our house at this time of night? I looked back to Dave. His blue eyes wondered around the bathroom and he held one finger up.

"It's the police." He'd heard them, and he was now leaving although he left his blue aura behind. The room was cold, and I changed into the jammies I had. Why were the police here? I didn't do anything. Then I remembered that my phone went off. I grabbed it up unlocking it.

Jason: Hey Sky I'm coming over I need to make sure you're okay.

"Sky, come down here!" Mom yelled for me, and I popped the door open. This was getting crazy.

Skylar: Sure, but the cops just showed up and idk why.

Heading on down the stairs with my wet hair dripping seeing two cops standing inside the living room, I had to act stupid. Looking over to my mom putting my best confused face on I could, she came over to me.

"You must be Skylar?" The one police officer asked me.

"Yes, did I do something wrong?" That wasn't my confession, that was me not having any idea what this was about.

"No, we are just going around to some of the kids

houses to see if they saw anything that had happened tonight, and since you were one of the students that got stuck in the building we were just wondering if you saw anything more." He pulled out a note pad ready to write. My mouth came open a little remembering it all. I shook my head taking a seat on the couch as my phone went off again. There was another knock on the door but this time it was Jason.

"That's–" I stopped for a minute thinking what to call him, "that's my boyfriend." I told them pushing my hair back.

"Was he there with you tonight?" The officer put his hands on his hips.

"Yes." I simply said as Mom let Jason in. I glanced up at him and he came over to my side. I stood up hugging him. I didn't see him after I got snatched away. He had his Blink-182 hoodie on with sweatpants. His hair was fluffy and there was the smell of a new fresh layer of his cologne. I took a deep breath feeling relaxed now that he was here.

"Jason, right?" The other officers asked, and his green eyes left mine.

"Yes, what's all this about?" Jason asked taking a seat beside me. The one officer whispered something into the other one's ear. I have no idea what all this is about. They say it's about everything that happened tonight, but the whispering had me wondering.

"Okay, since your both here, while you were in the

building did you see anything that didn't seem to fit?" The officer asked sitting down on the coffee table. Jason looked over to me and I lifted my shoulders.

"You mean besides the fact that the ceiling almost came down and crushed us, no." He told the cop. The other cop did not look amused by that answer.

"There was a shooter, did you see him?" The other cop cut in. I did see him. I knew him and he was a dead guy. There was no use in telling them. They would never find him. He made himself look like another person, but he wasn't. He was a devil that escaped his chains. The one thing I didn't understand was how was he supposed to be helping me by killing an innocent victim? Unless it was never about helping me, then again how does someone escape from their chains in Hell? I needed so much more explained to me.

"Ma'am you're not saying too much, are you alright?" The other cop asked me. I blinked away from my deep thoughts looking back up to him. Jason's hand came down on my back.

"Look officers it's late and these kids have been traumatized, don't you think it might be a better idea to let them sleep on it?" My mom cut back in saving us from whatever else this interrogation involved.

"As you wish Ma'am, but as it is still fresh in their minds, they might be able to tell us more info now than later." The cop rolled his wrist with the pen in it. Jason stood up from the couch leaving my side.

"How about I give you my side of the story and take what you have of hers, I mean you were here before I got here so I imagine you already have her story." Jason was trying to get them away from me too. Why was I being protected by everyone all of a sudden? I guess they just cared and maybe I looked tired? I had no idea. I smirked knowing Jason was here just a minute after them.

"We don't have much of a story, but I will ask you one more thing, where were you at the time the gun was fired?" He turned back to face me.

"I was on the dance floor." I remained honest, although I knew that it didn't really matter.

"And you were aware of the dead body of Stacy Anderson?" The other cop asked pulling a photo out of her. My hand rushed up to my mouth. I saw her bloody dead self, lying there once again. She never did anything to deserve this. Sure, she wasn't a nice person to me because she hung out with Abby, but that still wasn't a reason to kill her. I closed my eyes nodding my head yes. It was a terrible feeling to see the aftermath of someone who had been murdered in front of you. She wasn't killed in front of me, but I saw what happened. Something I never dreamed of seeing before.

The cops left after Mom jarred them away, seeing the picture that they asked about, but Jason stayed. It was about three in the morning now and Mom left us to go to bed. Neither of us said a word to each other, we just sat on the couch staring at a blank TV. Almost like both of us were too scared to move. I was at a loss for words, and he might have been too. I wasn't sure why he stayed but I felt safe. Jason turned toward me taking both of my hands. I watched as his lips touched my knuckles. I smiled at him as my hand came back down to my lap.

"You should probably get some sleep." He encouraged me, pushing my hair to the side.

"Does that mean you're leaving?" There was a place inside of me that wanted him to stay. Something told me that everything felt safe with him. My walls were breaking down and I trusted him more and more each day. Yet he never had anything to prove to me.

"Shhh... I'm not leaving, I want to keep you safe." He said, gently pulling me down on his warm muscular body. His scent went right up my nose. It was a dreamy rush of sweet woods. A blanket draped down over my back. His body rested beneath mine and I closed my eyes. He chose to stay down here to make sure nothing was awkward. He just wanted me to feel protected. I felt all warm inside as I closed my eyes feeling his lips touch my forehead. His heart thumped under my ear as my wrist rested against his chest; our hearts played the same melody.

Chapter 15
The Return

My eyes fluttered open as the smell of bacon and eggs surrounded me. I opened my eyes all the way, sitting up. Jason was no longer under me. The blanket fell from my body, and I twisted my head over my shoulder peering into the kitchen. Mom and Jason were both cooking. What was I witnessing? My hands came up rubbing my eyes still seeing the same scene. I realized I didn't have the nightmare that I've been having every night. I didn't wake up running through burning woods, my feet weren't muddy, and Jason wasn't screaming.

I stood up and felt a pain in my side. I looked down to where the bullet wound was. A scar was forming where the stitches once laced. I feel like the pain of this will never truly leave me. Not because I was shot but because my own father did this to me. The chuckling of Jason cooking beside my mom brought me back from the dark thoughts I was about to embark on.

"Hey sunshine!" Jason saw that I was up, and I smiled at him. I went walking out into the kitchen where Mom turned around.

"What is this some new kind of breakfast tradition?" I questioned having never seen my mom warm-up to strangers like this. Jason wasn't a stranger, but she didn't know him well enough to not call him one either. Mom laughed shaking her head.

"No, Jason just told me he knew how to cook." She said, setting a plate down in front of me. I was waiting for the embarrassing questions to come about last night. About Jason staying, me sleeping on him, it was all about to come out. Jason walked over setting coffee down in front of me. The warm strong smell swirled up to my nose. I closed my eyes taking it in. Then I felt someone move my hair back. Opening my eyes seeing Jason's smile as his hand moved away.

"You look so beautiful." His voice remained low so my mom couldn't hear. I felt my cheeks warm, and Mom called him away to get the eggs. I knew I was blushing and every part of me wanted to wrap my arms around him in a hug. I wanted to kiss his lips and lay back on the couch with him. A cozy rush of happiness blanketed my heart.

"So how did you sleep last night?" Mom sat down across from me sipping on her coffee.

"Just fine, there were no bad dreams." I confessed to her, feeling the awkward questions begin. Somehow, I felt alright with it though. The more I called Jason my boyfriend the more I was believing it. I never wanted anything to do with him, but everyone sees us as more than what we are. Jason, however, believes that it's all real. I told him the truth and I just don't think he's going to give up. That makes me feel whole inside for some reason. He was my boyfriend but what made it real was a lie. I would be leaving soon, and I would have to break his heart, I really didn't want that. I wanted this to be real.

"Do you two have anything planned today?" Mom ate her food and Jason sat a plate down in front of himself. I focused on him for the answer. Jason's mouth came open a little as he checked his phone. I smiled as he shoved scrambled eggs in his mouth.

"Well, I actually need to run home." His green eyes came over to mine. That meant he was leaving. I felt my heart drop and something inside told me to follow him.

"Just know you're welcome back anytime Jason, unless Sky doesn't want you here." Mom smiled, pointing her fork at me. I forced a smile shaking my head. I wanted him to stay. I didn't want him to leave. That sounded crazy of me. There was some sort of addiction I had inside that wanted to be with him. Everything about him was pulling me in.

"Thanks Mrs. Saxton and I will see you later." He gave me that world famous smile. I got down from the bar chair following him over to the door. I opened it and stood there as he walked out then turned around. Staring up into those green eyes, his fingertips ran down the path of my cheek. I broke into a huge smile resting my hand against his. He chuckled, coming in to rest his lips on my forehead. When he moved back my hands were still wrapped around his wrist.

"Come back later?" Something else was talking for me. It wasn't my thoughts, but it was my heart. His smile grew even bigger with a bright gleam in his eyes.

"Your wish is my command." His voice solid with trust, I let my hand slip away from his wrist. I watched as he got into his shiny old-school Mustang driving away. He waved his hand and I waved back. When his car was gone, I noticed a black sedan across the street. The smile on my face vanished not sure if that was the same car as before. I closed the door quickly, praying it wasn't my dad.

"Is there something wrong hun?" Mom saw my concern. I shook my head thinking fast. The stone on my necklace was cold. Dave was the person I needed to speak with.

"I'll be back." I said, sprinting up the steps. I ran into the hallway and straight to my bedroom. Dave was standing by my dresser with an unhappy expression on his face. Something told me he already knew. His blue aura left coming closer to me; his face wasn't necessarily concerned but I could see there was something more on his mind.

"You saw the car?" His blonde brows lifted up. I nodded my head glancing over to my window.

"Please tell me that isn't him." I was practically

begging. I was in fear of having to run again.

"Not quite but something a little worse." His fingers pinched together.

"Mystery man?" That was my next guess. There was nothing else that was worse, that I was aware of. Then again why was he in almost the same black car? I went walking over to my window peering down at the car. I saw nothing besides a black shadow behind the already tinted windows.

"Get dressed; we have some stuff to do." Dave left my side, and my mouth came open. What was I going to have to do? I rushed to put clothes on, and quickly ran my brush through my hair fetching my purse. I sprinted down the stairs and grabbed my phone. Mom's eyes were big watching as I moved quickly to get things together.

"Hey, where are you off too?" She came walking out of the kitchen. Dave did not prepare me very well for this.

"Uh, Missy wanted to see me, I will be back." I told her, going over to the garage door. I opened it going into the garage where only one car was parked. I sighed wishing I had my old car back. I didn't like driving my mom's car, it felt riskier. Even though she told me to use it any time. Dave sat in the passenger seat, but I was pretty sure Mom was not aware of his presence.

"When will you be back?" Her voice was frantic. I popped open the door tossing my purse in.

"A couple hours, don't worry I will be fine." Waving

my hand like it was no big deal. I started up the car and backed out onto the street. The black car was gone, and I looked at Dave. He squinted his eyes gazing around him.

"He's waiting down the street for you." He pointed to where the stop sign was. Why was I about to do the unknown? I was never the one to behave like this, say this, or even think it, but here it goes. I took off down the street away from my mom's view. My hands gripped the steering wheel tightly.

"Did you tell him something?" I wondered if this was some sort of meeting. Dave wanted to set things straight with him. Or maybe he thinks he's up to more than just bad.

"I didn't need to; Kyle is not a stupid man Sky." His hand went up gripping the car handle. Dave gave me some key information. His name was Kyle.

"So do I stop?" I was approaching his car quite quickly.

"No, just keep going, the mouse will follow." His blue eyes watched the car as we passed by it. Something inside made my heart started beating faster, there was a passenger. Who could be working with him? There was a slight gut wrenching feeling that it might be my father. That thought made me want to stop my car. I didn't want to be on some hell bound ride with my murderous father. I watched in the mirror and sure enough the black car was following. I had no idea where I was heading, I was just hoping Dave was going to instruct me sometime soon.

"Take a left up here." He pointed, never taking his eyes off the mirror. I did as he told me and felt the stone in the necklace become warmer. That alerted me that Kyle was the one tailing behind me. I glanced down to the necklace seeing the orange wrapping around the bright crystal blue.

"Dave, where are we going?" I saw and empty gravel lot coming up. I didn't know I lived so close to an empty gravel lot. I pulled in but never stopped.

"Here is fine." He assured me sitting back in the seat. He was no longer worried if Kyle was following or not. I stopped putting the car in park. Dave held his hand up telling me to be patient and wait. I unbuckled my seatbelt turning to look out of the back window. The black car stopped right behind us, and he killed the engine. My hand gripped the seat tightly scared of what I might witness. I saw something shine under the sunlight through his dark windows. There was a knot in the pit of my stomach that wanted to freak out and run.

"Dave, I can't do this!" I squirmed as my insides started to shake. His cold hand came over resting on mine. He looked deep into my eyes and faded out of the car. My mouth opened slightly, breathing in the frosty air. I watched, seeing Kyle fade out in front of his black car as well. Dave was speaking to him. Why wasn't I invited? I got a funny feeling it wasn't safe for me, but Dave would not have brought me otherwise, unless I was bait maybe. My eyes grew bigger, my heart pounded faster. Dave and Kyle were just staring at each other. I didn't want to wait and watch what was about to happen. I spun around opening the door. I jumped out catching Dave's attention like an eagle with its kill.

"Get back in the car!" Dave's voice was tense. Anger flushed across his face like someone had just told him the worst news. I tilted my head, having never heard him talk to me like that before.

"Now, now, there is no need to run the bait away after I've already got her." Kyle flashed to my side pinning my arms behind my back. I felt the fire rushing through my veins. The burn was awful. My legs trembled breaking out into a blazing hot sweat.

"Let go of me!" I screamed struggling against his tight hold. My arms felt like they were on fire and my flesh was melting off.

"Kyle, if you don't let go of her, I will be forced to imprison you back in Hell!" Dave's voice was strong and very stern. What did he mean imprison him back in Hell? He could do that? Why hasn't he already? This surge of power ran through my body shocking my insides. I felt as if I couldn't move.

"Like you have the strength or power to do that." Kyle laughed loudly in my ear making me close my eyes. I had to find myself. So, I closed my eyes trying to ignore the strong surge of power rushing through my body. I tried all I could to block out the pain of whatever he may be doing to me. I felt my heart take deep pumps like it was struggling against its own will. I coughed bending over. My whole body was stiff, no longer able to move. I heard Dave's voice, but it was all a blur. My vision was slipping away from me and I felt my breathing decrease. What was he doing to me? Why was Dave letting him kill me?

Cold surges escaped into my mouth. It felt like cold winter air. Crisp yet sore. The kind of cold air that could give you a cough for about a month. Nothing but dryness as my eyes plunged back open seeing Dave's face leaving mine. I blinked realizing Dave had his lips on mine. As much as I wanted to slap him I didn't. His crystal blue eyes were gazing right into mine as he stood back up. I sat on the gravel filled ground looking back to the black car. Someone stepped out of the passenger door. I rubbed my eyes feeling my body returning to normal. The powerful surge had gone but Kyle remained.

"No one is going to kill her." Hearing his voice sent chills through my body. The hurtful feeling of a bullet surging through my skin became all so real again. I saw the man that had shot me only a couple of weeks ago. I gasped, jumping to my feet.

"Get the hell away from me." I backed up running right into fire. Kyle still stood behind me. My father laughed, crossing his arms.

"Skylar, I didn't bring you here for you to get hurt." Dave told me, looking right into my eyes.

"Somehow I don't believe you." My bottom lip shook

as I walked away from the tiny circle of people. I wasn't sure if I could trust Dave. What if he was in on it with them this whole time and I have been doing nothing other than leading my mom back to the dangers mouth? I ran my hand back through my hair trying to keep my eyes from pouring water fountains. I was swung around quickly by Dave.

"I know you don't trust me right now and I know how dangerous this may be, but you need to talk with your dad." He encouraged me watching very carefully. I shook my head looking back over to the two people that could cost me my life.

"You're a jackass!" I retorted, shoving him away. I was never going to put my fate in Dave's hands again.

"Pumpkin, we need to discuss something." The monster came walking up beside us.

"If you *ever* think in your lifetime of living on this earth it will *ever* be okay to call me by that name again you have another thing coming to you." I threatened him, ready to leave them all behind in the dust. This was not a game I was in for. I saw a tremor of pain wash through my father's eyes. There was not one inch of mercy left in my body for this man. He showed no love, no mercy, and no fatherliness. I shook my head at him bracing myself for what was about to come.

"I must say that was pretty touching Sky, but I'm not here to hurt you, I never was." He smiled closing his hands together.

"If you were never here to hurt me then how come I have this?" I tugged my shirt up on one side showing the scar that was forming. It still stung with pain. The skin still tender to the touch and most of all the light pink flesh showing it wasn't healed completely.

"I never meant to hurt you; you should have never moved my arm and got in the way of the bullet." Richard sounded like he was negotiating with me.

"Excuse me, but I believe you were in our house to kill one of us otherwise that gun would have never been triggered." Anger was working its way up inside of me. I didn't want to fight with him. I didn't even want to look him in the eyes.

"No, no let me explain myself–"

"I don't need an explanation, what I need is for you to get as far away from us as you can and never *ever* show your face to us again!" The fierceness was rising in my veins. I wanted to attack this man and scare the living shit out of him. His head tossed back in laughter. I glanced over to Dave seeing he was on guard for what might come. I shifted my attention over to Kyle, and he too was ready.

"And you, who are you and why are you helping the man that shot me?" I walked right up to Kyle pressing my finger against his chest. His orange eyes lit up like fire.

"Well princess, I think that's a discussion for another day." He took my hand tossing it off him.

"Oh, no don't you dare tell me that–"

"Skylar, it's not you." The monster cut me off. I turned around looking back at him. I walked back over to Richard.

"Why do you want to kill my mom?" My fist formed ready to stand my ground.

"She has done things that you will never believe." His hands raised as he was speaking to me, wanting mercy. I gave him a smirk stepping backwards.

"Just like you have done things that I will never believe, I think we're done here." I said, going back to my car. I was not about to listen to my father tell me something bad that my mom has done. I wasn't about to believe a word of it anyway. I got into my car as Dave flashed in beside me. A scream of resentfulness came out of me, before biting down on my lip. The door came back open to my car. I gasped for air not expecting Richard to be standing there.

"Skylar, I know I'm always going to be the enemy in your eyes and there is no place for forgiveness, but I need you to listen to me." His hand rested over his chest. I laughed without smiling, slamming the door shut. I started the car taking off away from him. He was right, he was the enemy and a villain that would never be forgotten. I watched him stand on the gravel road and then disappear from my vision. I turned the corner and slammed on the breaks. Dave went flying forward and came back into the seat. I gave him a dangerous glare feeling the tenseness wrapping around my heart.

"Dave, get out!" Gripping the steering wheel tightly, not wanting him here. I saw the sorrow fill his eyes. He had broken my trust. I could not be friends with a man that promised nothing but protection and yet had led me to a murderer.

"I'm not leaving you, I had to do this." His cold hand came over resting on mine. I jerked away turning to face him.

"No Dave, you had to do nothing. You lied to me and for the most part I don't even know who you really are. I thought I did but I was wrong, a stupid, wrong teenage girl who put her faith and trust in someone that was dead. I mean how crazy does that sound? I thought we were in this to help each other, but you were never here to protect me or my mother, now get out of my car and do me a favor; don't come back." I said forcefully, averting my gaze from him feeling the tears fill my eyes. This awful heartache filled me with pain. I was letting go of someone that I thought I knew so well. I couldn't believe I couldn't even trust a dead man.

"I am so sorry Skylar; just know I will always be here." He left my car leaving his blue aura behind. It swirled around me. I breathed in the crisp coolness. I closed my eyes feeling the tears running down my face. Everyone I knew was betraying me. Stabbing me in the back like some kind of distrusted animal that didn't save their life, what was my world coming to? I became close with very few people, yet they showed me no faith. Commitment was a foreign language to most. The scariest part was, I believed their words, as if I'm the idiot taken for granted. I heaved, crying hard into my steering wheel wishing for all of this to be over! My mind was drained. My heart hurt from every piece of it being broken off. My body was numb from all the war-like threats. I was exhausted of this life. I wished for a new one, a better one. A life where I would be free.

Chapter 16

Only You

It was pouring down rain as I drove fast. Stopping in between lights and having no idea where I was going. I just lost my best friend. It's true what they say, you can't trust anyone. The only person you can ever trust is yourself. More tears came rushing down my face. The windshield wipers moved back and forth as the rain was pushed away. A car blew its horn, and I took off through the green light. I took another turn, and I was in an area of huge houses. I slowed my car seeing a bunch of black SUVs up the street. What was going on? I pulled over to the curb wiping away the cold tears. Taking a deep quivering breath, I glanced around myself. I was in the rich part of town. I saw a back alley that could lead me off the street. I turned my steering wheel noticing the people with the cameras in hand. Umbrellas were popped and flashes went off. I knew who I was close to. Sniffling in some more air I turned into the back alley. Driving slowly, watching the back of these mansions pass by. All the pools that were filled with light blue water being pounded by the rain as the sky cried along with me. All I could think of was Dave's blue eyes piercing through mine. I stopped the car as I saw the shadow of the man I wanted to embrace. He stood by a wall sized window with his back turned. Jason's figure was hunched over, reaching for something in the room. My eyebrows rose watching as he pulled his black T-shirt over his head. My lips curving into a smile seeing his sculpture-like body. The fuse inside of me was fizzling out sensing an odd comfort.

The sound of rattling metal pulled my vision over to see one of the press trying to jump a neighboring fence. He took a few pictures but wasn't getting what he wanted. I watched as his hands slipped from the wet bars. His hair dripped down into his face. His head swung back flipping it away. I sighed blinking away the tears of Dave's absence. I opened my car door getting out cautiously. The photographer hung one leg over the chain link fence positioning his body in a slant. His index finger and thumb smoothly twisting the camera lens. My lips separated getting a closer view of Jason in the paparazzi camera. My eyebrows shot up as Jason unbuttoned his jeans.

"Hey!" I interrupted, stopping the man from capturing that soon to be juicy shot. His body jerked from the fence fast, making it rattle. A quick picture was taken. I flinched at the sound of the shutter.

"You're the girlfriend." He said smiling, snapping a few more pictures. My hand went up covering my face.

"No, I'm the girl that's going to let you walk free and

not lose your job for trespassing." I told him, feeling the rain soak into my clothes. His mouth fell open looking up at the thick clouds in the sky. He nodded his head smiling at me.

"I understand why he cares so much about you; he's a lucky man to have such a loyal girl on his side. Thank you." The man, still smiling, turned his back walking away. I had a smile on my face thinking about what he had just said. I'm loyal. The word loyal means a lot of things but for me, I feel that isn't true. Jason has stood up for me multiple times in just the one month that I have known him. All I have to give to him is almost being shot. I turned resting my hands on the thick iron fence. I looked up into the window where I saw him talking to his dad. Jason was still partially naked with his hand scratching his head. Another man that decides not to take interest in me and just wants me gone, his dad. Something about it all just doesn't feel right. I am not a loyal person. I am nothing but dangerous to him. Yet he thinks he's the one getting in the way with his fame. I leant my forehead into the fence thinking about leaving him. If I left him, he might never forgive me… My feelings didn't matter at this point. All I had to worry about was keeping the people I care about alive. Jason was one of those people. He would do the same for me even if we didn't know each other that well.

I walked back to the car pulling it around the curve of the alley. I killed the engine staring up at the house that was bigger than I would ever imagine. I got back out closing the door. I walked up a path leading to a small gate. Opening it carefully, walking through the wet grass, I felt like some sort of criminal. Once Jason saw me though, everything would be okay. I jaunted along the sidewalk that leads to the huge pool that was being pounded by rain. I was soaking wet as I reached the back door. I took a moment capturing the back yard that was enclosed by a privacy fence from the alley I hid in. I sucked my lower lip into my mouth feeling nervous. My fist went up slowly knocking on the glass door. I closed my eyes tightly feeling my heart pound out of control. When the door came open, his dad stood before me. A confused expression said nothing more than 'why are you at my back door?' I sighed looking away from him. The door slid open, and we both analyzed each other in silence.

"You can't see him." He said in a tough tone. Water was dripping from my hair running down the inside of my clothes making me shake.

"Please let me see him." I crossed my arms feeling the cold breeze. He shook his head never letting his hand fall off the door handle.

"Look Skylar, whatever you may have going on with my son, it will end soon." He predicted, pressing his lips together. My lips broke apart hating dealing with this man. I was still nervous inside knowing I wasn't the type of girl to go knocking on some guy's door. I needed

Jason. As much as I didn't want to admit it, I did.

"Mr. Blackstone, I get it, you don't want us together but right now I need to talk with him." I felt tears welling in my eyes. I needed someone to talk to. Someone to hug me and rest my head against and someone I knew could hold everything I said. I don't know Jason that well but from all the looks he gave me, all the things he's done to be with me, I felt I could trust him. Jason wasn't the kind of guy to toss me off a cliff. He was brave. Strong as stone and yet he was still soft as cotton.

"Tell me what you really want from him." He crossed his arms assuming the worst.

"What?" I didn't know how to answer his question. What I wanted from Jason was nothing I could easily explain. It was something to feel inside, something to hold all of my broken parts together. I need his happiness just to make the fearfulness go away.

"I know what most girls want with my son–"

"And I'm not most girls." I cut him off not liking the fact I was being compared to some sleazy girl that wanted in his pants for his money. I shivered remembering Abby call me trash.

"Dad, what's going on?" Hearing his voice took the coldness away. A shock of warmth washed inside of me and his dad stepped out of his view. Jason stood there, our eyes locking onto one another instantly. He came over to the door quickly, leaving his father aside. Without a minute to waste I was off the ground in a hug. I closed my eyes laying my head down on his shoulder. My arms around his neck, I felt close. His scent went up my nose and my world felt full of comfort. My feet went back down touching the ground.

"Why are you here?" Jason moved my wet hair away from my face. His mouth moved with concern wiping the tears away from my eyes. His warm hands against my cheeks made my eyes go shut.

"It doesn't matter, she was just leaving." Hearing his dad's voice made my eyes reopen. Jason turned around looking at him.

"I highly doubt she was." He turned back to me. I saw the questioning gaze in his eyes. He wasn't sure if he should believe his dad or not.

"I came to talk with you." I said, listening to the rain pound against the awning. He nodded his head then gave another glance to his dad.

"I feel as if she should return home." His dad crossed his arms standing in the doorway remaining with the stern eyes.

"She's soaking wet, I'm pretty sure she didn't just come here for nothing." Jason rejected his dad's idea, taking my hand. The warmth soaked into my body making me forget about the cold rain that ran down my clothes. My small hand was completely lost behind his.

"Jason, you know you have other obligations right now." His dad's voice was strict like an old man wanting young kids off his property. Jason pulled me alongside him into the kitchen of their house.

"It can wait." He said simply, never releasing my hand from his. We escaped from the kitchen into the living room. I was in awe seeing the rich red walls with white paint finishing the edges. The huge couch that sat in the middle with a big screen TV that looked like it could swallow mine. We walked around to a winding staircase. I stopped before following him up. Jason turned halfway around on the edge of the step. He gave me a crooked smile holding his hand out again.

"Your house is amazing." I said in what was almost a whisper, as I placed my hand back into his. He chuckled a little and I watched my feet leave wet prints from my dripping clothes on the gray carpet. This made me feel ignorant, but I continued to follow.

"It's alright." He shrugged his shoulders and I looked at him weirdly. My house was nothing like this. Not even my house back in Florida was this nice. We walked past the round balcony looking over the living room. Cool breezes swept past me, it smelled like bubble gum. We both stopped and I looked over my shoulder. Abby was standing there with her mouth wide open – glossy pink lips and tense eyes.

"No, not happening get that thing out of here/" she said, moving her fingers up and down like I was some sort of trash he'd picked up off the street.

"One, she's not a thing, and two I think you should be a little nicer to a person that helped save your life." Jason raised his eyebrows never losing his grip on my hand. My eyes fell away from them then. I didn't want her to be nice to me for saving her life. That was the human thing to do. Then I thought more about Kyle and how he killed her best friend. I felt so bad for her. But I still did not want her kindness to be an act of debt.

"I'm so sorry about your friend, Abby." I gave my sympathy to her placing my other hand on Jason's arm. She gave me tiger like eyes. She wanted to kill me but couldn't.

"I'm telling Dad she's here." She swung around rushing down the stairs. Jason shook his head leading us up to a door. He opened it revealing this huge bedroom to me. He held his hand out telling me to enter. My body froze in time locking eyes with my reflection in the wall size window. My eyes shot back to him realizing his shirt was back on along with his jeans put together.

"I usually don't invite people into my room this easily but you, you are important." He smiled taking me inside. The door shut behind us and I watched the huge window leading to the backyard. It was so beautiful. I walked over, looking down into the glistening pool. The sky was starting to lighten up, but water kept pouring down. Jason swung me around facing the forest that captured me. My lips sank back into my mouth thinking about how to begin. Where to start and where to end. It was all happening fast now, even though he's always patient. His warm hands barely touching my cold wet shoulders, he smiled brightly kissing my forehead.

"I'm important to you?" The words slipped from my lips realizing how stupid that sounded. He laughed a little stepping back. His hands came down to cradle mine.

"Well, it's not every day I have a girl come knocking on my back door trying to convince my dad to let you see me." He laughed a little more, sitting down on his bed. I watched one of his legs slip under him.

"I had to do something, I needed someone to talk with and right now, the closest person to me is you." I blurted out, walking up to him. The smile on his face grew even bigger. He could see that I was welcoming him into my life in a deeper way than I ever had before.

"And another reason you are so important to me, hold that thought, I'll be back." He said gently pushing me down on his bed. My mouth came open as he walked over to another door opening it. I saw the edges of a beautiful bathroom open up. He left me and I was at a loss for words. I came here to talk with him, but he just walked away. My eyes went down seeing my bra right through my shirt. My eyes opened wide realizing he could see everything. Jason came walking back, I flew up grabbing a pillow to hide my boobs. His black eyebrows shot up.

"You could have told me!" I said ripping the towel from his hand. His smile went down a little.

"Well, you can't blame a guy for enjoying some things." His arms went up chuckling. I wrapped it around myself hiding from him. I gave him a scowl.

"Seriously? I came here because I needed someone, and you stare at my boobs?" I stood back up from the bed. He held his hands up in surrender.

"No, I'm here to listen. I'm just waiting for you to talk." His voice softened, walking over to another door. He escaped away from me.

"This is serious Jason!" I called after him watching my hair drip rain onto the towel.

"I never said it wasn't!" He called back from what I assumed was his closet. I sighed thinking about my dad. Thinking about how Dave just took me right to him. Why would he put me in the arms of danger as if there were no consequences? It was like he was giving his dog away because he simply didn't want it anymore. I felt sick inside and just wanted to tell somebody everything. I couldn't tell Jason about Dave. He wouldn't understand that I am able to see dead people. He would think I was crazy and would probably want to stay away from me. I couldn't just turn around and let him slip away from me either. Jason was someone close to my heart and I felt safe around him. I didn't want him pushing himself away from me because I sound like a crazy girl talking to a dead man who promised to keep me safe. He came walking back out of his closet with a shirt in hand.

"I have a shirt or a robe, whichever you prefer." He told me, holding the flannel shirt out. A warm smile returned, feeling the comfort I was searching for. I took the shirt, the dry softness of it rubbed against my skin, I stood up from the bed. Jason tossed the robe onto a chair.

"Thank you." I couldn't stop smiling as he took care of me.

"I can dry your clothes if you like." His eyes went down to my wet shorts. Moving my eyes to the side nodding my head. We will talk while they dry.

"I don't suppose you have pants." I laughed standing in front of the bathroom. His green eyes went to the side, and he held up one finger. He went running back into his closet. He was not about to bring me a pair of jeans out; he returned with pajama bottoms. His pretty white teeth showed themselves as he held them out.

"An outfit for the lady." He laughed, taking a seat on his bed. I walked into his bathroom closing the door. I turned around seeing the bathtub and the see-through shower against the wall. The mirror hanging on the wall with the rich gold designs, just everything about it, it was insane. My hand ran down the marble sink that sat beneath me. Little pieces of hair stuck to my fingers. I shook my hand off never understanding why men couldn't clean up after themselves. I fought with the soaked shirt peeling it from my body. I whipped my bra off ringing it out over the sink. I slid my bra and the flannel shirt on. My shorts flew off fast and I tossed them out the door. My eyes went over to the hair dryer hanging on the side of the wall. I whipped it up hitting the red button. Air came streaming out into my face. My hair was drying super-fast. I blow dried my underwear as well before pulling up the pajama pants that were way to long on me. I quietly laughed at myself wearing baggy pajama pants. My hand went down flapping the airy crotch. It was summer and I was dressed for a crisp fall night. I walked back out hitting the light switch. Jason was no longer in the room. My clothes were gone, and I went back over to the oversized window. I watched as the rain fell down beating against the pool, and all of the other houses enclosed in this tight neighborhood.

My hand went up resting on the windowpane. I sighed and when I did my breath was left behind on the window like it was the dead of winter. Chilly air swept around me, and I looked down to my necklace. The stone was lighting up in blue. I closed my eyes letting my head dip down. Why was Dave here? All I wanted was for him to leave me alone. I turned around to see Abby standing in the doorway staring me down. My mouth came open, her eyes searching up and down my body. She waltzed into the room until we were close enough to smell each other.

"What do you think you're doing wearing my brother's clothes?" She touched the collar of the shirt. My eyes looked down, not ready to fight this. Dave would have been much better.

"I gave them to her, better question, what are you doing in my room?" Jason folded his arms walking closer to us. Abby looked up to him. For a split second I saw Jason's father in him.

"That's gross, you know Dad is going to be really

upset with you." She shook her head.

"It will be fine, now if you don't mind." He said, taking her arm and leading her away from me. I grinned a little but also thought about the way his dad talked to me and for me. I wasn't fond of that idea but there was more to Jason than his family. He wasn't like them. The door closed before he came back over to me.

"Now about your important problem that I have to know about." He rested his hands on both my shoulders. I closed my eyes nodding my head. I took a deep breath, sitting down on his bed. It was time to pull my words together allowing the truth to finally expel.

"I saw my dad today, Jason." I told him, just throwing the words out of my mouth. Jason's eyes opened wide as he watched me. I saw the forest open up. His eyes left me and there was no smile left on his face. His hand ran down over his mouth, then back through his hair.

"What was he doing around you?" His eyes full of concern. I bit down on my lip thinking back to what Dave did to me.

"He uh, he kind of ran me off the road." I stumbled talking around the fact that Dave took me right into his hands. Everything would have been better if it was just Kyle.

"What? He didn't hurt you, did he?" Both his hands came up to my face. I closed my eyes shaking my head no.

"He was trying to talk to me, reason with me." My

shoulders went up remembering what he said about my mom.

"Reason what with you, the fact he tried to kill you?" His voice was panicky. I feel like I should have never opened my mouth. I couldn't just open up to my mom about this though. She would go off the wall. Jason is still keeping it together.

"He said he never meant to shoot me." Looking away from Jason feeling the bullet wound. Jason brought my head back around to meet his.

"Because he wanted me, Skylar please tell me you are not okay with this man after this." His eyes full of worried pity. I didn't want him to feel that for me.

"No matter what he does, I will never forgive him, nor will I feel free to welcome him back into my life but when he runs me off the road to tell me things and reason with me, I just can't Jason." My voice was weak as I let my face fall into my hands. I felt his hand rest on my back as tears ran down into the palms of my hands. Jason pulled me over to him. My head rested against his side. His hands ran down the side of my hair and I felt him kiss the top of my head. His warm body was comfortable.

"Shhh… It will be okay." His soft voice was a lullaby while his hand moved in gradual circles on my back. I had not one clue what to do. The police wouldn't bother. They never have before. Richard was always too good for them. I brought my head up from his chest looking into his eyes.

"He was the one that did all this at prom." My voice shook watching his eyes grow.

"Did he tell you that?" He pulled back from me some.

"He didn't have to, I'm not stupid to his games." I said, wiping the tears away from my face. He nodded his head looking over to the big window. The rain beating against it roughly. Jason got up walking over to the window not saying a word as he stared blankly away from me. He was thinking, but of what I couldn't tell. I heard a phone go off, but he didn't flinch. It wasn't my phone, so I assumed it was his. My head turned over my shoulder seeing the screen light up. I pulled my bottom lip back into my mouth picking it up. There was a lady on the screen under the name Emma. Who was Emma? It stopped ringing going to a missed call. I looked back over to him as his arms stayed folded. He looked millions of miles away. I laid the phone down getting up from the bed. I went over resting my hand on his back.

"I should have never told you." I said, feeling as if I should have just kept him shut out of my life.

"No, you need a safe place to stay, he knows where you live." He said, still not giving me a glance. My hand fell away from him thinking about running again.

"It won't matter where I go, he will always find us." There was no chance of losing him. Jason walked away from the window then.

"You should stay here with me." He suggested, gazing into my eyes. I gasp not expecting him to say that. I shook my head walking closer to him.

"I can't, there's no way I could leave my mom." I confessed, feeling as if she was the one in great danger and I was just along for the ride. Even though he said he didn't want to kill me I wasn't going to put anything past him. My walls were up, and they are going to stay guarded.

"Sky, I think you need to go home and tell your mom about this, we will figure something out." He knew I made a mistake telling him first. I nodded my head knowing he was right. My mom did need to know that Dad was still here. After all he was sitting in front of our house. He was waiting for me or my mom. Although he seemed to want to talk to me, more to convince me of what wasn't true. Then I got to thinking if he was already there trying to get to her. What if this was the plan to draw me away from the house knowing I would be upset after talking with him? He would expect me to run off then abolish my relationship with Dave leaving Mom and I separated.

"Jason, I have to go." I said, rushing over to his door. He ran quickly in front of me stopping the both of us. His hands lay against me.

"Let me get your clothes first." He said, and I saw in his eyes that everything was moving at a fast pace. Jason turned around revealing his dad standing before us. He studied me standing here in Jason's clothes. I swallowed heading back to Jason's room. This was about to get all kinds of awkward. With a short surge of surprise, Jason shut the door after I reentered his room. I heard a few words being exchanged between them before the sound of rushing footsteps left the hallway. I swallowed hard focusing on the door. *Please, don't come in here to lecture me,* I wished, not wanting a bantering conversation with his dad right now. I was beyond worried about my mom. My fingers fiddled nervously with my necklace noticing Dave's absence. He was here but now he had left.

Dave worked to his own agenda. If he felt comfortable with someone I was with, he would leave. If I was in the company of strangers, he would always linger around for my protection. Another baffling reason why Dave would throw me to the vulture. Dave always put so much effort into making things safe for my life, it didn't add up why he would jeopardize all of that. I wanted to believe Dave was not setting out to harm me, but things went south very fast. All I could wish for was that Dave was watching over my mom. Even if I wanted him gone from my life, he wouldn't leave. That was his loyalty. For right now though, the madness was still livid and raging inside of me.

Chapter 17

Get Out Alive

I drove away from the alley fast, leaving Jason standing in the pouring down rain. Turning back onto the normal streets where cars zoomed passed me. Avoiding all the rain was impossible but what I had to tell my mom wasn't. I didn't even know how to go about this. She was going to freak out. There was no way of hiding this though. There were many ways to take this and many solutions that wouldn't fix it. There was no fixing or getting away from a monster like that. We were fools to believe we could.

My light went green, and I took off. As I did a car came skidding through the red light. My heart went from ten to a hundred beats a second. The wheel turned under my hands without me doing so. We both came to a stop. Breathing hard and vigorously I saw my dad in the other car, my mouth dropped open. He gave me this evil grin making himself look like the Joker. My fist wrapped around the steering wheel tightly as horns from other cars were blowing. He waved at me taking off down the road. Where was he going? I followed close behind, but he was swerving in and out of lanes. What was his game?

"Let him go." Dave was sitting beside me. My attention shifted wondering why he was here.

"Get out of my car." I demanded watching the black car move to the far lane.

"Sky, listen to me following him is a trap, he set you up." He took the wheel from me pulling us over on the side of the road. My aggression wanted me to drive but my morals lifted my foot from the gas pedal switching to my brake.

"And you took me right into his hands, I don't believe either of you are worth trusting." I said, defensively glaring out the window. He was long gone now. My hand ran up through my hair that was now damp again.

"I know you hate me, but I will do anything within my power to keep you safe." He said, leaving those soft cold eyes behind. He left the car, and his blue aura was floating. I closed my eyes placing my hand over my face. He says he would do anything to keep me safe no matter what but then he just hands me over. I was so confused by how to feel about him. I pulled away from the curb heading back down the road. I couldn't stop thinking about Dave now. The things he says and does, it's all so sweet. Then after what he did today, it all just seems so fake.

I turned into the driveway. Before I got out, I looked all around me seeing no black car waiting for me. I picked up my necklace seeing no hint of orange. It was just a normal black stone. Dave wasn't here either. I got out of the car making a run for the door. Mom was there waiting with the door open. She smiled at me closing the door.

"How was Missy?" She asked sounding all cheery. I sighed looking back over to her. This was going to be a long discussion. Her smile went down seeing my face.

"I didn't exactly get to see Missy; I saw someone else." I said, walking over to the couch. I wasn't sure how to breathe with this horrifying news.

"Who did you go see, Jason?" She got more of a smile on her face. My bottom lip sucked back into my mouth as I shook my head. I had no idea how to spill this. Mom came walking closer to me. She sat down beside me resting a hand on my shoulder. We made eye contact, I tried to read what she must be thinking. I couldn't read anything besides her questioning eyes.

"Dad, he ran me off the road on my way over to Missy's." I came out and told her. The questioning look disappeared within seconds.

"What? He didn't hurt you, did he? What did he want?" Her voice anxious, wanting all the answers I could give.

"He didn't hurt me; he wanted to talk with me." I said, telling her everything I'd told Jason.

"Please tell me you took off away from him and called the police." She had a pleading look in her eyes, hoping I made the right choices. I shook my head not doing either of those. I did leave him, but I also listened.

"He told me he never wanted to hurt me." I repeated, needing to tell her the whole story.

"And you believed him?" She jumped off the couch like someone was at the door. I shook my head once more pulling my knees close to my chest.

"I would never do such a thing, he also wanted me to believe that you did bad things." I recalled his words wondering what he was talking about. I didn't believe him and realized he was just trying to turn me against my mom. She tilted her head with sorrow filling her eyes. She had a story behind all the fear. What has she done?

"What did he tell you?" Her hands ran down the white dress she wore. I lifted my eyebrows getting up from the couch.

"That's when I left; I didn't want to believe you had actually done something bad." I told her, feeling as if I didn't know her either.

"Sweetie, I haven't done anything that he might have tried to tell you." She said getting a sad look in her eyes. She wasn't feeling trusted, then again, I wasn't sure I should break down more walls.

"Are you sure there isn't anything you're hiding from me?" We stayed across the room from each other. I saw the tears welling up in her eyes. There was a secret.

"You want to trust a man that almost killed you? A man that was aiming a gun at your boyfriend and now just because he said something about me you want to turn your back on me now?" She laid her hand on her chest.

I closed my eyes feeling like such a worthless child. She was right, why would I take his words into consideration after what he left us with? I was crazy.

"I'm sorry Mom, it's just I feel like I don't know who to believe." I remained honest sitting back down.

"It's okay, I know how you feel, look if he came after you then we have to leave again." She said bending down on her knees. I looked at her knowing she would want to do this. She was just going to keep running and sooner or later it would all just catch up to us. She wouldn't be able to run anymore because he would have her exactly where he wants her. Right in the palm of his hand. Our initial move date from here was still pending as the new house in Florida was still awaiting our souls to fill its space.

"Are we still planning on Florida?" There was no way out. I felt as if she knew that, but she just didn't want to confirm it.

"I will call and make our definite arrangements." She patted my leg. Arrangements? What was she talking about? The last time we ran she did the same thing. She always had someone to call but I was never sure who it was. I was always lost. All I knew was our arrangements were the same, find a basic home, low-key. When we would arrive at the home it would be minimal, with a sofa, refrigerator, and beds.

"Do you think we could stay closer?" Realizing it was almost summer, missing the last two weeks of school could be crucial after missing pretty much all of last year.

"Look, just go get your things packed again and I'll call." She held her hand up walking into the kitchen. She dialed someone on her phone, and I stood up. We had to be very discreet about leaving. There can be no moving trucks and no packing things into a car. There can only be us leaving in one. We only came up here with two bags each. My life was never going to change.

I went sprinting up the stairs into my room. My shoulders slumped knowing the few pictures hanging on the walls would soon be taken down. My bags were set out and Dave's blue aura was fading away. I closed my eyes taking all this in. I was getting ready to leave two of the closest people to me. I haven't known them for very long, but I felt such a strong connection to them both right away. Missy was like a sister I'd never had. Jason was the crazy boyfriend that made me lovesick every night because I couldn't be with him. Now no matter what I couldn't have either of them. These actions were to keep them safe. Although my monster knows who they are to me, I could only hope they aren't his next victims. Knowing that I wasn't here to capture and make the target. After all he was going to shoot Jason instead of me. He said he was here for my mom. If he was here for my mom, why would he have aimed for Jason? Thinking rapidly about everything that had happened up to this point; he arrived when I was with Jason. The first time I had seen the black car, it was with

Jason, and he broke into the house on the same night that Jason had appeared at the house. Then today I was on the road when Dave took me to him. It all led back to Jason. What if this whole time he was after him instead of us? None of that made sense. Why would he use us to get to him? I grabbed my phone hitting Jason's number. I had to talk with him. I needed to put this puzzle together before leaving. Sitting down on the bed as the phone rang grabbing my computer up.

"Hey, wasn't expecting a call from you so quickly." His voice sounded amused.

"Jason, listen to me, I have to leave again, and I need to tell you something." I said, playing with my necklace.

"What do you mean you have to leave again?" His cheery voice lowered. I sighed staring at my own reflection in the computer screen.

"I told my mom and she's making plans to move away." My voice was faint finding it hard to even tell him. That warm place in my heart felt cold. Leaving someone you have feelings for isn't so easy. I was up against a new challenge.

"But you haven't even been here that long." He sounded more bummed than me.

"I know, but listen to me, can you come over?" I asked him, pulling the phone away from my face. I saw the options to end the call, and all the rest, light up.

"I'll be right there." He said, and my finger tapped the back of my phone. He hung up and I pulled the battery out. Scanning it, looking for any sign of anything that might be different. Any sign that he could be tapping into my phone calls. I didn't want him knowing any of our plans. Anything to mess up our escape. There was no sign of a tracking device hidden under the battery. I popped the phone back together and put it aside. The idea of always having an older phone just in case of having to toss it, bothered me. Walking over to my suitcase, the sound of the bag unzipping sent me back to leaving Florida. I was now returning, after so many instances of wanting to return to Florida; my head was spinning. The curious side of me wanted to know which city we would relocate to this time; it wouldn't be Miami, that much I knew.

Grabbing things up left and right tossing them in the bag, I didn't even care if they were a mess. I went over picking up a small box that has yet to be opened. You know it's bad when you haven't even fully settled in and you're on the run again. I just wanted to stay in one place. It would be a dream to not worry about dying. Not feeling like a criminal that just brought down the biggest bank in the world and was left running. I know we were far from the criminals, or even the accomplices, but still the similarities remained. Shoving more of my belongings into my bag I stopped when I grabbed my photo album. I just looked down at it running my fingers over the stickers I had covered it when I was a little girl. Back when everything was still okay, and my dad didn't want to kill my mom. To abominate every part of what was supposed to be a perfect life.

"Hey, Jason is here." Mom peeked her head in the door. I dropped the photo album turning around. She didn't have a smile on her face.

"Okay." I said, walking out of the room. Before we reached the stairs, she turned me around.

"I don't think this is the best time for him to be here." She said, giving me a gentle look. A hectic storm of emotions brewed inside of her.

"I need to talk to him, it's important." I went sprinting down the stairs. Jason's green eyes met mine right away. I smiled a little reaching him.

"Hey, what do you need to talk about?" His green eyes were questioning.

"I've noticed something over the couple of weeks since my dad has come back." I started, starting to confront him about my dad always popping up when he's around. He probably doesn't know anything about this. Nor has he probably put this together.

"Besides the fact that he's a creep, what is that?" He took a seat on the couch pulling me down with him. I glanced to my left seeing my mom in the kitchen. She moved stuff around as if she wasn't listening. That made me wonder if she was.

"Every time he came back for me or us, you were around." I lowered my voice, holding onto his hands. His head went back a little like he was in shock. His green eyes darted away from me as he was sucked into his own thoughts. He licked his lips moving his eyes back and forth. He looked over his shoulder to where Mom was packing.

"I remember the first time I took you out." He whispered, thinking back. I smiled a little bit, embarrassed by how short I was with him that day.

"What do you remember about it?" I had to know what he picked up on that day that I never told him.

"That you were highly distracted when we left and when I looked back, I saw the black car, the same one you couldn't keep your eyes off of, also the same car that gave you the worry of death in your eyes." His fingertips barely touched the tip of my chin. I nodded my head, hearing what it was he saw that day.

"I just wanted you to realize that every time you're around, he's around." I told him, glancing over to the window.

"Don't worry, we will be okay, you will be alright. You just need to get out of here." He said, pushing my hair behind one ear. I closed my eyes bowing my head. Hearing him wanting me to leave, it felt like I was being pushed away. Jason wasn't doing that he just wanted me to be safe. He lifted my head back up and I felt a tear rolling down my cheek. He pressed his lips hard together, wiping the tear away. His lips touched my forehead, and I closed my eyes once again. I felt his arms drape around me like a blanket. I was pulled up onto his lap making my body fall over on his. My arms wrapping around his torso, feeling his ribs move up and down as he breathed. His wonderful smell traveling up my nose. I didn't want to leave this.

"Jason, I don't want to leave." Reopening my eyes, I felt him sigh as we pulled back from each other.

"I know Sky, but it will be safer for you and your mom." His hands lay on both sides of my face. Shaking my head looking over to my mom, she came walking back into the living room.

"Honey, we have to do what's best, and I know we haven't been here very long but sometimes it doesn't take long." She breathed, squeezing my shoulder. My mouth dropped open for air as if I was suffocating from her words.

"Exactly, so why would we keep running from something that doesn't take very long? No matter what he will keep finding us and hunting us down. He will find us in a matter of days no matter where we run and hide next. Just remember that bullet went through me as fast as he's going to find us again." I said, jumping off the couch. I ran over to the stairs. I didn't want to listen to her try and make it better like all the times before. Weeks turned into days and days turned into hours, then Richard would show. This time might have been different because he sent an assassin first, but the motive was always the same. His motivation was like a tattoo inked within our skin. It might fade, but it would never wash away.

"Skylar, hang on!" Mom yelled after me. I just went on up the stairs.

"I'll talk to her." Hearing Jason's voice traveling not far behind, I stopped. Leaning against the wall feeling the tears falling down my face, breathing in hard. I went walking back into my bedroom picking up the photo album. I flipped through the pictures quickly until I reached one. Seeing my dad sitting with me by the Christmas tree. I was so little and in his lap with a big unopened gift. My smile was as big as the moon. Everything was so normal back then. Now it was just a mashed-up hell. Sobbing over the picture, I was turned around in his arms.

"Shh, it will be alright. The sooner we get you out of here the better." His rough voice made me move back away from him.

"How can you say that?" Sniffling in the air wiping my cheeks off, I heard the tender steadiness of his heartbeat.

"I'm not saying this because I want to, I'm saying this because–" He stopped staring into my eyes. I shook my head laying the album down.

"Because what, Jason?" I wanted to yell at him. He wanted me gone and was all for what my mom wanted. His head lowered as he bit his lip. Watching his green eyes go up to the ceiling and back down, the green forest was being drenched in rain. He blinked away the tears that grew on the surface. His hands ran back through his hair as he turned away.

"Because you mean something very special to me." He swung back around. I tilted my head seeing regret in his eyes.

"You don't have to lie to me." I said, fighting the tears.

"I'm not lying to you; if I was, I wouldn't be so wrapped up in trying to save your life!" His voice frustrated and his eyes full of hate.

"How would I know that? After all I'm just an obligation to you!" The tears were turning into a waterfall. I felt myself breaking inside because I was fighting with him. His green eyes held a look of hurt like a lion that had just been stabbed. I didn't want to bring any of this back up. It was better to get him away from me, though. To let him run away. I didn't like hurting him because it hurt me more.

"You know what maybe this was a mistake, I thought you were different than this, I guess all you are is just a little scared puppy running from the shadows of her father. You know when you're gone, lose my number, and lose my picture, my image, anything you will remember about me because I am nothing to you; it's obvious you only think of yourself as a goddamn obligation to me, but you are so wrong." He backed away from me blinking away the tears. My mouth dropped open and he went, walking away from me. Both his hands moved back through his black hair as he escaped out of the room. My hands went up over my face as I cried harder. I just let the most important person slip away. The pain that ached inside my heart was unreal. I've never felt this kind of agony before. I walked over to my open door seeing him leave down the steps. Either I chase after him or I let him go. Either way it wouldn't change how I just made him feel. I knew so much better than to speak those words because they were never true. Jason never saw me as an obligation, only his dad did. All Jason did was fall in love with me, the wrong girl. The love that grew for him overpowered most of my emotions but that was why I had to let him go. This whole time I thought I was Jason's obligation, but in the end he was my obligation. I was obligated to keep him alive because I loved him. Now I had to say goodbye for his own good.

I walked over to my window seeing him sit in his car. He wiped the tears away from his face. My heart felt as though it had broken into a million pieces. My fingers rested against the window as he backed out of the driveway. My forest was furious yet broken. His hand pulled his lips down remembering my painful words that had ended it. One last glance from his sorrowful eyes then he was gone.

"I'm so sorry." I cried, wanting him back already.

Chapter 18

It's Not The Same

We stood in the airport watching the planes take off. I couldn't stop thinking about how I'd just let Jason walk out of my life. There was this strong bond with him. I've never felt this way about anyone before and pushing him away was hurting both of us. I felt sick last night; I couldn't sleep because I wanted to apologize. He would never accept whatever I might have to say. I hurt him more than I've hurt anyone. Then something else occurred to me, Dave was also gone. I told him to stay away from me. I didn't want anything to do with him after what he put me through. I was losing everyone that meant something to me. There was always a price to pay for my own innocence.

"Sky!" Hearing a happy girl's voice, I turned around. Missy hugged me tight. My face was lost in her red hair. I smiled moving back from her. My mom smiled at the both of us as she stayed in her seat.

"Hey." I said not believing I was leaving my best friend so soon.

"Jason told me everything, I don't understand why you never told me, but I can't believe your leaving now."

She shook her head taking a seat. I watched all the faces around us. I couldn't believe I was leaving either.

"I didn't tell you because I just wanted to live a simple normal life, obviously I couldn't obtain that here." I said, feeling guilty for shutting another important person out.

"I'm sorry to hear about you and him." She glanced away with a shallow tone to her voice. I wasn't sure if she was talking about my dad or Jason. Either way none of this had to do with her.

"I'll be fine." I sighed, staring out the huge glass windows. I thought back to Jason's bedroom. One of the biggest windows I've ever seen in my life. The pool was as crystal clear as the rain pounding against it. His big backyard and the awkward moments between his dad and me. Everything about what had happen made me feel like I was a part of Jason, a part of his life. He was a part of me, a bigger part than I would have ever admitted to.

"Missy, I just want you to know, I appreciate all that you have done for me, in school and just welcoming me in general. You made it easy." I told her, looking back. She had this genuine look painted across her face. She was touched by my words.

"What else are best friends for?" She lifted her shoulders up. We both laughed and I heard a door open. I glanced over my shoulder seeing them getting ready to board us onto the plane. Mom stood up grabbing her carry on. I got up as well, and Missy came up beside me.

"Well, this is goodbye I guess." I felt the tears coming. They have been haunting me every day it seems. Missy hugged me tightly and the sound of her sniffling made the tears escape. We pulled back from each other, and I saw the sad yet happy smile on her face. It was a mesmerizing moment to realize the hold these two strangers had on me. Missy was the first friend I'd clicked with instantly. Her genuine personality that had positivity beaming from her soul, there was never a day she didn't make me smile. Jason was a whole different story on his own. The famous boy, I didn't want but fell madly in love with while trying to persuade him to stay away. His drive to always return, to be sure of my wellbeing was one passionate memory I would forever keep. The thoughts made me die inside a little bit more. Life was a road full of potholes, yet these two people made a fresh paved path for me. I would carry them with me forever, wherever I may go.

"Call me when you land, and it's never goodbye." She said, grasping my shoulders. I nodded my head as she assured me that this wasn't really goodbye, and we both wiped the tears from our eyes. I walked towards the gate and we waved at each other before it was time for me to turn away. I was once again on my way to a new home. A place I've never seen. Going onto the plane seeing all the people getting settled in, I glanced down at my ticket for the seat number. A tap on my shoulder, and my mom pointed to the seats a couple of rows down.

"We're right there, Honey." She said, and I walked on up as Mom took my bag. She stored them away in the storage compartment. I took the window seat staring at the men on the ground putting the bigger luggage under the plane. I looked back down to my ticket and noticed it said Key West, FL. I looked over to my mom as she took a seat beside me.

"What is this?" I asked showing her my ticket. She gave me an odd expression.

"Where we are going to live." She said not sounding pleased either.

"Why would we go back?" I didn't understand the idea behind this. It was going to make it easier for him to find us. Mom sighed shaking her head.

"It was the only place available, and he might not think to come back to a different city for us." She said, lifting her eyebrows. I couldn't believe she actually thought this was a good idea.

"So, you took it because it was easy, I don't know about you, but I am not for running my whole entire life away." My voice grungy, looking over to the guy that sat down next to my mom. She looked angry, as the man beside her was getting settled in. She didn't speak a word. I wanted to know if she even thought about things before agreeing. There was a part of me that felt I would be safer on my own. If we were split up, then we wouldn't be an easy target. Either way this was one of the most stupid things she has decided to put us through.

I wanted to know the person she arranges these things with. I wanted to know if they knew the entire story. She can't be this naïve to continue going back to the same state with just a flip of the city. Why did my mom love Florida so much? It might have been our home, but it was a death ticket we needed to let go of.

Watching the clouds roll under us. The sun was starting to set. Mom was talking with the guy sitting beside her. I on the other hand didn't trust anyone. I couldn't let my guard fall for one minute. There were so many thoughts going through my head it felt cloudier than this sky. Wondering if my father will ever catch back up with us, if Jason would ever understand why I pushed him away so harshly, if he would ever even give me a chance to explain, if Missy and I would ever see each other again; there was so much cramming together in my mind. It all ran together as one, like the clouds. Then there was Dave, the color of the sky could bring back everything about him. The coldness, yet the warmth of his heart. Everything he has ever done for me, held so close and on just one vibrant string attaching to my heart. I pushed him away too. He stabbed me in the back. Then I had to process if it was for a good reason or not. Nothing was settled that day besides my dad trying to turn me against my own mom. I also found out that he worked with the dead. Only Kyle was the bad side which proves there is a good and bad side to everything. There were still so many questions about how you can break out of Hell.

How Dave could even have the powers to send Kyle back to Hell. There was so much about the dead I had no clue about. Dave kept secrets from me, which urged the light of our friendship to grow dimmer.

Lighting my phone seeing a picture of Jason and me as we ate with each other. Clicking my fingernail against the screen just wanting to be back in his arms. Wishing I could turn back time, take back all the words I said. I was positive that the hurt I had caused him was more than that of myself. Letting go is never easy but forgiving someone takes strength. It takes a loyalty to trust that person would never hurt them like that ever again; they must have the power within them to be able to trust again. The power that I once had has become very weak. Trusting someone is now one of the hardest challenges I have ever faced. You think you know someone then it turns to ashes when the match hits the flame. They explode all these secrets that you never could imagine. A person that lies and never tells the truth makes the world a very colorful place. They give entertainment to some, while scaring others, and manipulating many. Unlike the innocent people, we live normal lives and just try to get by. We don't plot what our next move is, how to get revenge, or who will be the next target. Our lives seem so simple and humble compared to all the liars. We live in a very colorful world where we can't trust anyone but ourselves.

The wheels popped out of the plane as we hit the

runway. I watched out the window seeing the ocean was not too far away. I took a deep breath in flashing back to when I left. It wasn't all that long ago since I said goodbye to Joey. Now it was time to reconnect with an old friend. Not like we were ever disconnected, we just got separated. He said he was moving to Key West from Miami. A tiny smile tugged at my lips. The world was reuniting me with the one friend I had from my past.

"Oh, how nice it will be to get back on the beach." Mom's eyes were filled with joy. I couldn't help but wonder why she was so happy to be back. I knew this was our home for all of mine and her life. I just don't see how it wasn't bringing back horrifying memories. The fact was I enjoyed my mom's positive outlook; I just did not find it realistic.

"Is that why you chose here?" I asked getting up from the seat. She grabbed our bags out of the stowaway. She laughed a little pulling the handle up.

"Heavens no, but it is nice to be back where it stays nice." She said handing over my stuff. I followed behind squeezing between everyone getting their things together. Once off the plane and down the tiny walkway we escaped into the open airport. Voices flowed around you, noises of people's shoes clicking on the shiny floor. So much movement in the airport. Before I knew it, we were out in the warm summer air of Florida. My instincts told me it was close to 90 degrees. Intense sun rays were casting down before us making me pull my sunglasses out. My eyes locked on a palm tree being brushed by the light breeze. The saltwater smell took me back. I was in a new city I've never explored, once again. My school days were numbered, I continued to have the fear of failing again.

"Our car should be in the parking lot." She said examining a piece of paper. I closed my eyes taking in the air. A flashback of being a little girl running down the Miami beach collecting sand in my pale, before the ocean hit me knocking me onto my butt.

"What is it?" I asked searching through all the cars that were lined up beside each other.

"Oh, that one!" She pointed to a small black four door Ford. No idea what model but it seemed to be in the later years instead of earlier. That was always a good sign. Watching the lights flash as the trunk popped open. I tossed my things in and jumped in the car. It smelled new, as if it just came off the lot.

"How about we go get some food after that long flight?" She got in starting it up.

"I'm not hungry." I said, staring down at my black phone. Chewing my lip wanting to see it light up with a text message.

"How on earth are you not hungry after that?" She gave me a crazy look.

"I just want to go to the house." My voice was shallow, wanting to go back to Ohio. I wasn't sure how well I would handle the move back down here. I've lived in

Miami all my life and for the first time it just didn't seem right being back in Florida, it felt like something was missing. Someone was missing, whether it was Dave or Jason, it was someone. There was an empty gap in my heart.

"You know there is a surprise I didn't tell you about." She told me smiling. I rolled my eyes as we crossed roads loaded with people. It wasn't like Miami though, and that was way worse.

"Nothing surprises me anymore." My voice was grim watching all the people in their bikinis.

"But this will make you smile." She sang squeezing my arm. I looked up at the palm trees blowing in the wind. *Welcome back home,* was all I could think. I guess I should be happier to be back home however, my heart felt its home was now someplace else. Like it was hanging on a wire waiting to be ripped off. I felt stupid for leaving, stupid for not standing my ground. She would have never put up with my wishes, knowing that I wanted to stay there. All for a guy I met a month ago. Knowing people would assume it was because he was famous or because of the money. Honestly, I looked right through that with Jason. It felt like he wasn't one of them at all.

We took a turn away from traffic heading down a street. The sign read Water Front Ave. Seeing the huge body of water surrounding the properties, we pulled into a driveway. There was a small pink house sitting in front of us. It didn't look as nice as the old one, a little run down. Overlooking the small house, I saw the Seven Mile Bridge. The longest stretch of highway. A doubt occurred to me, if Richard found us, we would be on a hell-bent train to get out of here.

"We're going to live in a dump?" Looking over to my mom she gave me a hard smile.

"Don't look at it as a dump, besides a little fixing up and it will look great!" She got out of the car. I stepped out looking at the chipping pink paint, the gray roof with the shingles splintering up, and then the dirty dusty windows. I sighed shoving my door shut.

"Is there even any use in trying to fix something up if we will just be racing away again in a month?" I followed her up to the door. She turned around glaring at me.

"Now Skylar, I don't want to hear another word about running our life away. Things will be fine again once they catch that crazy animal of a man." She was optimistic, opening the door.

"I'm sorry if I feel like we're wasting time doing all this for a man that won't be caught." Walking into the house, I could smell the old dust that has been sitting for years. To my surprise there was still furniture in this place. I walked over to the couch that was still wrapped in plastic. A price tag hung on the side reading $380.87. I shook my head noticing how old it looked. How long has this place been sitting here empty? I flipped the tag over reading: order from 1989. My eyes opened wide turning back to my mom. She was walking back into the house with bags.

“Even if you’re not happy with me you could at least help.” She complained, setting the bags down.

“Hey, this couch said it was ordered back in 1989.” My thumb hitched over my shoulder. Her eyes popped open in surprise.

“No kidding?” She came walking over next to me.

“Never been opened either.” My hand ran over the thick layer of dust.

“Guess someone didn’t want their things.” She said, glancing over to the old tube TV that sat across the room. Right under the huge wall window. Flashbacks arose of Jason’s window in his bedroom. My eyes fell away then. I walked over grabbing my bags up. Heading back into one of the smallest hallways that could consume a person, three doors lined the sides of me. My hand didn’t go out two inches before reaching a handle. I entered a room with a twin bed, toys on the floor, and a beautiful view of the beach. Dropping my bags down on the bed walking over to the window, the beach was our backyard. We lived in a beach house. It could have been worse; we could have ended up in a meth dealing neighborhood. Surrounded by men eyeballing you all through the day no matter what you wore or what you might have been doing. This place was different. Small and quaint. One street over was million-dollar homes. I couldn’t help but wonder how we could afford this in such a prime location. I remembered passing the famous Duval St.

I grabbed the latch to open the window. When it didn't budge, I looked around the room for something that could be used for a good lever. Finding a hard toy, I turned and smashed it down on the rusty window latch. When it flew down, I tossed the toy aside. Opening the window, listening to the sharp squeal it made. The ocean breeze came right up through the room. I closed my eyes smelling the ocean all over again. A piece of me felt more like it was home now. My eyes came back open watching the water sparkle under the sun while people gathered on the beach enjoying the humid air.

Jason

Heading out of my bedroom slipping my phone down into my pocket, I didn't want to believe it was over. I never planned on something turning around and then coming back to lash out at me. She pushed me away. It wasn't like she hasn't been doing it before, it's just this time it felt different. Like she wanted me out of her life forever. There was a piece of me that wanted to go and confront her. There was another piece of me that said stand back and give her space. She will come around when she feels it's right. I was just worried by the time she did it would be too late, before she was gone and out of my life. I didn't have the first clue when that was going to happen. She was packing her things yesterday. I didn't have much time to catch her. Running down the stairs to the garage, Dad grabbed my arm. I looked over to him not having time for whatever he was about to say.

"Where are you running to so fast?" He smiled letting me go.

"Robby wanted me to hang, I'll be back." I said, opening the door. I hoped he wouldn't send Abby off to follow me. I hated how he would try to protect me. It was like I couldn't protect myself. Getting into my car I drove out quickly. The press had their cameras snapping in minutes. Zooming passed them, and down the road listening to my phone go off. Hitting the button on the touch radio answering the call hoping for her voice to come cascading through my speakers.

"Hello?" I didn't want to talk with anyone unless it was Skylar.

"Hey Jason, it's me did you get your invite in the mail yet?" I glanced down to the radio seeing Emma's name run across it.

"Uh, I don't know, this isn't a good time." I sputtered, taking a turn away from the street. Flashing myself out into busy traffic was never a good idea.

"Jason, you need to let them know you will be there." Her voice was anxious. I rolled my eyes driving up the hill.

"I will be there; I know I have to present but right now I have other issues." I passed by the high school and drove down what appeared to be a rather trashy street, I came to a stop sign. Emma sighed over the phone, and someone waved to me. Just another girl from school. Waving back, I rolled on passed them.

"Is this about the girl I saw a few weeks ago on the front of Touch magazine?" She asked and I rolled up to Skylar's house.

"Yeah, hey, I have to go." I said, ending the call and jumping out of the car. Walking up to the porch something didn't feel right. Glancing around making sure her dad was nowhere around to hurt me or them. There was no black car parked on the street, that didn't mean he didn't have eyes someplace else though. I knocked on the door and stepped back. She might have pushed me away, but I wasn't going to settle for that so easily. I had to talk to her I wasn't about to give up. Yesterday she was flustered, she just had to catch her breath. Today was different, I was anxious to see her smile while her eyes rolled at me. Just the right amount of annoyance, but not enough that she would send me packing.

"Excuse me, are you here to see about the house?" A man came walking up behind me.

"What? No, I'm here to see someone." I told the strange man dressed in a suit. He laughed pulling down on the suit jacket.

"You must have the wrong house; nobody lives here, boy." The heavyset jolly man laughed some more.

"No, just yesterday they were here." Shaking my head wondering if it was already too late.

"Nope sonny, no one has lived here in years." He said,

holding a gold key up.

"You're crazy, a woman and her daughter lived here for maybe a month or so, are you the real estate agent?" Pointing my finger at him really confused on who he was. I wasn't sure they could sweep up a house for being left empty in such a short matter of time.

"Why yes I am! Bob Shillan." He held his hand out. Lifting an eyebrow and shaking his hand, he was ready to sell me this house.

"It was nice meeting you." I said, walking away. A heavy cloud formed over me realizing it was too late. The house was just an empty shell. Even worse the realtor acted as if no one was even here. Skylar was a phantom of her short existence here.

"Now wait, there are some really good things about this house, the plumbing is in good–"

"I'm not here for the house." Getting back in my car seeing his expression tumble, I backed out driving away. She was already gone, the unwritten piece of today felt so pointless. My hand ran over my face, stopping. What have I done? Touching the radio scrolling through the contacts, I hit Missy's name. If anyone knew where Skylar went it'd be her. My fingers fiddling around the new car steering wheel. I should have drove my Mustang today, but it needs more work.

"Hello." She said, after it rang once.

"Missy, is Skylar gone?" Those were the only words that could escape my mouth. The only thing I could think of. My heart raced and my palms turned sweaty, staying hopeful there was still time.

"That depends, do you actually care now or are you just making sure she's actually gone?" Missy's voice was curious. Watching the cars fly by I couldn't help but wonder why she couldn't just give me a direct answer.

"I always cared, Missy." The truth was I had always cared; from the moment we had first brushed shoulders, and still now when she had pushed me away never wanting to see me again. That first moment when I'd seen the picture that she sketched of me, I had felt something. She wasn't like everyone else, she was different. She didn't care about the money, or the fame, or the people who I've worked with and the people I've met. She was just worried about herself and focusing on us; she lived such a mysterious life. I think that was the true reason she wanted to banish me from her life.

"Well, she is gone, and you didn't even bother to say goodbye, so I don't think I should tell you where she happens to be." She told me, and I felt this weird plunge in my chest. My stomach turned making a fireball ignite. She was not aware of the conversation we had yesterday, yet I was the bad guy.

"Listen Missy, I can never make things better unless you tell me." I said, trying not to yell.

"Then how about you call her yourself and talk it over?" She was mad with me for not being there when she left. I didn't even know she was going to be gone so soon. She didn't even tell me. Then I realized that's what hurt me the most. She was so different from everyone else, yet so cold hearted just like everyone else. She knew how to make things go her way. This whole time it has been nothing but running from a man who wants to kill her. She was scared and needed to feel safe. At the same time, she took a bullet for me. I was so confused by what her feelings for me were. There was one thing that was certain, I was never confused on the way I felt about her. I had to find her. I closed my eyes seeing her smooth chocolate eyes watching me, always skeptical yet flirty. A warning sign hung in those glossy windows of hers, yet I never paid it any heed. I saw love and devotion, but also fear coating her eyes almost everyday. I've seen her blue, I've seen her red, and I've seen the yellow. She was so beautiful, the way she would walk. She had a confident stride, yet she was very timid. Skylar never knew how beautiful she was. The way she would defend her own proved she was a warrior hidden behind her own scars. She didn't need a hero; she just needs someone to be brave with her. I had to find her.

Skylar

I walked down the beach watching the sun rise at the ocean line. It looked just like the perfect painting. The water was glazed over, and the ripples were making it shimmer. A sailboat was coming into the beach. There were people carrying wood in to make a bonfire. If only there was a piece of me that could go back and hang with my friends. Walking down the beach feeling the sand, cool as it rose through my toes. The wind blew my hair back as I climbed up onto a big rock. A small cliff hung over my head, and I watched the ocean. Birds flew overhead chirping. Most people would claim this to be their idea of the perfect life, but that was them looking in from the outside.

Lighting my phone up staring at Jason's contact number, his voice came back to me. He wanted me to say good riddance to him. I couldn't just delete his number. It wasn't that easy, it only made me wonder if it was that easy for him. If he could move on that fast, away from something that might have been growing? Mom always said she would never trust a Hollywood star if she was ever in a relationship with one. We used to joke about it all the time, the crazy thing is it's really happening. He wasn't just some snobby rich guy either; he actually seemed to have a heart. He fought for us against his own monstrous father. His demons were just as real as mine, but his seemed less dangerous.

Pulling my legs up into my arms I hit his number. Trying to call him had to be the next solution. There was no other way. Listening to the phone ring and ring, doubt started to take over. His voicemail came on and I hung up. Placing my face down in my hands; what have I done? A cold arm came down around my shoulder. Dave gave me gentle eyes. He held me close as I cried. I wanted to budge from his embrace, but my body fell victim as I allowed myself to get lost in my own mistakes.

Chapter 19

Old Friends, New Memories

I tossed my towel out over the sand listening to the birds fly overhead while children ran into the shore of the ocean and mothers sat around reading magazines, gossiping with one another. Men ran past me tossing a football back and forth. Teenage girls were giggling into their phones about whatever they were reading. It's been a week since I've been here. A week since I've talked to Jason. He never tried to reach me. Missy told me he went looking for me and wanted to know where I'd gone, but I didn't understand why. He never took one chance to call. It broke my heart but maybe the message became clearer to him. It was better off this way. When Missy said she told him everything, I wasn't sure what everything was. Jason knew more about my personal life than Missy. I slid my sunglasses up the bridge of my nose with a sigh. I haven't spoken to Missy in a week either. I might be the worst best friend there is. It was probably best to allow another fragment of my life to just fade away. Allowing it to become history was wise yet cold.

A man came running up to me. Seeing his palm tree trunks told me he was overly happy about the place he lived in. The mirrored shades he wore and his blonde hair that was spikey and pushed up like some new aged rock band style made my eyes squint. He smiled and I smiled back. A puzzle piece fell into place when he took his sunglasses off. I jumped up from my towel jumping into his arms.

"Hey girl!" His voice high and happy to see me.

"Joey!" I screamed his name in excitement. We both laughed and he held my hands.

"You know, not telling me that you were back was the meanest thing you've ever done to me!" He playfully smacked my shoulder. We laughed again before sitting down on my towel.

"Sorry, the move has been a little rough on me." I admitted, staring out into the ocean's white line. Where the water turned to foam, and little kids picked up seashells.

"I bet; you were only dating one of the hottest guys around!" His voice always showed he was the happiest person I could ever turn to. I laughed shaking my head at him.

"I wouldn't really consider us dating." Running my finger through the sand feeling my heart turn cold. That's all Jason wanted. He wanted us to be together and I ripped it to shreds and turned out the lights. Technically we were a couple, my heart fed off of that love, but my brain tarnished it with reality.

"How many people can you convince of that?" His

eyebrows rose questioningly.

"I couldn't even convince my mom, so not very many." Tilting my head, feeling the warm breeze blow up in our faces as the water got closer.

"You don't look nowhere near as happy as the Skylar I used to know." He looked stumped on why I could be so down. To be honest, it was mostly because of Jason. I missed seeing his black hair flow down over one eye. There wasn't a time that I didn't miss looking into his forest green eyes. The way he would wear his facial hair in his well-trimmed goatee. His arms when they would embrace me. I felt safe with him. Now I'm back to having nightmares in the woods and him burning over a pit of fire. I just didn't understand anything anymore. There was a piece of me that just wanted to fly back to Ohio and go running into his arms. Regardless of what his dad thought.

"When you basically leave someone to save their life and push them away so they won't come looking for you, then a week later you have the strongest feelings for them and there is nothing you can do, wouldn't you be sad too?" Looking over to him and seeing his lost expression. I took a deep breath of humid air, knowing that Joey never knew a word about my father.

"Girl, you need to call him right now!" He was trying to encourage me to get Jason back. I just couldn't.

"Joey, if I call him, he might answer; there is no place in me that feels it would be safe for him." Holding my hand over my chest feeling ready to cry. If everything happens for a reason, then I want to know the reason for this. Was it because Jason was bad for me? Was the high life never meant for me? Is Jason someone I should be warned about? I didn't feel as if I needed to be warned about Jason.

"Why wouldn't it be safe?" He kicked his sandals off lying back on my towel.

"Because someone tried to kill him, and I took the bullet." It was getting easier to talk about, but the vision and pain still came back. Joey popped back up within seconds. His eyes so big as though he'd just seen someone get hit by lightning.

"No way, you got shot?" He seemed more excited than worried. I chuckled a little shaking my head. If only he was there for everything that had happened. I nodded my head pulling the side of my shirt up. The scar was a white circle and a line from the stitches. His finger brushed the healed wound.

"Pretty sick right?" Leaving him with the good side and trying not to dwell on it. He laughed nodding his head. My phone went off and Joey's face got excited. Pulling it out seeing it was Missy, I answered.

"Oh, my god it's him!" Joey clapped his hands in excitement. I shook my head wondering what she wanted.

"Hey." I said, plunging my feet into the warm sand.

"Sky, get to a TV now!" Her voice rushed through the phone in happiness.

"Why?" Confused on why it mattered so much, I continued watching the water hit the shore. The last time she told me to flip the TV on I was the one we all were watching. It was entertainment news about Jason having a girlfriend one that ditched him and ripped his heart out just to keep him safe.

"Jason is on the red carpet!" Her voice full of enthusiasm, and my heart sank. Like it wasn't already as oceans deep as the Titanic.

"Okay I'll check it out." I said, in a low voice, pulling the phone away and hanging up. I didn't want to talk too much about him. Every time I did, it hurt me. The memories were just too real to ever forget. I collected my things and Joey and I both got up. He gave me a confused smile as he folded up my towel handing it over.

"What did he say?" We started walking back to the beach house.

"Nothing he's on TV being interviewed apparently." Taking the towel, tucking it under my arm, his lips pushed out. We walked up to the back patio of the pink house.

"That's exciting/" he admitted, and I pulled the glass doors back that led right into the house. Joey followed me in. I dropped my things turning on the old tube TV that just happened to still work. Flipping channels quickly, I reached the red carpet. Jason stood in front of the cameras with that gorgeous white smile. His forest green eyes, that captivated me so much, making me sit down. He looked so stunning in his black tuxedo. His hair was all done up and a black-tie lining from his chest to the tip of his pants. His smell was coming back to me as if it was seeping out of the TV. Listening to that rough laugh all over again, I wanted to be with him so badly. Chills rose on my arms just hearing that oh so familiar chuckle. The tube TV had static but that didn't flaw Jason's appearance one bit.

"Hello?" Joey's voice laughed as I blinked my eyes away from Jason. Joey shook his finger at the TV.

"Ya know, I didn't think you had such a thing for Robert Downey Jr." He cracked up in more laughter, falling back onto the couch. Looking back to the TV seeing Jason left the camera. My eyes fell back away seeing a small box pop up in the corner showing other arrivals, Jason was standing in front of camera's getting his picture taken. There was a dark-headed lady standing beside him. Who was she? Her skin toned color lips and the dark blue tight dress she wore. Her makeup done from ear to ear. They flipped to commercial, and I just stared.

"I don't understand." I said, pressing my thumbs into my temples.

"What don't you understand? How he's so famous and somehow you ended up with him or how you could ever let him go?" Joey leaned over his legs staring at me. Shaking my head pushing myself up from the couch.

"How he is with someone else already?" Frustration took over and I walked back and forth in front of the TV.

"Well, you left him." Joey said, giving me that 'how do you not get it' expression.

"Yes, but he did it so easily and fast." Trailing off into my own thoughts I went running into my bedroom, grabbing my computer up heading right over to Wikipedia. Joey walked slowly into my room, that I haven't yet got a chance to clean. There were still old toys and whatnot lying around. I searched Jason's name. I wanted to see what they had to say on his relationship status.

"Wow this room looks like a historical dump." Joey went down picking up a doll. Its hair full of dust and an eye was missing. Looking back to the screen, it had nothing under personal information. My hand went down on the bed skipping over to his secret Facebook page. Only a few people knew about this. It didn't tell me much, but maybe it would tell me something. It said Single. I sighed shoving my laptop aside.

"Who do you think she is?" Pulling my legs up to my chest feeling used but knew I wasn't.

"Well, she doesn't seem to have a name." Joey flipped the doll back and forth.

"Funny." Not laughing or even finding what he said funny. Joey sat down beside me tossing the doll back on the floor.

"It's probably nothing but if it is then maybe you should take your own words seriously." He lifted his shoulders up. Maybe Joey was right. Jason took them seriously enough to move on so fast. Maybe it was time for me to accept my own mistake. After all, if I wanted to keep Jason a person in my life, I wouldn't have said the words that I knew would cause the most hurt. I felt like a fool for having done such a thing, but I knew there was nothing I could do.

I walked back out into the room seeing Jason on the screen. He had a closed envelope in his hand. He was giving an award away. I was so focused on just seeing him again, I wasn't even listening to the words he spoke. I felt so distant from him. I wanted to be there on that red carpet, at that show. There was not one thing I could do. Walking away heading for the sliding doors, Mom stood outside letting the wind blow through her hair. A small smile came to my face walking the other way. If there was any piece of me that could control the way I felt, it would be amazing. I watched as Joey left waving to my mom. Comfort started easing into my heart at being reconnected with an old friend. I wasn't alone.

Dave sat on the couch as I walked back into the room. He looked over to me waving his blue aura to come sit beside him. The whole room was frozen. If it was really winter, there would be ice hanging off the TV. Taking a seat beside him, not saying a word as a cold arm came around me. He smiled running his hand through my hair. I jerked my shoulders not wanting to be touched by a man I still felt leery about.

"I feel that if you really are having a hard time with

this, then call him." He moved my bangs back behind one ear. I felt the tears threatening my eyes. A war reenergizing.

"I've already tried." My stomach felt worse after saying that. Dave's blue eyes now turning a different shade of blue. It was like the ocean, the darker water fading into the shore. It was one of the craziest things I've seen Dave's eyes do.

"He didn't answer?" He seemed more lost and confused.

"Or call back." Feeling my heart sink back into its dark pit. Tears came rolling back down my face. I couldn't keep doing this to myself. There was going to have to be a time when I let go. He was just a thing from my past. A very vivid thing. Both hands closing off my face from the world. Dave's arms wrapped around me.

"Sometimes things just aren't meant to be." His crisp voice whispering into my ear, chills ran up my spine. My body shook from the coldness, and he released me.

"Dave, I can't believe I'm saying this, but I think I loved him." My bottom lip shook taking in the salty tears. I went back to the first time I said that. Now I fully believed it. There was a strong piece of my heart that felt chained to him. I just wanted to know if he felt the same way. All I needed was one call back. To hear his voice rush over the phone, for him to tell me how he truly felt. That one last call to apologize. I didn't care if he would accept it or not; it would make me feel better.

"Love comes in mysterious ways and leaves us in the most heart wrenching ways." His blue eyes settled back into the frosted blue. He was staring away from me as if he was miles away now. Where was he? I took his hand holding onto it. It felt like a snowball melting in my hand.

"Have you ever been in love?" Asking that might have made things worse. Those blue eyes came over piercing into mine.

"A couple of times." His thumb skimmed across the bottom of his lip.

"What happened?" My legs came up, crossing them. I wanted to know where his past took him, and even why he's here now. Dave looked over his shoulder and patted my leg.

"Maybe another time." He gave me a smile, vanishing. My lips fell apart and Mom came back into the house. Either Dave didn't want me to know or there was just something too unreal about it that he still couldn't bring himself to tell me. Maybe he was still trying to cope with his own death. Maybe that was it, he had to leave the person he loved the most. Thinking about it just made me feel worse about leaving Jason. Moments ago, my anger with Dave dissolved making our relationship feel more like it did before. I fought with myself over whether or not I should forgive Dave for trapping me with my father. He was so loyal to my life, but that one action continued to play out in my mind.

Looking back to the TV screen seeing two more top A-list actors talking. They did a screen cut to the audience. Jason was still sitting by the girl with dark hair. Feeling my heart dip back into its dark cove I flipped the channel. I got up walking into my bedroom. Pulling my phone out, I brought his contact up. He wanted me to erase it like we had never happened. I shouldn't try to contact him. I didn't want to annoy him. Although I couldn't just settle for saying goodbye. For all I knew my dad might be out there now, searching him down. Wanting to hurt his family only because he thinks he's a connection to me. Realizing everything now, how many new mistakes I'd made. Only to keep heart crunching memories in my dreams, I couldn't leave the past as just the past. Dave was right, if I wanted anything I had to take the past and make it my future. The hardest part was, trying to create the future you want. Did I sound crazy for thinking something like that?

A diary sat on the floor across from my feet. Tilting my head and picking it up, feeling the thick dust coating it. The brown leather was old and cracked. I popped the diary open. The pages old but not too old, although they looked as if water had got to them. The writing was smudged but I could still read it to some degree.

7-13-93

Today I met someone, she was beautiful the most sensational eyes I have ever seen. Her curves were just excellent. I went to the bar with a couple of friends from work. It was a dare to meet her, to dance with her. I was hammered out of my mind. However, I think being drunk the other night was one of the best times of my life. I wish to see her again…

-Alex

I looked over to the next page seeing the following day. His name was Alex and he met someone he was really into. Apparently, he liked to drink. He started writing in this diary two years before I was born. Something about finding this seemed cool.

7-14-93

Well, it has happened again. I went on a date with Kate. She was one of the most wonderful women I have ever met. Her laugh is like a song to my heart. I couldn't stop staring at her smiling face across the table from me. It's a little fast to speak but it would be crazy if she was the one. If I didn't have to work, I would take her on a date every night of the week. She is just like someone that could be my light every night and day.

-Alex

I smiled flipping over to the next page. He skipped a couple of days. I'm guessing nothing exciting happened in that period of time. I sat back on my bed thinking about this. The lady's name was Kate. My mom's name is Kate. I feel like this is a bit of a funny coincidence. Also, my mom told me she met my dad two years before having me. There was no possible way that this man could be my father though. I know my father and he's a monster. Alex was in love with this lady though, and he wasn't about to give her up. He wanted to sit with her every night at dinner just to see her smiling face. Her laughter was the song to his heart. It was so romantic.

Picking my phone up staring at the picture of Jason, I flipped to his text messages. Seeing our old conversations, just wanting them to be real again. The screen popped up to message him. Dave wanted me to; he thought it would be a genius idea. I just felt like I shouldn't be running after him. When you break up with someone you don't beg for their forgiveness. You don't beg to get them back. You have to stay strong and move on. I shook my head pulling up the screen to text him. A nervous pit opening inside of me, breaking my own rules for a breakup.

Skylar: Hey I know you never wanted to talk to me again I just need to say some things. If you never answer back, I understand.

Laying my cell phone down, staring out the window to the beach. The sun was on its way back down and I was getting lost in my feelings once again. I sighed, gazing back down at the diary. At least I'd found something interesting. I opened it back up onto the next page.

7-17-93

It's been a real busy week. Work is off the chain, however Kate showed up at the workplace today. She was so shocked by the flowers I sent to her work. She came and brought me coffee. We went out for lunch and watched the birds in the park. I am so thankful for taking that dare a few nights back. I owe my pals a lot after that. Something else weird also happened to me the last night. I haven't had a chance to write about it yet, but I think I am getting into paranormal things. I had someone come to me a couple nights back. She was pretty, her name was Ashley. She told me she was here to protect me, whatever that might mean… She also told me she was dead which means I am talking to some sort of ghost? I can't tell anyone because they would think that I am crazy. Every time she leaves me this purple fog forms around me. It's so cold to every touch. Something about knowing her makes me feel insane. Until next time.

-Alex

My hand flew up to my mouth. He'd had encounters with the other side just like me. Only there was a woman that went to him. In that moment I had something in common with Alex. Who was Ashley? She was there to protect him from something as well. Now there was an even bigger question, what are we being protected from?

Chapter 20

Mystery

My arm was being shaken and I felt a breeze sweep in from my window. My eyes were just barely coming open, but they were open enough to see the blurry edges of my mom. What did she want? Tossing over on my side not wanting to see what she wanted; all I wanted to do was sleep, to forget about my loving memories that would haunt me until we meet again. For once I wanted to have my nightmare of running down the forest just so I could see him again. Yesterday, what I saw on TV, it wasn't enough. I wanted to hear his voice, feel his arms wrapped around my torso.

"Hun, wake up we have company coming over." Her voice was a light sweetness. The kind of day where she wasn't trying to pull me out of bed to go to school, she was much sweeter this time. I rolled back over looking at her.

"I don't care." Company was never my cup of tea. It was bad enough when I had to see all my family on the holidays. I didn't know if this was family, but I didn't feel like seeing anyone. The thought of more people to engage with made me feel sick. I'm too overwhelmed with my whiplash lifestyle to even give two fucks about who might be out there.

"Now don't be like that, I need your help." She said, moving the blankets back off me. She got up leaving the room. She knew she had me awake, that was the part that annoyed me. I sat up seeing the bright sun cascading down on the ocean. I winced blinded by the reflection. The sea birds flew overhead waiting for people to drop food. This was the dream to wake up to. Many people would give anything to wake up on a beach like this. Then there is me who just wants to go back and fix everything. Getting up out of bed and hearing the diary hit the floor, I picked it up sliding it into my shelf between two more books. I wanted to keep it safe. I bit down on my lip pulling it back out. I wanted to read more on Ashley. I wanted to see what he had to say about the earthbound souls. We both know what this is like.

7-19-93

Today I went to go meet up with Ashley. She wanted to see me on the south side of the beach. Where all the hut houses are, when I got there, she was with someone else. He was built and looked strong. Her purple fog was lingering with her but the man she was with, he was different too. Heat was steaming off him, this bright orange color just floating off his body. She told me that he made her let him come. I wasn't sure what part she had in what was going to happen. He never did anything the whole time. I felt tense, like we couldn't talk. I still feel very skeptical about this whole "ghost" thing, or so she calls herself. I felt like Ashley wasn't telling me everything she wanted to while he was around. On another note, today I haven't gotten the chance to see Kate, I really just want to get my grip on what is happening with the other side.

-Alex

I sat back against my bed. Every part of what he'd described sounded like Kyle. He met him and he was just as scared as I was. Kyle is a threat, but now this is different. I had to keep reading to see what he had to say. If Kyle did anything to him or this Kate lady, something had to have happened. Unless Ashley wasn't on the good side. I felt like it was time to talk to Dave about all of this. I also wanted to go to the south part of the beach where the hut houses are. I recalled Dave saying Kyle wasn't like them. Who was 'them'?

"Dave!" I called for him needing his advice on all this. The room turned cold and icy. His blue glow was wrapping around me. My door closed the rest of the way allowing his full body to come into view.

"Yes, my dearest." He gave me a bright smile. I held out the diary for him to read, he looked confused.

"I found this last night and this guy named Alex writes in it." I explained, still wondering where all this connects and if it involves me somehow.

"And why does this concern me?" He flipped it over running his hand down the cracked leather. When his blue eyes dropped, I knew something odd was tumbling through his brain.

"Because he is friends with one of your people and also knows Kyle." Shoving my hands down into my shorts not sure where to take this. His blue eyes were shocked as he looked back up to me.

"Which one of my people?" He opened the diary flipping the pages.

"A girl named Ashley; it says she is one of you." I explained stopping him from flipping any further, pointing to what I read. His blue eyes flew over the writing quickly.

"You want to go to the huts?" He said already knowing where my thoughts were heading.

"Dave, I have to know what all this is and how we connect." I told him, grabbing some clothes quickly.

"Wait, how do we know that you are connected with something some guy wrote back in 1993?" He held the diary out questioning what it was I wanted to go see. I shook my head changing into my clothes quickly. Dave turned away from me like he usually did. He gave me the respect without me even asking. His devotion still stood strong.

"We don't know but if we don't go looking then we might never know." I said, turning back around, snatching my purse up.

"So, you're feeling adventurous; you do realize you can just read more, right?" He smiled holding the diary back up for me to take. I grabbed it shoving it down into my purse.

"Are you in or are you out?" I asked him, heading out into the other room. Mom came running over to me quickly. She stopped, seeing that I had my purse and sandals on.

"Oh, no you are not ditching me." She shook her head like I was leaving her on one of the busiest seasons of the year.

"It won't take long, then I'll be right back." I assured her, grabbing the keys off the wall. She gave me those eyes, as though I betrayed her on the side of the road like she was a puppy. I sighed walking over to the door. For once she wasn't going to try and stop me.

"Skylar, you better be back here soon!" Her voice was a warning.

"Promise." I smiled darting out the door. Getting into the car and leaving the tiny beach house behind, Dave came in next to me. Not saying a word as we passed down the road going past dozens of palm trees and the beautiful ocean shore. People walking around in their bikinis and men not wearing shirts - Florida was the place to be. A bright red car came rolling up next to me. An older guy sat in the convertible. He waved smiling at me. I smiled back and took off. Lucky for us the hut houses weren't too far down the road from our house.

Pulling into the parking lot seeing all the bungalow looking houses sitting by the ocean.

"And which house are we looking for?" Dave gave me a gaze of wonder.

"We're not looking for a certain one." I said, getting out of the car. Pulling my sunglasses down and locking the car, I held the diary.

"So, why are we here?" Dave stopped beside me.

"Just to check it out." I said, walking to the path that leads from the parking lot to the houses. I stopped when I saw the man from the bright red car. I grabbed Dave's arm holding him back from walking any further. The guy walked into one of the bungalows. Dave gave me that look that said, 'don't you even think about it'. I smiled at him walking away with ease. Dave flashed in front of me giving me warning eyes.

"What did he do to ever be the target of why ever we are here?" He asked folding his arms.

"Better question, what didn't he do not to be?" I asked walking around him.

"Sky, you will only embarrass yourself." He said, running after me. I laughed thinking about a ghost running after me. I ducked down at the window peeking in. He just turned on the TV and grabbed a beer from a mini fridge. Who has a mini fridge that close to them when their fridge is like three steps away? My eyes swept the other way seeing the kitchen. Nothing looked weird there. Dave's cold arm swung me away from the window and onto the sand.

"There is nothing there." He hissed in a stern voice.

"How do you know?" I asked brushing the sand off my clothes. He sighed rolling his eyes. He started to walk away, and I followed swiftly behind.

"Because I know who Ashley is." His blue eyes never meeting mine. I stopped us both then.

"Then why haven't we spoken to her yet?" I asked, wanting to talk with her.

"I haven't seen her since I got assigned to you." He explained as he flashed back into the car. I went around jumping in.

"So now we both have goals, you find her, and I keep reading to see what I can find out." Something about this whole thing was exciting to me. Dave shook his head opening his mouth, but no words came out. He didn't seem like he really wanted to talk with her. That made me wonder if they had some sort of past that I wasn't aware of. There was so much of Dave's life that I would like to know about, but I just haven't got the guts to ask. The urge to explore earthbound spirits ran high on my to-do list.

"Sky, what if you don't want to know something?" He asked me moments later as I pulled up in front of the house.

"What do you mean?" There was something I didn't want to know? That left a worried pit in my stomach.

"Like what if I find something out that could hurt

you?" His blue eyes glanced up to the house. A car pulled up behind me and Dave left the car. What did he know that I didn't? How long has he known about whatever it is that might hurt me? That left me cold inside all by itself, without Dave's disappearance needed. There was a tap on the window of the car. I saw my aunt Lisa smiling at me. She had a bowl of food in her hands. Forcing a smile and waving back, I jerked the keys out of the ignition. It's been so long since I've seen my aunt. That told me one thing and that was that April was around somewhere.

"Hey there doll." She sang, always calling me the weirdest names ever.

"Hi." Keeping my voice low with the same shyness as I always did when it came to family gatherings.

"Oh, my god, Skylar!" Hearing April's excited voice made me cringe inside. Trying to keep my face normal and happy instead of annoyed and wanting to dart away.

"Hey Ape." Trying to still sound happy as we walked up to the door, Mom looked up surprised at seeing they were here already. She put down the food that she was prepping once she saw my aunt, running over to her. Hearing the joy come from the both of them made me smile. My mom was reunited with her sister.

"So, it's time to lay down the deeds about the hot Jason you nailed." April turned me around. Lifting an eyebrow up; I never nailed him. Jason was right, word gets around everywhere. Tabloids spread words like fire.

"I have no idea what you are talking about." I sat

down on the couch not even wanting to talk about him, expressing my feelings right now wasn't a good idea. It made me feel sick inside. Love certainly does make you do weird things.

"Right, like you can hide what these say." She laughed, tossing a magazine at me. I grabbed it up seeing a horrible picture of me on one side, from when I left the hospital, and a normal good picture of him on the other. Between us sat a lightning bolt. On the bottom it read in big bold letters 'A Harsh Break Up'. My eyebrows lowered wondering what this was about. How could they even get a hold of something like this? There was no way, unless he told someone he was dating that girl I saw him with at the awards the other night. My heart dropped ten feet deeper.

"We weren't ever a couple." I grumbled, handing it back over to her.

"And that sad expression on your face tells me you're lying." She pointed out my emotions. I felt the tears threatening my eyes again. Coaching myself to be strong was the hardest part of it all. There was a piece of me that just wanted to go hang out with Dave. Joey would also be a good solution. I needed someone happy, someone that wouldn't think about Jason or even bring his name up. That person did not exist.

"Look April, what Jason and I had, it was–" I stopped, not sure how to put it into words. I wasn't sure April knew all the details of what my father has done to us. Glancing over my shoulder seeing Mom in deep conversation with my aunt, she probably knew more than April. "We were not much of anything." I said, getting up from the couch. April stood up, following behind me.

"You are such a liar!" Her excited voice almost made me crash and burn inside. All I wanted was to be back with Jason but talking about him wasn't helping.

"I'm not a liar, furthermore, why do you even care?" I lashed back at her not wanting to start a fight.

"Because I watch the entertainment news and *hello,* Jason is blowing up like a mad house and you are always in the conversation." She smiled giving me that, 'I know you're with him' look. I sighed loudly just wanting to lock myself in my room to get away from her.

"Okay, yes we were together what else could you possibly want to know?" Feeling minutes away from exploding into tears; watching her get her pleasure of truth, there wasn't a piece of me that didn't want to smack her.

"Why did you let someone so hot like that slip away?" She got closer to me. Not only was I feeling the pain taking over my heart, but I was also feeling anger. Why did she care so much about my love life? I couldn't care one minute about hers. Blinking back my tears; trying to keep it all together until I was away from them.

"He didn't slip away, okay? We broke up because of some personal reasons and that doesn't concern you nor should you even care! Do I miss him? Yes, like crazy!

If I had the chance to go back and run into his arms, I would take it in a heartbeat, but I can't, he's gone. What more do you want to hear from me? Did I love him, yes but that doesn't matter now, so just shut up!" I yelled making my mom and aunt Lisa stop their conversation. Everyone in the room was staring at me. I went running back to my room slamming the door shut. My hands covered my face realizing I was crying that whole time. I might have just acted like some young teenage girl that broke up with a boy she was recently dating for a week, but I didn't care. Jason meant more to me than I think even I realized. How can you fall in love with someone so fast? How can you fall out of love that fast?

I sat down on my bed staring at the text messages on my phone. Moving the messages up and down that we sent to each other, my finger skimmed over the delete button. I closed my eyes biting down on my lip. The sooner I let him go the easier life will get. I lost what I had, now it was time to leave it in the past. Looking back to his contact I hit the delete button just as he had asked. The conformation came up asking if I was sure I wanted to delete it. A tear dropped down hitting the screen. I shook my head wondering if there would ever be a chance for us again.

"Hey, I found Ashley." Dave's cold body flew into the room right before I hit okay. Looking up to him feeling the icy coldness cover my face from the tears. He saw that I was crying, and he came over to me within seconds.

“Who did this?” He questioned wiping my tears away with his snow like hands. I shook my head sitting my phone aside.

“Myself.” Saying it only made the pain worse. A thick layer of regret still poisoned my heart.

“I don’t believe that, did he call you?” His crystal blue eyes glanced down at my phone. I shook my head again wishing that’s all it was.

“If it was him, I wouldn’t be crying.” Pushing my hair back wondering if there was any chance of him feeling the same as me, there was a high chance that he did not. After all he’s been through, he’s learned how to let life slip through his hands just to get away from the tabloids lined with rumors.

“Then who?” Dave wanted to rip apart whoever might have hurt me. Truth was April didn’t really hurt me; it was my own memories that left me standing there like a fool.

“April had a magazine, and I was on the front of it with Jason. It was talking about the break-up, and she was asking millions of questions and I reached my breaking point; I went off on her and now we’re here.” I said, falling back onto my bed. My head hit the diary that I’d left lying under my pillow. I pulled it out tossing it back down on the floor. Dave’s cold hand rested on my leg. He pulled me up into a hug. My eyes fell shut.

“Don’t worry, everything will be okay, the pain will leave and before you know it, he won’t even matter to you anymore." He told me running his chilled fingers through my hair. My tears felt like they were turning into icicles, and I pulled back from him wiping the tears away. He gave me a smile that said, 'you're stronger than you think you are'. I had to shake away the hard feeling of heartache. I've never loved someone before; now I knew what it was like to let go. It almost felt like the day I found out my dad wanted to kill my mom. There was no love there anymore nor was there trust. I feel as if the same has happened here. Only this time I was the heartbreaker. How could I have behaved in a way that is similar to how my vicious father would have? I tore a guy's heart out because of that monster. I knew there was no way of apologizing now. Jason was a free bird. The only piece I had left was a feather from his unbroken wings.

The bedroom door plunged open revealing Mom with an expression of hurt on her face. She wasn't hurt, but she mirrored my pain. She didn't speak as she came over blanketing me with a loving hug. Out of the corner of my eye lingered Jason's contact. His smile remains warm in my heart, his forest green eyes a tattoo in my brain, and his scent miraculously stained on my clothes. I wasn't going to delete him.

Chapter 21

The Unexpected

The awkward moment of my mom coming into my room and asking what that was all about happened. She has been sitting here talking to me about her first relationships. There was a piece of me that just wanted to ignore all of what she was saying. All parents do this once you go through your first break up, they act like it is their job. In all honesty we just want them to leave us alone. It is awkward telling them the things we are most hurt over. Even my mom doesn't understand the pain of losing someone and falling for them over the same short period of time, like I have. She never fell in love while engaging in a game of cat and mouse. The horrific part about the game was, she is the mouse. She lived through one of the most vulgar eclipsing relationships I've witnessed. I was just the hell-bent child who was along for the ride. I knew my mom would feel the abuse from the blunt hits, body tosses, and strangling for the rest of her life. Just like I would from touching my scar. Turbulence was our story, yet Jason made me feel so grounded.

"Are you sure you're just not gushing over how cute

he was?" She sat back against my wall. My mouth fell open, feeling the anger kicking back in. If I was obsessed with his hotness, then I wouldn't be worried about being with him. It was hard to tell someone that though.

"It wasn't because of any of what you think it is. It doesn't matter about the money, what his job is or even the fact that other girls gush over him, he was different." I said staring out into the ocean. Maybe I was the one that needed to get away from all of this. It was driving me insane and that wasn't good. None of this was good. It was like I was waiting around for something that would never happen. Hell, for all I knew love didn't even happen. Maybe Jason was just some passing by guardian who helped me through a rough patch. I was allowing my brain to become toxic with thoughts of what ifs and lost love. A blunder decision I could have walked myself out of, yet my heart won. I've never had a war so strong between my brain and heart.

"Well, I think you should go back out there and apologize to April for going off on her." She said getting up off my bed.

"No, she pushed it there!" I argued, still feeling the anger from it fizzle inside my stomach.

"Now Sky, I know it isn't what you want to do but she is our guest, and you have to be the bigger person." She told ne, walking out of my room. The bigger person ins. However, I didn't feel like the bigger elt like the little one that got stepped on and had her heart run over by a truck.

I picked up the diary that was lying there. Mom didn't say a word about it. I opened it up going back to the page I was on. I had to see what Alex had said for that day. I needed something to get me away from all this chaos. Whoever Alex was, his life was my escape.

7-23-93

Today I saw Kate. There is some sad news I must say, and it wasn't easy for me to digest. Kate told me that she was thinking about moving away. That only made me wonder if we weren't meant to be. I can't say how hard it is to hold the tears in. She didn't even tell me why she was moving away, just that she couldn't see me anymore. There was a part of me that wanted to talk her out of it. I just couldn't get the words out to say anything to her. I can't express how heavy my heart feels right now. Almost as if a piece of me was taken away. It was crazy of me to ever think that she could have been the one. Well until next time.

-Alex

I blinked back the tears, feeling now what he was feeling then. He lost someone he loved because of some unknown reason. I wanted to tell Alex not to give up hope on her. She might have to go for another reason that she didn't feel comfortable talking about. There was a huge piece of me that felt like I knew Alex. Like we were almost the same person. I wanted to believe I could help him, but chances are there wasn't a chance of me actually being able to find him. I put the diary back under my pillow and got up. Walking back into the living room and seeing everyone sitting there. The feeling of the awkward silence was setting in. Why did everyone have to watch me? Just because I made a normal person look like a looney. It's not like they haven't loved someone before.

"Skylar, I'm sorry for pressuring you into telling me." April apologized as I took a seat next to Mom. I shook my head holding my hands up.

"It wasn't your fault." I counteracted, trying to ignore my feelings. I wanted to talk with Alex. He shared things in common with me. He knew about the dead, he lost love like I did. I knew he was older than I was but that didn't mean we haven't shared the same experiences. Alex had a ghost savior, Ashley, while I had Dave. Dave told me he knew Ashley but seemed stumped at Alex.

"Good, so how about we all get ready and head to the beach for some fun?" My aunt stood up smiling as big as ever. My mom got up as well.

"Sounds like a good time." They both walked away, and I got back up again. April followed me back into my bedroom. Her mouth fell open seeing my big window that leads out into the ocean view.

"So, is it okay if I want to steal your bedroom?" She asked pulling out her bikini from a duffel bag she'd brought with her. I laughed a little lifting my eyebrows. Did they have plans of staying here with us? I would give the bedroom to anyone if I could take back time. I might sound a little desperate, but it was all because of love. Maybe I'm a psycho for wanting to be back with him so badly. Some people would tell me I'm too attached and need to move on. Then I wondered if this is how I would live out the rest of my life. Wondering, waiting, and not sure if anything will ever happen. With that conscious thought I felt sick. Mentally sick. I would not spend the rest of my life waiting on Jason Blackstone to return to my life. That would be moronic.

There was a knock on my door and April and I both turned around. My aunt peeked her head in the door and smiled at me.

"I think one of your friends is here to see you." She told me, and I was confused. It could have been Joey, but he usually tells me before stopping by. We all went out into the living room and Mom was sitting on the couch putting things in her bag. I stopped where I was standing when my aunt let him inside, opening the front door. My heart skipped a beat when I saw his black hair draping down over one eye. All I needed to see was his snowy white smile and those perfect green eyes. I screamed not wasting a minute. I ran into his arms within seconds of seeing him standing before me. His smell went up my nose. I was home. His strong arms embraced me, circling my body. My feet went back to the ground as he pulled back from me. My arms remained around his, seizing the moment of getting lost in the forest. The iron gates were wide open allowing me access into the wanderlust world, that I wished to be in.

"What are you doing–" he cut me off placing his lips down on mine. Feeling the movement of his soft lips taking over, I closed my eyes. Both his big hands came up cradling my face. Our lips moved like clouds connecting into one another. The minty taste he left lingered in my mouth. My heart was racing out of control. When his lips left mine all I could do was keep my eyes shut. My hand naturally reacted to his movement nudging his head back forward. My lips plunged back out catching hold of his again. The lowest rough chuckle crept up his throat. His warm hand slid to the arch of my back. Memories froze lassoing me back to my bedroom where our lips first met. His warm breath was like passion evaporating the poison. My hand slid up through his black hair never wanting to let go. My heart was latched to his. No words could explain the love I felt for Jason.

"This is not happening." I heard April whisper to herself from across the room. I felt so warm inside. Everything felt complete now that he was here with me. Jason moved back away from me gazing down into my eyes. I started crying from happiness. He shook his head pushing my hair away from my face.

"You have no idea what I went through day and night trying to tell myself to forget you." He was breathless pressing his lips back onto my forehead. I smiled, letting out a sigh of relief. I shook my head grabbing his face letting my lips rush back to his.

"Yes, I do, because I couldn't do it either." I whispered to him, watching his forest green eyes gaze down into mine. He wiped the tears away from my face.

"I promise you that I will never let you slip out of my hands again." His low rough voice was all I needed. I couldn't try to leave him even if I wanted to. Our hearts are together, we're like links of chains. Chains that could never be broken. No one could break us free from what we felt for each other and that was stronger than any truth that could be told.

"Jason, what are you doing here?" Mom chuckled in amazement, walking over to us. His green eyes left me for a few seconds but then returned. His smile never left as he looked over to my mom taking my hand.

"I'm sorry if I interrupted anything but Mrs. Saxton, I couldn't stay away from your daughter anymore, yes we broke up but there is something about her that kept drawing me back, I had to come and be with her." His words melted every inch of ice that had formed over my heart. I watched my mom's face glow with a smile that couldn't be forgotten. Her hand lay over her chest as she got tears in her eyes as well.

"Jason, I don't know what to say." She was in complete amazement just as I was. April came walking up behind Mom. She came over even closer inspecting his body. His gray jeans and black V-neck shirt, his sunglasses that were pulled up onto his head, she lifted his arm up. He laughed a little giving me an odd look.

"I just have to make sure he's real." She said, laughing awkwardly. Jason gave her an odd look and laughed a little.

"Who is she?" He whispered to me, seeming a little creeped out.

"Someone that has never met a famous person before." I told him, taking his arm away from her. I gave April big eyes, imploring her to act normal. There was too much to catch up on with him, to be involved with them.

"You're right and I would sure love to see this on the beach." She said, flexing her eyebrows at me. His green eyes wondered back to me as things became more awkward. I blushed, remembering him taking his shirt off in his bedroom as I watched from the alleyway. Jason had no idea that a paparazzi man had almost got explicit pictures of him.

"That's right we were heading to the beach, Jason would you like to join us?" Mom asked him, holding out a towel. He laughed a little running his hand back through his hair. He glanced back over to me, then to the window.

"I really don't think that's a good idea." He said, acting nervous about something.

"Like hell it ain't." April was eyeing him up like he was the sweetest candy in the shop. I was annoyed by the way she wanted to take things from me. I also remembered why I stopped hanging out with her. Ever since we were children, she took, or thought she owned, specific things I had.

"I just don't want to draw a lot of people around." He explained. looking at everyone. Jason put himself in an awkward spot by surprising me, but I wasn't complaining. I was mesmerized. Mom nodded her head like she understood right away. She saw all the press that followed and waited outside of our house before.

"Okay, well I guess we will see you two in a little while." She said, heading over to the door. April's eyes stayed on Jason the entire time until she was out the door.

"Be safe." My aunt said with a wink of her eye. In that moment in time all I felt was my cheeks becoming warmer. They left the house and Jason turned back to me. He didn't say a word, he just wrapped me back up in his arms. His lips kissed the side of my head once more. He was more than happy to see me. I pulled back from him staring into the forest. The forest I ran down every night trying to save his life. Almost like I was trying to find him again. My hands held both sides of his face as my thumbs skimmed the tips of his black hair. I closed my eyes letting my head lower. He lifted my chin back up, making my eyes reopen.

"Don't look away from me." He pleaded, running his finger down over my lips. A small smile came back to me, missing his touch.

"I just can't believe you are here." I confessed, feeling my heart begin to blaze once again, rather than freeze.

The chains of poison vanished; it felt like my heart was whole. Although, I still had a lot of things to ask him, things I wasn't sure he would want to answer.

"After letting you go, there was something I learnt and had actually learnt a long time ago, once you have something that makes you feel complete, something that embraces you so strongly, like a page in a book you can't read yourself out of, you should never ever let that go because once you do, you may never find it again." His eyes were reading me so deeply. His words were so sincere, almost like he was speaking words out of a book. I felt my entire body tremble; all I managed was a cheesy smile. Wrapping my arms around his neck once more, as he lifted me up off the ground. We just gazed into each other's eyes. He walked us into my bedroom and sat me down on the bed. He was the first person that didn't look at my window and look mesmerized within seconds. His full attention rested on me, only me.

"Jason, I am so happy to see you but there is something I need to know." I said, already feeling weird and awkward about it. He sat down right beside me letting the sun catch his beautiful green eyes.

"Whatever it is you want to know I will answer." His hand rested on my leg. My eyes left his, watching the birds fly over the ocean. How was I even going to ask about the girl I saw him with? How was I going to even start asking why he didn't answer my phone calls or texts? There were too many why's and how's and not enough answers. I needed to be brave and ask.

"You never answered my calls." I said, feeling a darkness cast over now. His lips retreated back into his mouth as if I'd asked something extremely out of line.

"Honestly, I didn't want to seem like the weak one that was going to come running back to you after a breakup and every time I saw it was you, I ended up letting the fear overtake me instead of being a man and swallowing it. I'm sorry." His answer was genuine. He didn't want to seem desperate, to come running back into my hands. I understood him, I felt the same way when I broke down and called him for the first time. I was the one who broke him, and myself.

"And the other night, the girl you were with on the award show, she was who?" Lifting an eyebrow just spitting the questions out instead of hesitating, I always felt that was bad. His smile grew bigger than ever. He laughed at me pulling his legs up onto the bed. I watched his shoes tumble to the floor.

"You watched?" He seemed taken away by the fact that I paid attention to him, rather than the important part.

"Yes, but who was she?" Getting back on topic so he couldn't shift things. He laughed again shaking his head at me.

"No one that you need to worry about, I knew this would come up sooner or later. She is my manager — Emma." He told me, leaving a grin on his face. Emma was the woman that kept texting him that night in his room. Suddenly my feelings simmered down and were no longer a gauntlet of fire. I haven't seen who Emma was, nor met her, but all I had was his words to trust. I recalled the short research I did on Jason and the name Emma did come up for his manager along side his dad. I nodded my head thinking back to my dad then. What if he followed him down here?

"Jason, no one followed you down here, did they?" Everything was falling into a more serious aspect. His green eyes shifted from me as he smiled.

"Well, I'm pretty sure no one can follow me onto my own private jet so..." He laughed again tilting his head to the side. My eyes opened, not ready for those words to be used so loosely.

"Your own jet?" Feeling like I was just now waking up to how famous he was, he laughed once more. The sun shimmering over his eyes that were full of amusement.

"Yeah, I'm not just going to take any normal plane, do you know how many people would be around me?" His black eyebrows lifted up like he was telling me some sort of joke. His sigh was happy as he pulled me into his lap. We stared at each other, and his arms wrapped around me. Feeling the air from his nose brush across my face as his forehead leaned down against mine. I felt a spark of coldness emerge into my chest. I sucked in air pulling back. Seeing my necklace turning vibrant blue, Jason looked at me with concern.

"What's wrong?" He straightened his back letting his

hand fall on my leg. I shook my head swallowing down the chills that burst through my chest. Dave needed to talk with me. I could always tell when it was important or urgent. I got up from my bed.

"I'll be right back." I said, going out of my room and right into the bathroom. Shutting the door behind me Dave stood leaning against the sink. His blue eyes sparkling, he unfolded his arms.

"Looks like Mr. Hot Stuff is back." He said, not sounding very impressed. I laughed a little still feeling amazed inside.

"Yeah, it was something unexpected, I can't believe it!" My voice excited and still not believing how easy it was for him to find me. Then again, he was rich, he probably could pay someone to find me. In a way that scared me inside. Dave came up from his leaning pose and let his arms fall.

"Well, I have some very interesting news for you but first I must know what drew you to that man earlier?" His head cocked to the side as if he was waiting for some explanation. Looking away from him thinking back to the diary, Alex and the older man we followed into the bungalow. There wasn't anything suspicious that I saw. Dave found something out and he was getting ready to spill it. That guy is someone important I can feel it.

"Who is he?" Was all I could ask.

"No, first off you knew something was up with that guy, now I want to know how." He held a finger up.

There was no explaining. I didn't know why I wanted to follow that man. It was just like my legs took me there.

"Dave, I can't explain what happened today or why I followed him. I guess it was just that I thought he could be someone important." I said, not sure if he was or not. I remembered him from the road though. He watched me like I was someone important or someone he knew. Maybe I just wanted to get a better look at him. It meant nothing because I found nothing.

"Well, he seems to be someone you will be excited to hear about, that man was Alex." It was like he waved a magic wand handing over a piece of paper. Seeing his name next to his picture, my mouth dropped open looking back up to him.

"But how can we be sure it's the same Alex?" I asked him, glancing back down at the paper. It had all his personal information on there. Everything down to how tall he was and his eye color, Dave shook his head, lifting his arms up.

"That's for you to investigate." He told me, fading out of the room. Why did he leave me? I wanted to know so much more. I had to go search Alex out. First, I would have to explain to Jason what was going on. He would be lost and confused. I opened the door walking back out into the hall. Jason stood in the opening of my door. I looked back to the paper folding it up and shoving into my pocket. I needed to figure out who Alex was. He knew a woman named Kate; they dated two years before

I was born. My mom told me a story very similar to that one. Then there was Jason. How was our life going to be placed together with all that is happening? He has explained everything to me, there was just some strings that were still dangling in the wind. Then there was my father. Only time would tell for how long it would take him to find us again. Now that Kyle is on his side all hell is about to break loose. It's up to us to fight this and stay alive while trying to figure out all the mystery that still lies inside. I sucked in some air, realizing that this crazy life has only just begun.

"Is everything alright?" Jason's eyes told me that he was worried. I smiled at him walking back into my room, shutting the door.

"Nothing could be more perfect." I smiled, full of bliss as I wrapped my arms around his neck. He smiled resting his hands down on my hips and his lips came down covering mine. I closed my eyes taking in the feeling of his lips. I flew back to when he kissed me for the first time. I was sitting on my bed explaining my life to him and for some forsaken reason that made him kiss me. Dave ruined that kiss, but our lips still brushed together. My lips moved out before he broke the kiss, moving back to my bed. When he sat down, he pulled a little black box out from his back pocket. The smile on my face disintegrated, watching the jewelry box. My stomach flopped, nervous of what was inside that box. The smile on his face was whole, like it was in the movies that made millions of girls want to smile back, including me. He reached out taking my hand and placing the small black box down in my palm. I swallowed hard, while panic consumed me. I heard my heart pounding anxiously. The velvet box felt like it weighed 800 pounds but in reality, it was just under a pound.

"I came across this the other day. All I could think about was you and that's when I made my decision to come down here." He started explaining, sucking nervously on his bottom lip. I grinned opening the box up. I sucked in air quickly, seeing a heart necklace blanketed in diamonds. Small bursts of rainbows dashed across the room, covering it in a kaleidoscope filter.

"Jason, it's beautiful." My voice was low just taking it in as the sun coming in from my window caught every edge of the diamonds making it shimmer. I saw the smile warming his face as he took the necklace out from the box. Watching his actions made me want to kiss him until there was no more daylight. I pulled my hair up into a ponytail and he hooked it around my neck letting it lay just above the colorful ghostly necklace Dave once gave me. I watched as he licked his lips slowly flipping it over. My eyebrows rose seeing words engraved on the back of it. *Will love you forever.*

"Skylar, I know this sounds crazy, but you light up my whole world with the sun light that casts down from your smile, you make me feel so different and there's not a day goes by I can't stop seeing you in my mind, everywhere

I looked, I saw you in some way whether it was your smile, hearing your laugh, or even hearing your stubborn attitude, it all brought me back to you. This last week has been a living hell for me, my head was never straight I couldn't even look at my fans because I knew deep inside there was a girl out there that was so unlike them. That girl brought happiness to my world even though she pushed me away every day until you finally accepted me but then you were gone. I'm sorry that I ever told you to just leave and forget about me and to delete me from your world. I was a fool to think I could just let you go because I can't, nor will I ever do so again unless it's really what you want. Although, right now I think what you want is the same as what I want, Skylar I will love you forever, even if that means someday letting you go." His hand rested gently on my cheek and his thumb skimmed my bottom lip. Tears rolled down my face from the words he spoke, and the ones engraved inside the necklace. I shook my head leaning in and pressing our lips back together as one. He just told me he loved me. Now I knew everything I was feeling wasn't just some stupid heart aching emotion. I was in love with him, but the crazier part was he was in love with me too. Every day that I kicked my own ass, he equally was kicking his.

"Jason, I am so, so sorry I ever hurt you." My voice cracked admitting to my own faults in hurting him. Deep down, Jason wasn't so tough. At least not when it came to me. I was his weakness, his kryptonite.

"Don't apologize, you only pushed me away to keep me safe. I'm the idiot for not seeing through those actions. Just know, as long as I'm around, you will always be safe with me. That is my eternal promise to you, my love." He promised me love forever and with his undying love came eternal devotion.

"Please don't ever let me go." My voice was just a breath as I was crawling into his lap. He pressed our lips back together holding his strong arms around me tightly. We held each other and I knew my life was about to change forever with him. I didn't care if I had to be in the spotlight, I would do it just to be in his arms. I didn't care if I had to fight with his sister every single day of my life just to breathe the same air he did. I didn't care if I had to jump hurdles of crudeness from his father to assert my profound love for his son. He found his way back into my heart only because I was missing from his. This was our world now and we were in this together. They say if it's true love it will always find its way back. I was not sure if this could be considered finding its way back, but it was something that made me feel alive inside. A magic feeling I've never felt before with anyone else. I wanted to start my life over, and maybe being with Jason was starting over. He didn't care if my father was a murderer or even the fact that I had to live my life behind a curtain just to stay alive. His own family could not even stop his decision to fly down here to find me. All he saw was us and that meant the world to me. I never pulled away from his lips, his touch, or even that amazing strong hug he would embrace me with. He said forever, writing the word *eternity* in my heart.

Acknowledgments

I want to say a special thank you to my team, who have helped me build my book, enlightened me further in this literary world, and who I have built special friendships with. Thank you to my editor Jessica, and my graphic designer Matt and his wonderful wife, Aimee, and my personal assistant Frankie. Each one of you means so much to me!

A special thank you to my ARC team for providing your undivided attention to my book. I appreciate all your kind words and love.

With all my heart, I want to thank my parents for always being my two biggest supporters. Mom, you have encouraged me to follow my dreams since day one of me wanting to be a rock star, your outlook has always made me believe that no mountain is too high to climb even if reaching the top may be difficult. I know Dad is smiling from ear to ear, witnessing my accomplishment of becoming a writer, he knew my destiny before anyone else did.

A gracious thank you to a few teachers throughout my years of school, "Big" Mrs. Bailey – without you allowing me to participate in your English class for a special writing project, I'm not sure I would have discovered my passion for writing. You allowed my dreams to spark in 7th Grade by giving a special needs student an opportunity, I am forever grateful for that. Mrs. Coyle and Mrs. King, the both of you carried this overwhelming support for me all through high school, you both believed in me, pushed me, and stood beside me in ways that other teachers never did; I appreciate the four years I spent in both of your classes.

Lastly, I want to thank my best friend Devin, you have been beside me with this crazy journey. You instantly click with my imagination, which is truly refreshing. You've helped me make final decisions and given me your input when needed. I am thankful that I have you to lean on, the never-ending support, and the dirty jokes that follow; never stop being you.

About the Author

When Estalyn isn't writing her next book and engaging with her characters, she spends her time playing video games with her husband, walking her Chihuahua, and taking pictures. Estalyn is not only a writer, but also a photographer. She studied Journalism at school to become an entertainment news reporter, but her love of fiction overpowered the non-fiction side of life. She resides in Ohio, continuing her journey with the next book!

 Estalyn - Author

 Estalyn_Author

 estalyn_author

 estalyn_author

Coming Soon!

Heart Shock

Printed in Great Britain
by Amazon

10709406R00189